BOOK TWO

LOST *and* FOUND

Megan Carr

LOST AND FOUND

A PACIFIC NORTHWEST LOVE STORY
BOOK TWO

MEGAN CARR

LOST AND FOUND

Lost and Found, A Pacific Northwest Love Story - Book Two

For anyone who has ever felt lost

CHAPTER ONE

MIKE - MAY OF THIS YEAR

H ERE'S THE thing about Georgia: she's too goddamn naive.

It's not her fault, really. She was raised by good parents. Good parents that, frankly, loved her too much and protected her from everything scary in the world. They tried to shield her from me, but that didn't work, did it? She chose me anyway. She chose me, and we've been happily married for years...despite what her so-called divorce papers say.

But the reality is, Georgia grew up with no grasp on how things really work out here in the real world. Life is shit, and the sooner people figure that out, the better.

Me? I was lucky enough to learn that lesson at a very young age — at the hand of my ol' man. He'd come home late, already tanked. He'd hit the scotch and then hit me, his belt turning my skin beet red. I used to cry and hide and try to run away, but it didn't change my circumstances. Didn't make me any stronger. No, I learned pretty quickly to take it, and take it like a man. Hell, that's what *made* me a man. It's how I learned to use my God-given brain to get through this life.

1

Now, some kids would take that set of circumstances, and let it ruin them — they couldn't handle it, couldn't grow from it. They become the scum that I clean up off the streets every day, high as fuck on meth, and begging for money so they can go and buy more. But I used those beatings as a way to learn. I learned how to defend myself, how to be invisible, and how to read people. Above all, I learned street smarts, how to be self-reliant, and how to rely on number one: me.

My mom didn't hold my hand — didn't shield me from anything. She made me fight my own battles, and look how I ended up — a fucking detective for the San Diego P.D. Talk about struggle. No one gave me this job. No one helped me. I had to work hard as hell for everything I have. Extra shifts. Late nights. Hell, *all night* shifts, shitty beats, and even shittier partners. I put in my time, and I climbed the ladder.

And what does my wife do while I'm putting in all this time, working so hard? What does the one person I love more than anyone or anything, do? She fucking cuts bait and runs. She takes the easy way out, tries to escape, and hides like the scared little girl she is.

We were supposed to be partners in this marriage, and things were going so well, too. Sure we hit a bit of a rough patch after Jason, but nothing that got us off track too far. I had a few drinks after work, just like Jase and I used to — just to relax — and she starts whining about how I'm an alcoholic. Ha! What a fucking joke. If she even knew my real past, the real story about my family, she'd rethink throwing around the word *alcoholic*. But she doesn't. She never did, and she never will.

Which brings me back to how naive she is.

She thinks she made a clean break with this so-called divorce. But she's my wife, and I intend to get her back. She has no idea how much I don't give one pitiful shit about a piece of paper that says *Judgment of Dissolution*.

2

What I *do* care about is this file I've got on Mr. Fireman here.

This guy. Even looking at his face in this stupid surveillance photo makes me want to rip his heart out.

The burn of the straight whiskey fuels my rage as it slides down my throat, and I slam the empty glass down on the table. Yeah, Ol' Benny boy here's got balls, man. He thinks he can swoop in and fuck my wife? *My* wife?

No.

No way in hell.

And Georgia. What did she wait, like four hours before she wrapped her skinny legs around him? Jesus. How could she betray our marriage like that? Did it mean *nothing* to her?

Well, it means something to me. It means everything. And there's no way I'm going to let some loser like this guy put his filthy hands on her gorgeous body.

Ben's face begins to blur as I stare at the photo. I drop it back into the file, pick up my bottle and pour another shot, shooting it hard and fast. Shaking my head to clear the burn, I reach for my prepaid cell phone and begin typing. Yeah, he's got quite the interesting past all right. Georgia's going to come crawling back to me, begging me to take her back.

It's going to be fun to watch this prick squirm.

CHAPTER TWO

GEORGIA

H E'S GONE. HE'S REALLY GONE.
I don't want to admit it, but the more time that passes, the more I can't ignore this possible truth. Ben didn't just drive around the block. Half an hour has passed, and he's still not back.

I haven't moved from my chair in the living room; too many thoughts swirling around my brain have kept me planted here, unable to find a clear direction. My legs start to cramp, and I decide to get up and get something to drink at least. I slowly crutch my way back to the kitchen, grab a glass, and a bottle of San Pellegrino, and sit down at the counter. Ben's cell phone stares at me from the corner. The fact that it's still here gives me hope he's coming back, but as I pick it up and re-read the awful text messages, the small lift I feel dissipates; replaced instead by a distinct wave of nausea. The knowledge that someone was watching and following me makes me sick.

I notice the time the last text came in, and also realize it came from a different number. I bring my laptop to the kitchen and type this new information into Google. The search brings up several sites dedicated to complaints about telemarketing calls coming from the number, with warnings to block it. Reaching for our new house telephone – *thank you Scott for installing it right away* -- I decide to talk to Lieutenant Dickerson. I scroll through the cell phone call history to pull up his number, and dial. After a quick transfer at reception, he picks up the line.

"Dickerson."

"Lieutenant Dickerson. It's Georgia Marks."

"Well, what a coincidence. I was just about to call you."

"Oh?"

"Yeah. I had Roth check into that solicitation company a little farther. Unfortunately, he didn't make any headway. No one knows anything there, or if they do, they're not talking. The manager says they place thousands of calls and text messages every day. It'd be impossible to try and track down which particular employee sent the message without going through reams of paperwork, and even then I don't know that we would get anywhere."

"All right, well thanks for letting me know," I say, feeling let down.

"Sure thing. So with that dead end, I'm going to close my — "

"Lieutenant? I'm sorry, excuse me. I just thought I should let you know. I've received another text. Well, I guess *Ben* received another text. It's from a different number this time, but it's the same type of threat."

"Oh? When did that come in?"

"Late yesterday afternoon. We didn't notice it until this morning though. It was late when we got in last night."

"Hold on," Dickerson interrupts. "Ms. Marks, are you still here in town?" His voice has jumped in volume, and I suddenly realize I've forgotten to let him know I left Bend.

"Uh...no, I'm calling from my house in Silverton. I apologize. I forgot to let you know — "

"Ms. Marks, I assume you remember our conversation where

6

I specifically told you to be sure and report any changes in your location while we're investigating?" he says, point-blank.

"Yes, sir," I reply. I don't have the energy to fight with him. "I apologize. We left suddenly due to a family situation here."

"And by 'we' I assume you mean yourself and Mr. Harrison?"

"Yes, Ben and I came to Silverton together."

The phone line is quiet. Somewhere in the distance, I hear the small sound of a telephone ringing. Dickerson coughs and clears his voice.

"Ms. Marks, is this telephone number a good number I can reach you at? I'd like to follow up on the new text — if you don't mind passing me the information?" He's calm again, and I pick up the cell phone and relay the number and the context of the message to him.

"Hmm. All right. And Mr. Harrison doesn't recognize this number either I take it?"

"No." This time I'm not lying.

"And what is your home address so I can update your file, Ms. Marks?"

I rattle off my address along with the house phone number.

"All right. And do you have family in town or nearby there? Someone that could check on you from time to time? With your injury and all, until we get to the bottom of this, it would be good to know someone is available to you."

"Yes," I say, quietly. "I live with my sister and brother-in-law, and his parents are just across town. I work at a local antiques shop here, and I've known my boss Ed for the last eight months or so. I can give you his number too if you'd like?"

"Yes. We just want to make sure our file is complete."

I give him Ed's telephone number and address and the contact information for Scott's parents, as well as their respective office numbers. When I've finished, he wishes me luck and makes me promise to check in with him again in a few days.

7

Meanwhile, he says he'll look into the new text, and see what he can find out.

By the time I hang up, I realize over an hour has passed, and there's still no sign of Ben.

I decide to distract myself by taking a shower and cleaning up the mess in the kitchen. My shower is short because I keep getting freaked out, ruminating on the fact that I am alone in the house. Visions of the movie *Psycho* run through my head as I stand in the old claw foot bathtub. Scott and Sylvia retrofitted it to a shower with a curtain — just like the movie. I hurry through washing and switch the water off as quickly as I can, ripping back the white fabric curtain and trying not to think about crime statistics.

After I'm dressed, I clean the kitchen and make myself a small lunch. I'm not really hungry, which is a blaring sign that something is definitely not right with me. I love food, and I love to eat. I'm lucky enough to have been blessed with a metabolism that acts like it runs on a 24-hour supply of cocaine, so the absence of hunger in me is like a fleet of police car sirens sounding outside my house.

Nearly three hours have passed, and still Ben hasn't returned. I would call him, but he left his cell phone here. As I run through different scenarios of how I can reach him, I keep hitting the same brick wall: I really don't know him very well. Maybe he knows someone here he went to visit? Or maybe not here, but Salem, or Stayton, or any of the small towns along the highway. Maybe he grew up around here or something. Maybe his wife was from here, and that's how he knows people in the valley. His wife.

Ex-wife, I clarify to myself.

This line of thinking brings thoughts of Charlotte back to my mind. Did Ben fall into intimacy with her as quickly as he had with me? My thoughts spiral down a very dark hole, and I feel the self-recriminations begin. Why hadn't I been honest with him from the beginning? Why hadn't I just told him about the text message right away? I was so confused and worried about what answers I might hear, but now look at me: facing the fact that he might be gone for good. The embarrassment of allowing myself to even consider falling in love so quickly fills me with shame, and that shame instantly turns to anger.

I pound my fist on the kitchen counter and sit down hard on the stool at the bar. I chide myself for being so naive, for jumping into a sexual relationship so quickly, never even taking the time to get to know him, or his past. And yet, when I think back to the way he described what happened with Charlotte, it feels truly genuine. I don't get the sense he was lying or exaggerating. I remember Annie gently telling me that Ben had been through some very hard experiences in life. At the time, I assumed she meant his divorce, or maybe a work issue. Now it's clear she was talking about Charlotte. And Matt, adamantly telling me Ben had never hurt her, standing up for his character like Ben was his own child. These people couldn't both be wrong, could they?

I check the clock on the kitchen stove, beginning to worry. Maybe he was in a car accident? He was so distraught when he left.

Where could he be? A small voice in the back of my mind suggests he's gone back to Sisters. Could I blame him? Look at the mess he wandered into with me. He had a nice quiet life, beautiful home, great job, and then all of the sudden some crazy woman shows up, breaks her ankle and needs taking care of. I shrug at these thoughts. Really, do I have the right to be upset? Maybe it's actually best if we just stop whatever this is, right now, before it goes any further — before someone really becomes invested and gets hurt.

CHAPTER THREE

GEORGIA

B Y THE TIME EVENING ROLLS around, I just want to make sure Ben is physically all right. After that, if he's gone back to Sisters, I decide it's probably best anyway. As much as it hurts to admit, I don't ever want to try and convince someone to stay when he would obviously rather leave.

———

Sylvia phones the house, and we talk briefly. I make excuses about what happened with Ben and why I couldn't meet her at the hospital. Although she politely listens, it's clear her focus is on Guthrie. Can I blame her? We agree to talk again when she and Scott come home for the night.

In the meantime, I prepare a full dinner for our little crew: roasted chicken with lemon, potatoes, steamed broccoli with a garlic and bacon aioli, a leafy green salad with cilantro dressing, and a loaf of hearty garlic bread. I'd made this meal many times before, and even without a broken ankle, it took me a good deal of time and attention. This time around, cooking requires my utmost concentration, which, after all, is the reason I chose to make it. Distraction can be a very welcome friend.

As I pull the chicken out of the oven, I glance at the stove clock: 6:53 p.m. Sylvia and Scott should be walking through the door any moment. I set the roasting pan down on the stove and turn my attention back to the oven to check on the garlic bread. As my hot pad touches the aluminum foil, I think I hear Ben's cell phone ring. I freeze, listening intently.

There it is again.

I withdraw my hand and slam the oven door shut, turning to pick up the phone from the countertop. A number I don't recognize displays on the screen, and I wonder if it might be Ben calling. More likely it's the same person that's sending the messages. Either way, I don't think it's a smart idea to answer. I set the phone back down, and watch to see if the caller will leave a message.

The phone stops ringing, and a moment later the voicemail button lights up. I open the menu and press play, waiting for the message to begin.

Ben's deep voice sounds in my ear, and I swallow hard.

"Georgia, if you get this, it's me...Ben." I hear the rattling of dishes and mixed voices in the background. It sounds like he's calling from a bar or a restaurant. "I want to apologize to you. I'd hoped to talk to you in person, but I can understand why you didn't pick up. Listen, today, talking about what happened in my past with Charlotte..." He pauses, and I hear ice clinking in a glass.

"Well, it brought back a lot of hard memories. Anyway, look, I've been thinking all day about you and me, and whatever it is we have, and I think it's probably best...I think it's probably best if we just don't become romantically involved...any longer, I mean." He mutters a curse word, and it's a moment before I hear his voice fully again.

"I'm not good for you, G. My past is just too messed up, and you don't need, or deserve, that in your life — especially after everything you've been through. I think it's best if I stay away. I seem to attract danger to you."

"Obviously, someone doesn't like us being together, and I don't want any harm to come to you. I'm heading back to Sisters in the morning. You can call Annie to make arrangements to pick up the Jeep. Any time is fine, Georgia. It will be there as long as you need. And don't worry about returning this phone. Just keep it."

He stops talking. My chest hurts, and my palms are sweating. I hear random noise in the background, and I know he hasn't hung up, but he's not speaking any longer.

Another moment passes, and then he adds, "I wish you nothing but the best in life. Take very good care of yourself. Be sure to follow up with the police about those messages. They are obviously aimed at me, so I don't think you're in any danger anymore, but still, please just be careful. Goodbye, Georgia."

And then he's gone.

I set the phone back down on the countertop and absent-mindedly crutch back to the oven in a daze, removing the bread and distracting myself with the must-do tasks of right now. *I will think about this later*, I tell myself, biting my trembling lower lip.

I grab three plates out of the cabinet in what feels like slow motion and set them on the counter next to the rest of the meal that's already waiting. I throw a handful of silverware and napkins out and sit down on a barstool. My body feels heavy and sluggish, and I have zero appetite.

God, how did this happen? I thought I could handle him leaving, cutting this off, going back to Sisters.

My heart lied to my head.

13

Outside, the sound of a door shutting grabs my attention. A moment later I hear another one, and I lean back on my barstool, turning my face toward the living room and front door. I hear a key in the lock, and I grab my crutches, slip Ben's cell phone into my back pocket, and make my way toward the living room.

Sylvia bursts through the door first.

"Gia!" she says loudly as we see each other from across the room. I register Scott coming in the door behind her just as her arms wind around my neck, and we hug each other tightly.

"I've missed you so much!" she says, her face buried in my shoulder. She is shorter than me, even in her heels, and I lean down from my crutches and embrace her, closing my eyes as a wave of emotion runs through me.

"God, I've missed you, big sis." My voice cracks and she immediately pulls back, both hands planted firmly on my shoulders. Her eyes are intense as she scans my face.

"What? What is it? I know something's wrong so don't bother trying to hide it. Out with it." I have no chance against her. She's married to a lawyer for God's sake; she's been trained by the best.

I drop my head and bring my hand to my forehead. I am suddenly furious with myself for this ridiculous display of emotion.

"Um," I begin, "uh, it's just been a really, really stressful four days." I pinch my nose and blink, knowing any moment the tears will spill over. "Hey!" I perk up quickly, changing the subject. "How is Guth? Please tell me some good news." Sylvia's hands slide from my shoulders down to my wrists. We clasp hands and squeeze each other tightly.

"The vet says he's going to be ok!" The concern on her face immediately vanishes as a wave of relief visibly washes over her. "He's going to stay in the hospital for the next few days, but after that, as long as he doesn't have any problems, the doctor says he can come home to heal."

Scott drops their bags on the living room floor and walks up behind her, laying his hands on Sylvia's shoulders.

"Hey there, Georgia. It's really good to see you home again. I'm glad you could be here for this good news." He steps toward me from behind Sylvia and gives me a strong hug. Scott is the brother I never had growing up, the brother I have come to love so much. Their marriage makes me honestly happy.

"Thanks, Scott. I'm glad to be home. And I'm really happy Guthrie is going to be okay. I can't wait to see him," I say. "Hey, I made a huge dinner. Let's go and eat!" I turn my crutches and head toward the kitchen.

"Christ, Georgia! I didn't even notice your crutches. Are you in much pain?" Sylvia asks. Turning to Scott, she adds, "I'm a terrible person. How could you let me not say anything to her?" Scott just shrugs as I shake my head at her.

Over dinner, I explain what happened during the hike. Sylvia has tons of questions about the injury and immediately asks about Ben, while Scott sits quietly listening. I try to keep the discussion of Ben very low-key, hoping I won't need to do much explaining. I skip over the hotel break-in, and the threatening text messages. They both have enough on their plates, and I don't want to add to the likely, already toxic levels of cortisol in their systems. I wrap things up by explaining that Ben graciously drove me home for moral support with Guthrie and that my Jeep is still in his barn in Sisters.

"I'm afraid I'm still going to need your help to get it home," I say, my focus on my plate in front of me. I'm embarrassed to ask for help.

"Oh, that's no problem. We — "

" — Georgia," Scott interrupts. "Sorry, Sylv. Georgia, where is Ben now?" I look up at Scott. He doesn't miss a beat, this guy.

"He's...he, he had to go back to Bend. Fire season. Work. You know." I pick up my fork and begin moving minuscule fronds of broccoli around my plate.

Scott just slightly nods. Of course, he knows I'm not telling the whole truth, and I can feel my face begin to flush.

"Well, I hope we get to meet him soon!" Sylvia gushes and then turns to Scott. "When can we get over there to get the Jeep?"

Scott holds my eyes a moment too long before sliding his gaze to her.

"I'm actually not sure, honey. I've got the partner retreat this next weekend, and then we're going to that CLE class in Washington, remember?" He lays his hand on top of hers on the table, and she looks over at him and smiles. God, they are so in love it makes me physically ill sometimes.

"I'll need to look at the calendar after that," he says, "but I do know we are getting pretty close to the Tate trial then. I might not be able to get over there for a month or so. I could send my law clerk though."

"It's totally okay, guys," I interject. "It's not like I can drive anywhere, anyway. There really is no rush. I'm not worried about anything worse happening to it between now and then."

Shit. I quickly try to change the subject, hoping Scott won't pick up on my slip.

"So do you want to hear more about the bear?" I ask, excitedly.

"If you're comfortable talking about it, absolutely!" Sylvia chimes in.

"What do you mean, *anything worse?*" Scott asks, narrowing his eyes.

Me and my stupid big mouth.

"Oh, just that it had to be towed off Black Butte. Flat tire, wouldn't ya know, and now it's being stored in Ben's barn." I laugh it off like it's no big deal. Lying. To my sister and brother-in-law. Yeah, I've sunk to new levels of low.

"Ah." Scott's brow furrows as he looks at me. "Okay, well, we've had a long day. I'm going to take a shower and go to bed. Thank you for dinner, Georgia, it was great."

He stands up from the kitchen table and clears our plates, rinsing them and stacking them in the dishwasher. I have to hand it to him — he is a great husband. I smile at Sylvia, so happy she's chosen such a good guy. On his way past us, he stops and leans over the top of her head to give her an upside-down kiss.

"Don't be too late?" he coos.

"I won't, honey."

Ugh. I really need to get my own place.

Once Scott leaves the room, Sylvia looks at me, her sappy smile instantly vanishing.

"You can cut the crap with me, Gia. Where's Ben?" The look in her eye can't be more intense.

"Jesus, Sylv, I told you. He had to get back to work." I smile, but I know it's unconvincing.

"Yeah yeah, but he could have taken tomorrow off, right? It's nearly a three-hour drive from here to there, and he's already made the trip once today. That's six hours of driving, not counting traffic." Her voice is hushed as she leans in across the table. "So why don't you tell me what's really going on."

"You know, it really sucks having an attorney for a brother and a flippin' claims investigator for a sister." I swat lightly at her hand, forcing myself to laugh and smile, both of which unexpectedly and immediately backfire as I feel my forehead crease, my eyes filling with tears. I pull my hand to my mouth as everything crumbles around me.

"Oh, Sylvia, it's so screwed up now," I whisper, crying at the same time. "There's so much going on. I don't even know where to start." I drop my forehead into my hands on the table. Sylvia comes around and sits down next to me, resting her hand on my back, soothing me.

This routine between us, perfected in childhood, never fails to make me feel safe. Before I know it, I'm telling her everything that's happened — the vandalism, the hotel room, staying with Ben at his house, the two text messages, Charlotte, and finally, Ben's voicemail. By the time I'm done, I've gone through half a box of Kleenex and Sylvia is crying too.

"This is awful, Gia. All of it!"

She gets up and checks the lock on the front door and closes the curtains.

"You know I have to tell Scott, right?" She blows her nose and wipes a stray tear from her cheek.

I nod at her and close my eyes. "I know. It's fine. I guess I'd feel better if he knew anyway. After all, this is your house." I look up at her standing next to me at the table and reach to touch her hand. "Just be sure and let him know the messages were aimed at Ben, not me, and that Bend Police are aware of everything. In all honesty, sis, I'm really not that frightened anymore. I'm more concerned about Ben." I consider this for a moment. "It's funny because in the beginning, I think I was more interested in him than he was in me. Then I think it shifted. He became really at ease with telling me his feelings — "

"—Which made you back off."

"Yes, it made me really back off. Like, I got scared or something. But, in all fairness, that was also about the time I first heard about this Charlotte person." I feel a scowl cross my face. "Just when I start admitting to myself I'm beginning to care for him, I find out he might have a sketchy past with some crazy woman. And then, when we do finally talk about it, he freaks out and shuts down. Finished. Finito." I blow my nose and shake my head, searching Sylvia's eyes. "I'm just so confused."

She rubs my shoulder empathetically. "Well, how do you feel about him now?"

I silently study my nails as I sit at the table.

"I'm really sad that he doesn't want to see me anymore. I feel guilty that I've been too much of a burden, and I feel responsible for making him feel like shit again over his past," I say, sniffing.

"But I also feel like maybe it is a good thing he doesn't want to see me anymore." I think for a moment. "Sylv, I was starting to get scared. Letting someone that far into my life ...well you know; it's just not something I do. I promised myself..." My voice grinds to a halt as I swallow back the emotional pain of my failed marriage.

"Shhh. I know. You don't need to say another word. Here, let's get you to bed. Tomorrow's a new day, and I'm sure you'll have a lot of phone calls to make. I know Ed has been asking about you. He's wondering if you can come back to work while you're on crutches!" She laughs at my boss's lack of manners, and I smile at her. I do so love my big sister.

And it is so good to be home.

CHAPTER FOUR

GEORGIA

T HE NEXT MORNING, ALL THREE of us are up
early. Scott leaves first, the bottom half of a toasted bagel
hanging out of his mouth as he shrugs his suit jacket on and
pushes his way out of the door. Sylvia's next, running over a small
list of to-do's with me, including instructions to call my auto
insurance agent right away.

"They might cover part of the towing costs from the butte to
Sisters, and maybe even from Sisters to home."

I stared at her blankly. I feel like the world's greatest fool.

"Really? I guess I should have thought of that, huh?"

"Well, I just thought of it now, and I *work* in insurance. I
think we've both had too much on our plates lately." She smiles
and purses her lips together. "So are you sure about these tasks,
it's not too much for you?" She doesn't wait for an answer as she
grabs her briefcase and sunglasses off the counter. "You know
what?" she continues. "Whatever you feel like doing, that will be
great. If you feel like doing absolutely nothing today, that's fine
too, sweetie." She gives me a quick hug as she turns toward the
door. "We'll talk tonight, ok? I'll be home after work to pick you

up. We'll check on Guthrie and then come home to talk. Sound okay?"

I smile at my sister and nod. "Yes, absolutely. It all sounds great. I'll have dinner ready when you guys get home." I slowly crutch behind her to the door. "Can't wait to see Guth!" I yell after her as she runs toward her Audi in the driveway. She waves her hand at me as she slides into the driver's seat, and a moment later, she's off.

The smile fades from my lips as I shut the door. Being alone with my thoughts is dangerous territory. I crutch over to the living room window and take a look outside. The day is just beginning, but already the sunshine is warm on my skin. It's going to be hot today.

After a shower and starting a load of laundry, I make my way to the kitchen and prep the salad for dinner. I slice up leftover chicken to put on top of the greens, throw a handful of almonds into a pan to roast, and grate some carrots. After halving a lime and squeezing the juice over the salad, I cover the bowl with plastic wrap and slide it into the fridge for later.

I clean up the breakfast dishes and toss the vegetable scraps, turning the dishwasher on as I grab my crutches and sit down at the kitchen table. My calendar is open next to the phone, and my cup is full of lukewarm coffee. I take a sip and dial the number of my family doctor, determined to heal myself and get back on track with my life.

Fifteen minutes later, I have an appointment with my doctor and a referral for four weeks of physical therapy, starting next week. As soon as I hang up, I dial the PT office and schedule my appointments. Never one for sitting around, the thought of doing nothing for the next five to six weeks is enough to make my palms sweaty.

Next, I call my auto insurance agent, and speak to his assistant, Vanessa, telling her everything that's happened to my

Jeep as well as relaying the case number from the Sisters' Police Department. I explain my injury and how the vehicle is still there. She puts me on hold for a moment to review my insurance policy, and when she's back, she has good news.

"Thanks for holding, Georgia. Your policy actually allows for towing reimbursement for up to ninety miles, so we can definitely cover the tow bill from Les Schwab. And we can get you an estimate for repair after we see the damage. I have a claims adjuster in Sisters that can go out and take photos tomorrow. Can you give me the exact location?"

Shit.

"Well...sort of. It's currently in a barn at a friend's house. And I don't know his exact address," I say, cringing. It sounds like I'm lying.

"You don't have the address?"

"Um, no. I can tell you how to get there but...you know what, hang on, I have his business card. I can give you his work telephone number, and you can make the arrangements. Would that be ok?" I cross my fingers.

"Of course. Go ahead when you're ready."

I give her the number, and she takes my statement about the damage to the Jeep.

"Okay. Now as I said, your policy allows us to reimburse you for towing up to ninety miles. From Black Butte to Sisters is about fifteen miles, and from Sisters to Silverton...hang on." I hear a drawer open. "Let's see, Sisters to Silverton is approximately one hundred and eight miles, so you would be responsible for about thirty-three miles of the cost. Would you like me to have a towing agency bring it back for you?"

I sit stunned in my seat for a moment.

"Ms. Marks?"

"Sorry. Yes, definitely, thank you. I'm sorry, I just wasn't expecting this issue to resolve so easily."

"Yep, it's covered. A lot of people don't realize what their plan actually entails, so I'm glad you called. And again, I'm so sorry this happened to you. I'll make the necessary phone calls, and let you know how everything turns out. Sound good?"

"Sounds great. Thanks again, Vanessa. I really appreciate all you have done for me."

I hang up feeling like a weight has been lifted from my shoulders...until I realize I won't have a reason to see Ben again in the coming weeks. I am simultaneously relieved and then saddened. I guess I was quietly holding on to the idea that our paths would cross again in the near future.

Needing to focus on something else, I pick up the phone once more and dial my work telephone number. Ed answers on the first ring.

"Good Morning, Red Barn Antiques, how may I help you today?" Ed sounds as though it's his utmost joy and privilege to answer the phone.

"Hi, Ed, it's Georgia. How — "

"Georgia! Oh my word, how are you feeling? I spoke to your sister. Was it yesterday? I think it was yesterday. I heard all the details about your ankle. How are you doing? Do you have crutches? Do you think you could come to work on crutches?"

I smile. At age 67, Ed talks faster than anyone I have ever met. He's a living run-on sentence; never slowing down enough for the listener to fully follow along. He can also be one of the crankiest people I know.

"I'm feeling okay, thanks for asking. I'm home now. I've lined up an appointment with my doctor, and I'm supposed to start physical therapy after that."

"Will your therapy appointments interfere with your work schedule? You know we're getting into tourist season now, and the store has already seen a lot of traffic these last four days. You know how people are: word gets out and then *bam*! We're swamped! I'm gonna need your help as soon as possible, Georgia, as soon as possible, but I don't want you to feel rushed," he says, taking a deep breath.

"Well," I begin, "I don't anticipate the appointments will conflict with work. I've scheduled them all on Wednesday afternoons. I think I can start back part-time for now, if that's ok? I could come in tomorrow and answer the phone and do the front counter work. I just can't be on my feet all day...I'll need to sit down a lot."

"Oh, that would be just absolutely fine, Georgia. Just absolutely fine. You can stay up front and take care of the phone and the cash register, and I'll be happy to do the rest. Say, I might have you place another order with that wooden sign company in Portland. Those sure sold quickly last week. We're all out! A group from Seattle came through and they just all fell in love with those Oregon-shaped signs. Not really antiques of course, but they sure look rustic and old. Rustic and old; I guess that's all we need and we can still call it *antique*." He chuckles at his own humor.

"Okay, well thanks for understanding, Ed. I'm looking forward to doing a little work tomorrow. I'll see you in the morning."

I'm pulling the phone away from my ear to hang up when I hear him, still talking away. I press the phone back to my ear and roll my eyes.

"—And it's just such an inconvenience to have a broken ankle. Why, I remember when I was younger I had a broken ankle. Or maybe it was a sprain. Did you ever know that I played football when I was high scho—oh, Georgia, I've got to go now. Customer here." I hear him issue a greeting in his usual friendly tone before the line goes dead. I raise my eyebrows and hang up my end of the line, shaking my head in disbelief.

I chose this job with Ed because it was exactly what I needed after leaving Mike: no pressure, so stress, no overbearing boss...it was a cushy job where I could basically make my own schedule — the perfect fit for someone that needed time and space to get back on her feet. The trouble though, is that after this weekend, and experiencing strong feelings for someone for the first time in a long time, I'm now feeling oddly like I'm ready to move on. It's as if I've been on temporary hold for the last several months, and now, finally, I feel ready to move forward again.

Surprisingly, even though what happened with Ben is apparently now over, I still feel like I've had a steroid injection into my emotional musculature. It feels very odd, but also very freeing, to experience feelings of love again. Even though my heart is bruised, and already I miss Ben tremendously, it's nice to know, deep down, that I seem to be crawling out of the cave I've lived in for the last several years.

Instead of ruminating on a love that I've managed to lose, I decide to get up, make my bed and clean up my bathroom. On my way there, I stop at the laundry room and start another load, removing the wet clothes from the washer and throwing them into the dryer. It turns out to be pretty difficult to balance on one foot while moving wet clothes around, and I nearly fall twice, grabbing the dryer door to catch myself.

I am so ready to be over this injury.

———

After my minimal chores, I'm ready to put my feet up, and I head toward the living room to sit down. Earlier in the day I had a chance to upload the photos from my camera, and with my computer now in my lap, and my feet on throw pillows, I'm excited to go through them and play with the editing.

Scrolling through the images, I am instantly flooded with memories of the pine trees on the butte, and their delicious vanilla scent. It's so easy to remember the cool morning air on the hike, the adrenalin surge when I first stepped out of the Jeep, the feeling of exhilaration as I reached the top — it all comes back so quickly. Too quickly.

The sunrise photographs take my breath away. They are even more stunning than I recall — the colors so vivid it's hard to believe they are even real. I click through the series and discard the few that are out of focus or have alignment problems. Then I select the twenty or so I have left, and open them up into a full-screen view, looking at the images one by one, checking every aspect for inconsistencies or visual blemishes. The light is incredible in these photos. The shocking pink sky, vibrant against the deep blue of the early morning light, the trees across the valley barely outlined, looking like thin ghosts drifting across the landscape. Across the valley the Three Sisters mountains perch in soft hues, their white peaks dusted in an alpine glow. My smile grows as I look at the pictures, and after several rounds of comparison, I finally select the best two, saving them to a separate file.

I move on to open the photos of the lookout tower, the cupola, and finally, Ben's cabin. A heaviness settles in my chest as I stare at the morning sun reflecting off the front window of the cabin. God, it seems like so long ago already. How can it have been only a few days ago that I was there? My eyes travel over the details in each of the pictures: the front porch planks, the bird's nest above the stool I rested on, a close up of the log walls...I can almost smell the fresh air and pine floating in the breeze. I remember lounging on the stool, feeling the warm sun on my face as I closed my eyes, relaxing. I felt so confident, so proud of myself for hiking the two miles alone, in the dark, and then reaching the top to capture these gorgeous photographs.

I click back to the photo I took from the top of the butte, looking down the small hill toward Ben's cabin, focusing on the stool. This is the angle the bear would have had, coming down toward me. I look over the entire picture, my eyes traveling over each detail. The outhouse, the woodpile, the axe sticking out of the stump — I take it all in. I glance to the left side of the cabin, knowing that on the other side of that log wall is the bed I lay in for almost sixteen hours, and I remember Ben's kindness toward me. He took such great care of me, bringing me water, cooking for me, making sure I was as comfortable as possible. On top of it all, he was a true gentleman; he never tried anything or even hinted at a romantic interest. I shake my head as I stare at the photo, the heaviness sinking down deeper. It feels like a hole is slowly opening in my heart as I realize how much I miss him. I close my eyes for a moment. Maybe this wasn't the best idea — looking through these pictures.

I move the mouse arrow up to close the window when my eye catches something in the background near the cabin wall. Leaning my face forward toward the computer screen, I squint my eyes. What is *that*? Something light brown is sticking out of the small, moss green bushes that extend along the side of the cabin. It occurs to me that had the sun not been angled in that precise way, I would never have noticed anything.

I place my fingers on the computer touchpad and inch them apart, the screen automatically zooming in on the photograph. I move the picture, as a whole, to the right and increase the zoom again, bringing the focal area to the center of my screen. And then I see it.

"Oh my God!"

I sit back hard against my headboard — my hand over my mouth in shock.

There, in the photograph, peeking out from the tops of the bushes, sits the very distinct face of a young bear.

Holy crap, I was right *there*!

Ben was right: the bear was a female with a cub. No wonder she had attacked. No wonder she was so relentless. It all made sense now. The mother must have been on the other side of the butte when I was making my way down to the cabin. It was just pure, stupid luck that I hung out to eat and fall asleep, just as mama was coming down after her cub.

I smile and cross my arms in front of my chest, hugging myself gently. I feel somehow relieved knowing there is a *reason* the bear pursued me. The fact that I hadn't done something ridiculous to cause the encounter is of enormous relief to me. My feelings of inadequacy and shame — driven into my psyche by Mike — are suddenly squashed dead in their tracks.

I have to tell someone.

Reaching across my bed, I snag the telephone extension. Ben is going to die when he hears this, and I am beyond giddy thinking about his reaction. I press *talk* and listen for the dial tone. My thumb pauses over the keypad as I realize with dismay that, not only do I not know what number to reach him at, but more importantly, even if I did, he doesn't want to hear from me anyway.

My shoulders drop, and I press *end*, setting the phone down on my comforter and leaning my head back against the headboard, closing my eyes.

Why does this have to be so hard?

He is more than just a random romantic hookup, I quietly realize. He is my friend. He's the first person I thought of to share this exciting news with, and I desperately want to hear his voice. No matter how many paths I travel in my mind, I can't rationalize a reason to reach him. He made his position perfectly clear, and I don't want to bother him or embarrass myself.

———

Sylvia and Scott come home in time for a quick dinner, and afterward, we all pile into Scott's Durango and head to see Guthrie.

On the way to the hospital, I tell them the story about the photograph and the visitor I found. They are beyond stunned that I accidentally captured proof of why the bear attacked me, and we laugh lightly about the odds versus my luck. Sylvia and I chat like teenagers about the bear sighting and all that occurred afterward, while Scott drives us along the traffic-congested streets in silence.

We finally pull into the parking lot of the hospital and park the truck. Scott turns off the ignition and twists his body around to face me in the back seat.

"I've been thinking," he says, glancing over at Sylvia. After an awkward silence, she widens her eyes and raises her eyebrows, making rapid *move it along* circular motions with her hands.

"All right, all right, I'll get on with it," he says, smiling at Sylvia before turning back to me. "I've been thinking that you should submit that photo, and maybe some of your other ones, to the newspapers in Sisters and Bend. You might have a story of real interest to the locals there. No," he says, reacting to the look on my face, "I'm serious. You've not only got the story, but you've got the perfect pictures to go with it. And, think of it this way: you'd be doing the locals a favor by letting them know about the bears on the butte." He turns back around, pushes his door open and hops out. Sylvia looks at me and winks.

"Something to think about," she says.

———

We arrive home from the hospital with Guthrie in tow. Scott carries him into the house while Sylvia helps me crutch in behind them. It's late — around 8:00 p.m. — and we are all tired, but also a little wired by the unexpected news at the hospital that Guthrie would be coming home with us tonight.

And poor Guthrie is a mess. He's on heavy pain medication and unable to walk. His left leg is in a cast and his right in a splint. He looks as though he's gotten into a violent fight. His fur is shaved off in large circles across the back of his left hip and belly, and in two rectangular strips on each forearm. He's come home with several bottles of medication to be given each day, and strict instructions that he's not to be left alone for more than just a few hours — and placed in his crate right away if he refuses to lie still.

Scott brings him into the living room and lays him on the couch while Sylvia makes up a spot for him near the fireplace, layering a few plush blankets over the top of his large, square bed. Even though it's warmer weather now and we don't use the fireplace, it still feels like a cozy place for him. I sit on the couch next to Guth while Scott brings his crate in from the garage and sets it on the other side of the hearth. The poor guy just lies on the couch, eyes glazed over. I pet his head and run my hand down the side of his face watching his eyes gently close. He's always loved when I scratch under his chin, and I try lightly pressing my fingers into the white fur there. He responds with the smallest lick of his tongue, the sweet gesture nearly breaks my heart, and I bend over him and kiss the top of his head.

After further consideration and the realization that their bedroom patio is closer to the backyard, Scott and Sylvia decide to move Guthrie into their room for the night. We also decide, since I obviously can't lift Guthrie to take him outside, Sylvia will come home at lunch to check on him, and Scott will leave work early to be home no later than 5 p.m. We further strategize that in the morning, Sylvia will give me a ride to work and pick me up on her way home at lunch. It's our battle plan for the time being, anyway.

We say goodnight, and as I lay in my bed, emotion overwhelms me. What if I can't make my therapy appointments? What if my ankle doesn't heal correctly? How long will I be unable to work full time? The weight of it all is heavy on me, and once again I find myself wishing my parents were here. It's been a long time since I've cried over losing them, but for some reason, the memories feel fresh tonight. Their deaths happened so long ago, fifteen years now, and most of the time I honestly just block out the tragedy of it all. But on a night like tonight, and after the last four days, well, I just feel completely alone, and I really miss my mom. My heart is broken, and I just want to curl up in her arms and listen to her tell me that everything will be okay. I lie there with my hands folded over my chest — trying to keep the hole inside from growing any larger.

CHAPTER FIVE

GEORGIA

THE BELL CHIMES ABOVE ME as I unlock and push open the large, glass-paned door. The *Closed* sign tilts sideways as the door swings wide, and it takes me a moment to maneuver inside. Once I'm in, I turn around and flip the sign to *Open*, push the door shut behind me, and switch on the overhead lights.

It's good to be back in the antiques store. The smell of old wood and furniture polish lingers in the air as I make my way across the creaky, wide wooden floorboards, to the break room in the back. I hang my lightweight jacket on a hook and set my purse inside the desk drawer alongside Ed's ever-present box of Altoids. Turning to the small counter across the back wall, I pull the coffee pot toward me and fill the carafe with water. Even though I've had coffee at home this morning, it's always nice to begin my day at the store with a fresh cup.

Once the pot is happily gurgling away, I turn my crutches and head to the large desk at the center of the store. As I make my way around the side of it, the bell above the door chimes again and Ed walks in — his black cane tapping on the wood floor as he lumbers toward me. He removes his fedora and holds it, and his cane, in one of his outstretched hands as he motions for an embrace.

"My Georgia! Oh my goodness," he says, crushing me with his large, heavy arms. "It is *so* good to see you again! I've missed you tremendously! How are you feeling today?" He steps back and holds me at bay, looking down at my ankle. Even though it's a gorgeous, warm morning, he's still wearing a thick overcoat.

"Thanks, Ed, I've missed you too," I say, smiling back at him. "I'm doing well. Better every day. I see an orthopedic surgeon next week for a follow-up, and depending on how that goes, I'm supposed to begin physical therapy. These things though," I pull my crutches out from my armpits, "these are the worst!"

"I'm so glad you're back to help. We've been so busy and, well, I've done my best to enter everything correctly, but you know how difficult it is for me to operate that thing." His eyes narrow as he points a thick finger at the computer screen behind me. "Could you please check to make sure I've done everything right? I sincerely detest that piece of machinery." He turns and walks off, yelling over his shoulder as he heads toward the break room, "Coffee ready?"

———

Ed has made a genuine mess of the cash receipts while I was away, and it takes me all morning to sort and correct the transactions in the accounting program. Time flies by and after what seems like only an hour, Sylvia calls.

"I'm double parked out front, can you come out? I don't want to get a parking ticket."

I say goodbye to Ed and give him strict instructions not to foul up any more transactions while I'm away. I kiss him on the cheek as I leave, promising to return in the morning.

34

He's grouchy and not very sensitive to others sometimes, but I still like him. His demeanor is somewhat fatherly, and even though we've never had anything resembling any kind of familial relationship, I still have a soft spot in my heart for him.

———

As soon as we get home, Sylvia carries Guthrie outside to go the bathroom. Between the both of us, we coax him to eat a few bites and have some water before he falls back to sleep on his bed, exhausted from the simple activities.

"Hey, do you think this weekend we could make a quick trip to Salem? I need a new cell phone," I say. Sylvia is packing up her things to go back to work, and she answers without looking up from her bag.

"Definitely. Scott will be gone all weekend so it'll just be us anyway." She pulls out her keys, looks up and tucks a strand of hair behind her ear. "Okay, see you soon. Call me if Guth needs anything before Scott can get here." I nod, and she blows me a kiss as she closes the door. I stretch out on the couch and put my ankle up on a pillow. I hear Guthrie snoring quietly on his bed below, and when I lay my head back on the throw pillow, I'm overwhelmed by just how tired I am.

———

A rattling sound at the door draws me out of my light nap, and I quickly sit up and turn toward the noise. The lock flips, and a moment later Scott shoulders his way inside, briefcase in one hand. His folded coat and tie hang over his forearm, and several thick books balance in the other. The stem of his sunglasses hangs from his mouth. He looks over at my forehead and eyes peeking out over the sofa and tips his chin at me.

"Ehllo."

"Hey. Sorry about not unlocking that for you. I must have dozed off." I sit up slowly and push myself back against the arm of the couch. My head is splitting, and it feels like I've got knives in my eyes.

"How's Guthrie?" Scott calls from the kitchen.

"He's good I think. Slept most of the afternoon," I say.

I hear him set his briefcase on the table and open the creaky cabinet door, which can only mean one thing.

"I'll pay you good money to make me one too, big brother," I holler.

He chuckles in reply, and I hear the cabinet squeak open again.

A moment later Scott walks into the living room, ice clinking and popping in the two tumblers he's carrying.

"Here you are, luv," he says in a thick British accent, handing me the glass and sitting down in the armchair next to me.

"You will forever be my most revered and distinguished hero," I reply.

"Cheers!" We say in unison and clink glasses, each taking a long, satisfying drink of the gin and tonic.

Scott lifts a finger from his glass and points toward Guthrie, still sleeping on his bed at my feet, his white cast jutting out from his body.

"Has he really been okay today?"

"Mm hm. Like I said, he's pretty much just done a whole lot of this," I say, motioning with my glass in a wide horizon over Guthrie. "But Sylvia and I were able to get him to eat a little, and drink more water, and she did get him to go to the bathroom."

"That's good. The vet said it might take him awhile to get

back to normal. The pain medication takes away his appetite and knocks him out, too. Poor fella."

Scott purses his lips together and lowers his head slightly.

I stare at him for a moment.

"Scott, there was nothing that could have been done to prevent this from happening. You know that, right?"

He stares down at his drink, swirling the glass slightly.

"Yeah...it's just, I don't know that I'll ever forget the sound of the brakes, and seeing the impact. It was the most horrible thing I've ever witnessed. And then the crying and whimpering..." He takes a moment. "I just feel like I should've been paying more attention to where we were in relation to the road. How much traffic there was— "

" —These things, they happen all the time, Scott. Even to the best-trained dogs with the most responsible owners. It's life, you know? Shit happens. But it's not your fault. Let's just try and be positive and grateful that Guth is here, that he made it through surgery, and from the sound of it, will be back to normal in no time. Kinda like me!" I laugh, but the smile fades from my face almost instantly.

Who am I kidding? It's going to take me forever to get out of this brace, and I didn't even need surgery.

"Hey, speaking of you. How are you feeling today? Did you go back to work this morning?"

"Yeah, I'm doing okay, just really tired. Ed screwed up the books again." I smile at him and sip my cocktail. The fizz of the carbonation makes my nose tickle as I raise the glass to take another sip. The smell of the gin and the lime juice is heaven, and I nearly close my eyes to breathe it in — it reminds me vaguely of the scent of Ben's skin. I could get lost in the memory of how he smells, and I begin to envision the hollow at the center of his collarbones.

"So, have you given any thought to publishing that bear photo?" Scott's question tears me away from my daydream.

"Uh...yes. Yes, I have, and I think you're right. I'm going to look into it. Maybe tomorrow, after my doctor appointment. Oh, that reminds me, would it be totally against your firm's policy if I hired one of your law clerks for a few hours each week? I need a driver to take me to the doctor tomorrow, and physical therapy appointments later." I bat my eyelashes at him, and we both laugh.

"Actually, I was thinking we could all use *someone that can walk* to come and check on Guthrie twice a day." He kicks my good foot with his own as my mouth drops open in mock offense.

"Well you're right; we could totally use some help around here. Do you think it would be okay with the firm?"

"Absolutely. I'll run it by the other partners to be sure, but shoot, we use those clerks for every mundane task imaginable. Last week we had one doing yard work around the office building, and then," he chuckles, "then we had him clean the bathroom. Damn. I hated being a clerk." He smirks and then lifts his glass to mine. "Cheers to killing two birds with one law clerk."

"Cheers!"

We're in the middle of our celebratory toast when Sylvia comes through the door. She glances over at the two of us — now obviously feeling very relaxed — and drops her briefcase to the ground.

"All right, damn it to hell, where's mine?"

We all laugh as she navigates the living room furniture, and flops down next to me on the couch, her gray pencil skirt inching up as she sits. Scott stands and leans over to plant a long kiss on Sylvia's lips as her body slowly reclines.

"Ugh. Get a room you two." I bury my face in my drink and remind myself to check listings for apartments as soon as I can.

Scott pulls himself off Sylvia's now-liquid body and makes his way to the kitchen. I glance at my sister. She looks back at me, wide-eyed.

"Wonder where that came from?"

"He loves you. That's where." I smile at her and sip my cocktail. Condensation is building on the outside of the glass, and a few droplets of water slide off and fall to my lap.

"How's our boy doing?" Sylvia asks, getting up to sit next to Guthrie on the floor. As she pets his fur, he opens his bloodshot eyes and rolls his head toward her hand, his tongue peeking out for a quick lick of her fingers. She gives him a few more pets, and he slowly lowers his head back down and closes his eyes again.

"He's doing okay. I think he could probably go outside again? Maybe you can convince him to eat a little more?"

Scott hands Sylvia her cocktail and moves toward Guthrie.

"I was just going to take him out," he says, motioning for Sylvia to stay put.

"Okay, thank you. Mmm, I needed this," she says, taking a sip of her drink. A moment later she leans forward and sets her glass on the coffee table. "Okay, I'm up. Let's get Guthrie taken care of and then we can figure out something for dinner. Leftovers?" She glances at the two of us. Scott and I look at each other and screw up our faces.

"Thai takeout!" we both exclaim in unison.

"Good call. Gia, I'll bring you the phone. Call in the usual?"

"On it."

This is one number I know by heart.

———

"Oh my God, this is so good," I say as I scarf down noodles with coconut sauce. Sylvia and Scott both nod, as twisting ends of noodles disappear into their puckered mouths. We are sitting at the kitchen table eating straight out of the takeout cartons, our chopsticks hovering and diving past the short triangular flaps.

Over dinner, we talk about the plan for the next several weeks. A law clerk will drive me to my doctor and physical therapy appointments, and, we decide, will pick me up from work on his way to the house. He will also take care of Guthrie until he can bear weight on his legs again.

"Good news," I begin. "My insurance agent is having the Jeep photographed and making arrangements to have it towed back here."

"Yay! That *is* good news sis!"

"I thought so too. And, you'll be happy to know I plan to contact the Sisters and Bend newspapers and send in my photographs." I stir the noodles in my box contemplating whether I should say the next part. "And, I've given it some more thought, and I think I will contact Lieutenant Dickerson again and follow up on that second text message."

"Good, Georgia. That's a smart decision," Scott says.

"In my own time, though," I interject. I don't want to get everyone riled up over something that's probably nothing.

"Of course," Scott replies. "It does sound like the person sending the texts was really just trying to get Ben to back off."

An awkward silence falls as everyone realizes that is exactly what has happened.

"Well," I say, breaking the silence, "whatever the reason, I'll talk to the Lieutenant and just let him know. Now," I say, raising my empty tumbler, "another round?"

"Uh, do you even need to ask?" Sylvia and I pass our glasses to Scott as he rises.

"One more," I say to Scott. "And then I'm going to bed. I'm actually tired again."

Although I truly am tired, I really just want to give them their space. We've been living together now for a full year, and although they've never made me feel uncomfortable, I am always careful to give them plenty of alone time. I'm good at going to movies and taking myself out to dinner or hiking early on weekend mornings.

At least I was, anyway.

Scott brings us our drinks and clears away the empty cartons of food, throwing them in the trashcan and rinsing his hands under the faucet.

"Dishes are done," he says, laughing.

He sits down at the table again as we sip our new drinks. Mine seems stronger this time.

"So, Georgia..." Scott begins, looking at me and then at Sylvia. "Do you wanna talk about what happened with Ben?"

I look at them, one and then the other; they aren't being malicious. They're my siblings, and they care for me.

"Uh, sure. I guess so. There's not really much to talk about though."

"Except that you slept with him. Numerous times I might add." Sylvia stares at me coyly over her glass. I look at Scott. His mouth hangs open in mock surprise. Suddenly we all start laughing. If I can't be open with these people, my only family, then who *can* I talk to?

"Yeah, I guess that's true." I blush and then lower my eyes a bit. It hurts to think about him. "The thing is, I know it happened so fast between us, but it just seemed really right. I mean; he truly is a good person. Probably the most caring, decent man I've ever met, actually." I pause, searching for the right words. "But he's not perfect. He has a past, and it's painful. And I don't even know the whole story. I think he's afraid of opening his heart too much. No one wants to sign up to be kicked in the chest. Lord knows I should understand that..." my voice trails off as I raise my glass and take a long sip.

"You are very deserving of love, Georgia. Don't ever doubt

41

that fact." Scott reaches over and puts his hand on mine. "Perhaps with some time, Ben might come to realize that facing his pain, with the help of someone that cares by his side, is indeed possible, and not only that, it's the only way to put it behind him." He looks at Sylvia who nods in agreement. "I wouldn't give up on him just yet," he finishes.

"Yeah well, he made it pretty clear he didn't want to continue with whatever this is. Correction — whatever this *was*."

"Give him some time, sis. Things might change. You never know."

I look up at Sylvia — her hopeful eyes shine brightly at me.

"Remember when I told you to get away from Mike? Remember?" I nod at her, my jaw automatically clenching. "I didn't tell you to give it time, did I? I knew. I knew the moment you told me what happened that he was bad news. Well, this is different. My gut is telling me something completely opposite with Ben." She starts laughing. "And I haven't even met him yet!"

I look at them both: silly and soppy in love with each other, and I can't help but feel cynical. What if I really do love Ben? The thought scares me to death. Here I am proposing that *he* is the one that doesn't want to face the pain of his past, but the truth is, neither do I. My past is filled with hurt and fear and anger; the last thing I want is to go back there. *Besides*, I mentally pat myself on the back, *I've already been through therapy. Everything is sorted out.*

I push my half-empty glass to the center of the table and scoot my chair back.

"All right, you two lovebirds, I'm off to bed. Don't stay up too late now. We've all got school in the morning." We smirk at each other and after quick hugs, I crutch off to the privacy of my room.

Pulling on a pair of cotton shorts and a soft tank, I crawl into bed and turn on my computer. My head is a little dizzy from the alcohol, and I feel just the right amount of creativity in my system. I pull up the website for the Sisters' newspaper and click around until I locate the name of the editor and an email address. Typing quickly, I prepare a short letter about myself, and my experience on the butte with the bear. I include a brief explanation of how Ben stopped the situation from worsening, and then took care of my injured ankle. I finish by attaching a few photos of the cabin, the sunrise, and finally, the picture with the bear cub in the background. All of this goes into an email to the editor, and after a quick proofread I take a deep breath and hit *send*, repeating the process with the Bend Bulletin as well.

Feeling very constructive, I set my alarm, shut my laptop, and snuggle down into my warm bed, burying my face into the pillow that haunts me with the lingering scent of Ben.

CHAPTER SIX

GEORGIA

H E HOLDS OUT HIS HAND toward me, a broad smile across his face.

"Hello there. Calvin Dorsett. Pleased to meet you in person."

I reach over the long wooden counter at work and shake his hand. His appearance doesn't match the law clerk image I had in my mind from our brief telephone conversation a week ago. In fact, he reminds me of a J Crew model from the late '80's: young, cropped blonde hair that's slightly messy, tanned skin, and a mouthful of perfect teeth that probably cost his parents a small fortune. I look him over; he's wearing slightly tapered khaki pants and a patterned, button-down linen shirt. He is east coast seaside come to life.

"Hello, Calvin. It's nice to finally meet you as well. Thanks again for giving me Scott's phone number. See." I wink at him. "I told you I was family."

We drop hands, and I crutch around the side of the counter. "Let me just grab my things, and we'll be off." I point to the back of the store and turn to head in that direction.

I grab my bag and shove my book inside, crossing the leather strap over my body and heading back toward the front of the store. The crutches don't even bother me any longer; in fact, I'm becoming pretty quick with them.

"Ok, all set."

I tilt my chin up and search for Ed in the store, spotting his head near the armoire of books in the corner.

"I'm off to my doctor now, Ed."

He raises a hand in the air and tips his fingers at me, clearly busy with something more important.

Calvin steps outside and holds the door open for me. The day is warm, and the sunshine instantly heats my skin. A light breeze floats by and ruffles the sleeveless silk blouse I'm wearing. I crutch a few steps onto the sidewalk and halt, looking at Calvin to follow his lead to the car. He hasn't moved from the door. In fact, he's still holding it open, staring at me with a blank expression. Neither of us says a word.

Finally, I raise my eyebrows at him. "Um, which way are you parked?"

As if snapping out of a daze, his expression changes to complete surprise.

"Oh! Right, I'm uh, down this way and around the corner." He gestures over his shoulder. "Is that too far? Should I bring the car around?"

"No, not at all," I say. *What's up with him?* "Lead the way." I move to follow him, and we start off down the sidewalk in silence. The street traffic noise around us provides somewhat of a conversation buffer, for which I'm glad. Small talk always makes me feel uncomfortable.

We turn the corner and Calvin jogs ahead of me to a silver car parked alongside the curb. I sigh as I continue toward it. Cars are so much harder to navigate with crutches. Oh well. I'm grateful for the chauffeur.

Calvin opens his door and hops in. He's nearly closed the

door when he realizes I still need to put my crutches away. I smirk as he jumps back out and pulls the rear passenger door open, leaning in to grab the ends of my crutches as I angle them into the back seat. I've become pretty proficient at balancing on one foot, so it's not very hard to negotiate this task; although I can feel the breeze on my chest as I stand there, bent over. I have a feeling I'm probably showing cleavage, and I glance over at Calvin across the seat. Yep. He's staring at my chest. Jesus. Is he fourteen? I roll my eyes and clear my throat, and his eyes snap to mine. I purse my lips at him and raise my eyebrows.

"Shall we get going?"

"Yes! Yep, no problem!" he stammers, closing the door behind him. I help myself into the front passenger seat, give him directions to the doctor's office, and we're off.

After a few blocks of total silence, I can't handle it any longer. "So...do you live in Silverton?"

"Nah," he says, too loudly. "I live in Salem now, but I grew up here, and my parents still live here."

"How long have you been clerking for the firm?"

"I've been with this firm since the end of January. Before that, I was with an office in Salem for the fall semester. But I'm hoping this will carry me through the summer." He turns the car toward the outskirts of town and glances down at my ankle. "So, how'd you hurt yourself? Broken ankle, right?"

"Yeah. It's a long story," I sigh. "Basically, I fell through a porch, and my ankle landed sideways on a huge rock underneath." Calvin grimaces. "It didn't require surgery though, so that's a good thing."

"So now you get to be on crutches for a while?"

"I guess so. This will be the first time I've seen a doctor here about it, but the doctor in Bend said it would probably be about six weeks of recovery time, depending on how quickly I heal." I glance over at him. "So don't think you're getting off easy driving me to this appointment. You'll be my taxi for probably the next month."

Calvin smiles at me. "That sounds fine to me, Ms. Marks."

I nearly choke.

"Calvin, if you ever call me 'Ms. Marks' again, I will eviscerate you. I am not an 80-year-old, feeble woman. I could kick your ass right now, even with this broken ankle." My index finger is needling toward his face. We both stare at each other for a moment, straight-faced, until I break into a smile, and he visibly relaxes.

"I solemnly swear never to make that mistake again, Georgia." He grins at me — a little too long, actually — and as I turn my head away, I can't help but wonder if he's flirting.

———

We pull into the clinic parking lot, and Calvin drops me off at the front entrance, helping me get situated with my crutches. Since we aren't far from home, I hand him my house key and ask him to go and check on Guthrie.

"Do you want to text me when you're finished here?" he asks.

"No, I actually don't have a cell phone right now. Can you just come back in about an hour?"

He nods as I swing the strap of my bag across my body and turn toward the entrance.

"See you then, Georgia."

———

After another round of x-rays and an examination, the doctor surprisingly declares I am able to begin a very light regimen of physical therapy on Monday. He verbalizes and simultaneously records *marked reduction in swelling in the affected area* in my chart and decides to remove the splint I'm wearing, fitting me instead with a rigid walking boot. I'm still instructed to keep using the crutches, with the understanding I can begin *very* light, weight bearing. His nurse schedules a follow-up appointment with the doctor in two weeks.

After checking out, I turn from the front desk and glance at my watch. It's just after 1 p.m., so Calvin should be here any minute. I head toward the sliding doors and peer through the glass just as Calvin's silver sedan pulls into the parking lot. Even though the entryway is covered by a long overhang that provides shade from the sunshine that is now out in full force, I dig for my sunglasses inside my bag and push them onto my face. The memory of Ben buying them for me hits me like a sucker punch. How can it seem so long ago already?

I wonder if he's in the cabin right now, or maybe in the fire lookout.

I wonder if he's chopping wood again, swinging that axe up and over his chiseled body.

I wonder if he has a shirt on. *Damn it, Georgia, knock it off!*

———

Movement catches my eye, and I look up to see Calvin jogging toward me. He stops a few feet before me and whistles long and low, staring at my new boot.

"Dah, she's a right bonnie," he says in a mangled Scottish accent. I'm reminded of Scotty from Star Trek, except Scotty was incredibly cool. Calvin is just making me think about alcohol.

I smile politely and start off again toward his car, walking very awkwardly in my new boot. It feels as though I have a robotic leg that's not working correctly. I'm sure it looks that way too, and I secretly dare Calvin to say something.

49

Thankfully, he doesn't.

———

"How's Guthrie doing?" I ask as we drive toward home.

"He's good," Calvin replies. "Scott said he would probably be out of it, so I wasn't surprised at his lethargy. I carried him outside, gave him his pills, and even got him to eat about four big bites of food."

"Really? That's terrific. Sylvia and Scott will be so happy to hear this!" I unconsciously reach over and touch his shoulder, emphasizing my point. I immediately realize my error as Calvin looks surprised, and then relaxes into what I can only define as *flattered boy face*. I remove my hand and try to make light of it.

"Thanks for taking care of him. We all really appreciate it."

"Absolutely, Georgia," he says, his voice suddenly low and deep.

Ugh.

We're nearly home when an idea occurs to me.

"Don't take this the wrong way, Calvin, but do you have plans right now?" I know I'm treading on dangerous ground.

He looks at me, a hint of skepticism and excitement in his eyes.

"No, no," I say, holding up my hands. "I'm not asking you on a date." His smile fades slightly, and I can't help but laugh. "No, what I mean is, I really need to get a new cell phone, and I don't want to bother Sylvia to take me into Salem."

"You need a ride? Sure, no problem. I'm all yours." He smiles at me, suddenly looking about seventeen years old, which makes me feel ancient.

"Great, thank you. I just need to go inside," I say, motioning to my house up ahead, "for a moment and then I'll be set. Hey, while I'm in there will you call Scott and let him know the plan?"

Calvin gives me a military salute as the car comes to rest in the driveway. I roll my eyes at him as I open my door and gingerly place the heel of my boot on the ground, holding my breath. No pain. I place more weight on the boot, gradually flattening out my foot. A tug of pain radiates around my ankle, but it's nothing that takes my breath away. I lift the weight off my foot and reach back around my seat for a single crutch. I'm able to stand up and balance on one foot — well, the very edge of my heel is on the ground — and I use my single crutch to make it to the door, only to remember I'd given my key to Calvin. I turn back toward him and mime turning a key in the doorknob. He's on the phone already but hops out at once. As he approaches, I hear him telling Scott our plan to head to Salem.

I grab two apples from the kitchen, take out some chicken from the freezer, and check on Guthrie. He's awake but clearly drowsy in his crate, his head resting on his paws. His eyes look better than they did the day before, which makes me feel good.

"I'm going to Salem, buddy. Be back really soon, okay?" I say, stroking his nose with my finger. He blinks once and stares at me without expression as I close the door behind me.

———

We eat our apples on the drive to Salem, and Calvin tells me all about his first year in law school. He's attending Willamette University on an academic scholarship and has wanted to be an attorney ever since he took a debate class in high school, winning first place in a classroom competition. He tells me his parents were not surprised in the least.

"I've always been an arguer."

I take a bite of my apple and look at him while I chew, my eyes widening at his statement.

"Really?" I ask, incredulous. He reminds me of a Labrador

51

retriever: Always wanting to please and be petted. The idea of him arguing all the time seems ridiculous.

"Yep. Once I set my mind to something, I never let go. I'm like a Pitbull when it comes to winning an argument."

"How does that work in relationships though? Gotta compromise, right?"

He grins at me as he pulls a hand from the steering wheel and places it behind my seat. "I wouldn't know. I'm completely unattached at the moment." His voice is ridiculously low as he pauses and then touches my shoulder with his index finger, "Georgia."

I flinch in disgust, and then immediately choke on a piece of apple, which results in a violent coughing fit. The chunk of fruit flies out of my mouth and lands on the dashboard in front of me. Calvin physically recoils in horror, his suave demeanor changing to utter repulsion. I can't stop laughing and coughing, and I'm simultaneously trying to cover my mouth and wipe the apple off his car.

This kid is absurd.

"Calvin..." I swallow, still trying to regain my voice. "Calvin, I wasn't asking you because I am interested in you. I'm thirty-three years old. I'm old enough to be your mother!" I cough again. This conversation is forming a horrible taste in my mouth. "I was asking purely to get to know you."

"Hey, don't want to rule out any options. You might change your mind." He winks at me, and I turn my attention back to my half-eaten apple, deciding I've had enough — of both of them. I lower the window and throw my apple core into a field as we pass by. Calvin gasps like a teenage girl.

"What?" I say. "It's totally biodegradable, and we are surrounded by farms out here."

"Isn't there a fine for throwing something out of a moving vehicle?"

"Oh, for Christ's sake, Calvin, live a little. It's not like I threw out a lit cigarette. It's an apple. An *organic* one at that. Think of all the animals it will feed."

"True," he concedes, quietly. "I'm gonna look it up in the law library though just to be sure."

"I'd be disappointed if you didn't, Calvin."

CHAPTER SEVEN

MIKE

SHE MUST HAVE TAKEN OUT an ad on the Interstate that says, *I'm single, come and get it* because I cannot believe my goddamn eyes when I see yet another guy walking next to my beautiful wife.

I finally get Benny boy to take a hike — I seriously cannot wait to deal with that asshole later — and now, now I've got this idiot strolling into Georgia's work, and walking out with her like he's taking her on a date.

Oh, wait just a goddamn minute. This guy is eyeballin' her! He's not just walking next to her — he's checking her out. Who is this guy anyway? He looks like he's about fourteen. And what the hell is he wearing? I would have pegged him to swing the other way based on that ridiculous outfit alone, but here he is, opening a car door for her. Hey, you ain't no man, buddy! You're just a tall teenag—Holy fuck, he's staring at her tits!

I rip my seatbelt off and am halfway out of my car before I realize it's midday in this backass town. I could be seen. I duck back inside the car and grip and twist the steering wheel till my forearms burn. She could still recognize me here, even in this undercover car. I slink down in my seat and pull Bob's baseball cap down lower, shading my eyes. It was good of him to loan me this car. So much easier to blend in than that huge Ford of his. Sure, he pulled a few strings at work but we're all cops, right? Besides, I'm sure no one in Bend will miss it.

And I'll have it back soon.

Just as soon as I get this new bastard out of the way.

CHAPTER EIGHT

GEORGIA

T HERE IS NOTHING DULLER than buying a new cell phone and waiting around the store while it's set up. Watching the sales associate stare at a computer screen for twenty minutes, and then press various buttons on my new phone feels a bit like I'm undergoing a background check; as if I'm trying to buy a handgun, or apply for a passport, instead of simply buying a device that makes telephone calls and accesses the internet. Idle time makes me anxious. I hate not having something to do. Unless, of course, it's the end of a very productive day, in which case I love nothing more than curling up in my yoga clothes and relaxing.

Calvin apparently has no issues with idle time. He's sitting on a navy blue, hard plastic chair positioned by the door, cell phone in hand, his head in text message position: tilted slightly from the top, neck extended, eyes gazing downward. One leg is crossed over the other, and I notice he's wearing penny loafers. I roll my eyes. He probably has real pennies in them.

After what seems like a small eternity, the salesman looks up from his computer, finds me across the room and smiles, holding my phone up in front of him. *Finally.*

We leave the store and much to Calvin's chagrin, I ask him to head straight for home.

"What, no stop for happy hour?" he says, his eyes dancing with excitement.

I laugh and look over at him, quickly realizing he's serious.

"Oh. No, no happy hour, Calvin." I consider him for a moment. "Are you even legal?"

His mouth drops open as he pulls onto the main road, checking traffic on his left.

"Geez, I'm not a fetus. Of course I'm old enough! Can't you tell?" I swear he sticks his lower lip out. "If you must know, I'm almost twenty-three."

"My mistake," I say, holding back my laughter. "It was really just a joke, but if I offended you, I apologize. I'm a terrible judge of age."

"Apology accepted," he says, sitting up taller in his seat as we head toward Silverton in relative silence.

———

"Would you like to come in for a bite, or a glass of wine?" I offer as we pull into the driveway. Sylvia's Audi sits parked in front of us, or I never would have made the proposition.

"Normally I would say yes, but I actually have a few things to take care of back at the office," he says.

What is he, suddenly a grown man with a mortgage?

"Ok, well, maybe next time then." He perks up noticeably, so I quickly add, "When *Sylvia and Scott* are here, too." His face falls a little. "Bye, Cal. Thanks again for taking me."

"My pleasure. You have my number, right?" I start to tell him that I do, but he reaches into his wallet for a business card anyway and hands it over to me.

I reach for the handle and push my way out of the car. I can tell he's waiting for me to get to the front door before he leaves, and as I reach it, I make sure *not* to turn around and wave at him. As soon as I'm through the door, I hear him reverse out of the driveway. Closing it behind me, I lean back and sigh. The last thing I want to do is lead this poor kid on.

"Sis? Is that you?" Sylvia's voice echoes from the opposite end of the house.

"Yeah, it's me."

I make my way into the kitchen and plop myself down at the island, setting my purse on the seat next to me. Sylvia has started dinner, and it smells heavenly. I lie my head down on my outstretched arm and yawn.

"Scott's not with you?" Sylvia's hand passes across the back of my shoulders as she comes around the island, and walks toward the oven, pulling it open to check inside.

"Huh? Oh, no. That was Calvin The Law Clerk."

She giggles and turns around to face me, closing the oven door with her hip.

"That great huh?"

"You seriously have no idea. I'm exhausted."

"Your appointment took a long time?"

"No, no. My appointment was easy. In fact, look!" I sit up and raise my leg to the level of the counter, showing off my new boot.

"Whoa! What's that?"

"This gorgeous thing is my new walking boot. It's big. It's blue. And it's all mine." I smirk as I bring my foot back down behind the island.

"So this is a good thing?" Sylvia asks.

"Yeah, I guess so. It's one step closer to not having crutches, anyway. And the doctor said I can begin physical therapy next Monday. Apparently, he liked the way my x-rays looked."

"Enough about me though. How was Guthrie this afternoon? We checked on him before leaving for Salem—"

"You two went to Salem?"

"—Yeah, we did. Sorry. You don't need to take me to get a new phone. Figured I would just have Fabio take me. Seriously, Sylvia, he flirted with me, and hit on me the whole time! The guy must be desperate."

Sylvia's face looks like she's just eaten a lemon and we both burst into laughter.

"Anyway," she continues. "Guthrie is doing much better. He was awake when I got here, and I took him out, and he actually pooped! And then he came back inside and ate a half a bowl of food!" She pads softly behind me and around the corner to pop her head into the living room. "Yeah, he's asleep now. But really he seems to be getting stronger every day."

I clap my hands together softly. "I'm so glad!"

"I know. I'm so happy too. Hey, dinner will be about another half an hour. I'm going to find a good movie, wanna join me?" She waits in the doorway for my reply.

I consider her offer and then decide against it.

"Rain check until after dinner? I want to check in with the police department in Bend. Now that I have a new telephone number and all."

"Sounds good. I'll pick something we haven't seen before." She gives me the thumbs up and disappears into the living room.

I pick up my bag and gingerly set my boot down on the ground, the majority of my weight on my opposite foot. I shift a tiny amount of weight onto my right foot and pause, waiting for the shooting pain. Nothing happens. I allow a little more weight, this time hanging on to the island for support. I feel an aching in my foot and ankle but nothing that really resembles pain. I take a deep breath and decide to try and apply full weight on my foot. I grip the edge of the island, my knuckles white. I am so hesitant to bear weight that I can't actually do it. Breathing deeply in through my nose, and out through my mouth slowly, I attempt to calm myself as I try to release my weight onto my foot again. I feel the familiar ache and press past it. My ankle is stinging, and the pain begins to move through my ankle and into the ball of my foot and toes, radiating up into my shin. My upper lip starts to sweat, but I press on and realize, with complete surprise, that I'm standing with full weight on my right foot. Without crutches!

"Sylv! Come in here quick!" I yell.

I hear a commotion in the living room before she runs into the kitchen.

"What? What is it?' Her mouth drops open as she looks at me standing freely in the room. "Oh my God, Georgia!" She rushes over and throws her arms around my shoulders, squeezing tightly. "Does it hurt?" She asks, holding me back at arm's length and looking down at my foot.

"Yes. But not even close to what it felt like before. But I won't lie: this hurts."

"Can you take a step?" She asks, her eyes opening wide.

I shake my head at her. "Maybe? But to be honest, I'm too worried about messing this up. The doctor said I could gradually begin to apply pressure but not to begin full walking until I've seen the physical therapist."

"No, yeah, don't push yourself at all, sis." She steps toward me and hugs me again. "This is so exciting! Good for you, Gia."

The physical touch and her full display of love for me brings a lump to my throat as the full realization of how much I miss Ben hits me.

"Hey, you ok?" She pulls away from me, still holding me by the shoulders.

I swallow before answering. "Yeah. I'm good. Just a little

overwhelmed I guess." I smile at her for good measure before shifting my gaze to the floor.

She runs her hands up and down my arms and looks at me with complete seriousness. "You've been through a lot, Georgia. It's perfectly okay to break down, so don't you feel guilty for that all right?" Her index finger brings my chin up, and I look directly at her. "You've been so strong. It's okay to let it go now. Things are going to get better going forward."

We both know she's not talking about my injury any longer.

———

I sit on my bed leaning against the headboard, my legs outstretched, and my boot propped up on a pillow. My laptop rests on my thighs, and I hold my phone in my hand, still connected to the computer by the long white lightning cord. How many of these cords have I misplaced over the last two years? Probably at least five. They are like socks in a dryer, always disappearing.

Uploading my photos from my computer to my phone had been simple. Too easy, really. And as I look them over now, it takes only a second to find the ones I want, play with the filters, and post them to my site. I wonder if Ben ever uses social media. *Probably not.* He doesn't seem the type to be the least bit interested in using his time to see what's happening in cyberspace. The truth is, I don't really like it either. I only use it so I can enhance my photographs with the supplied filters.

I look over the pictures once more — the sunrise at the butte, and the pictures of the fire lookout from underneath — the huge metal beams crisscrossing up the tower, providing support for the platform at the top. I can almost recall the morning dewdrops standing to attention on the metal as the sunshine touched and warmed each one, eventually causing the tiny circles to evaporate into the breeze.

I scroll further through the collection and come to the photographs taken at Sparks Lake. The mountains in the background of the lush valley are majestic, especially against the vibrant blue background of the sky. The pictures of the stream and the army of frogs along the water's edge make me smile at the memories of my time there with Ben. I know the next shots will be of him, and I argue with myself about whether or not I want to look. After all, it's why I never progressed past this point last night. In the end, my own sick sense of torture wins out, and I swipe across the screen to see the next picture.

And there he is.

Standing in the distance facing the mountains, his back to me, hands in his pockets, elbows outstretched but relaxed. I pinch my fingers together on the screen and then slowly spread them apart, zooming in. The image expands, and I can see the rigid outline of Ben's trapezius muscles through his clothing; they come together to form a small valley that runs down the center of his back. He has one leg stretched out to the side, and this stance perfectly outlines the right side of his rear. My mind wanders back to the two of us in his shower, my hands running along his naked, muscular backside, the contours of his hips, the way in which he used them so well against me...

Thinking about us together only reopens my wound, and like a true masochist, makes me want more of the pain. I remove the zoom and look at the picture as a whole, trying to redirect my thoughts.

I try to focus instead on the balance of the scene in front of me. It's impressive, and not just because of the hunk prominently featured therein. Ben's standing off-center with the stream in the far left of the picture. The mountains in the background aren't completely in focus, and the position of the sun creates a slight shadow from his body, casting some shade on the tall green grasses around him. From my perspective, albeit very biased, this photograph is really good.

"Hey, Sylvia? Can you hear me?" I tilt my chin in the air to carry my voice across the house.

A moment later a small voice calls back. "Yeaaaah?"

"Can you come back in here for a sec?"

She appears in my doorway. "Hey. What's up?" She holds a blue linen dishcloth in her fingers as she wipes her hands.

"So, I'm just looking through some photos from my hike, and wondering what you thought of this one?" I set my phone down and bring the picture up on my laptop, swiveling it toward her as she sits down next to me.

"Is that him?" She leans in and stares at the screen, stilling the movements of her hands.

I stare at the screen too. We're both silent for a moment.

"Yeah, that's him. Well, the back of him anyway." The hole in my chest begins to ache again, and I look over at her for distraction. "But what do you think of the photograph. If you didn't know it was...I mean if you were just an anonymous person looking through a collection of photographs?" I cover my mouth with my hand. Even saying his name out loud seems too difficult.

She silently studies the picture for a moment.

"I think it's stunning. I know nothing about photography, but I love everything I see here. The mountains — Jesus, did they really look like that?"

"Yeah. Even better, actually."

"And is that water on the left? It's beautiful. Look at all the color and texture here. And I love that we can't see his face. He certainly doesn't look like he's posing for anything."

"He wasn't. He doesn't even know I have this picture."

Sylvia looks over at me. "He doesn't?"

I shake my head. "It just randomly happened. I was taking

some pictures before we left to go back into town, and I looked over and saw him standing there and...just snapped a few shots." My eyes begin to sting.

Sylvia puts her arm around my shoulders.

"He kissed me for the first time there, just a few moments after this picture, actually," I say, my voice cracking.

"Oh, honey. I'm so sorry." She pulls me closer, hugging me tightly.

"This is so stupid, but I think I might've slightly fallen in love with him. Is that even possible in such a short amount of time? It's probably infatuation, right? Not love. Because who could fall in love in, what? Thirty-six hours?" I'm crying and blubbering, and my nose begins to run. Sylvia disappears from the room for a moment and returns with a handful of Kleenex. I blow my nose and talk to her through the tissues. "But how can it hurt so much if it's only infatuation?"

"I think it is one-hundred percent possible to fall in love that quickly. There's no minimum waiting period, you know. There's no magical equation for the exact amount of time it takes, and I would say that love changes as you progress through it. You go through different feelings of love. So, while the beginning part may feel like infatuation, I don't know, I think that's normal. It can still be a form of love." She picks up my hand and holds it tightly. "If your heart is hurting so desperately, and it clearly is, then why punish yourself even further by denying what you are feeling?"

I can't answer her. I just tuck my head into her shoulder and let the tears fall.

"Hel-lo? Anyone home?" Scott's voice booms through the house. "Oh, hey, Guth, buddy. How ya feeling, big guy? Sylvia? Georgia?"

"We're back here, honey," Sylvia hollers back. She turns to

65

me. "Hey, chin up now. I'm going to go and finish dinner. Come out in a minute and get some food, ok?"

I nod and sniff loudly. "Love you, sis. And thanks." I raise a handful of crushed tissues at her and smile, a meager display of victory.

I hear Sylvia and Scott greeting each other lovingly in the hallway, and I close my eyes against the fresh onslaught of pain.

CHAPTER NINE

BEN

"YOU DON'T UNDERSTAND, ANNIE. IT'S not that I don't want to be with her. I do. I really do. It's just...well, it's just I guess I'm—"

"—Afraid."

I stare at Annie's face for a minute. How does she know these things about me?

"I can tell by the way you're grippin' the back of your neck, Benjamin. You always do that whenever you're unsure about something. I seen it enough times to know, by God."

I smirk at her and slide my hand from the back of my head. How can I argue with this woman? She knows me better than I know myself most of the time.

"Benjamin, she's not Charlotte. Now, just stop right there," she says, clucking her tongue and putting her hands up in front of her as I start to argue. I close my mouth and cross my arms over my chest.

"Now Georgia may have brought up some old pain that you don't want to deal with, but by God, son, can you blame her? She needed to know the truth. And it's best to get it out into the open now. The longer secrets are locked up behind closed doors, the stronger they become. I seen it happen, for pity's sake, and that kind of thing can destroy, Benjamin. It can destroy everything you are, and everything you have."

I hang my head and look at my boots. I know she's right.

"But Annie, what if something were to happen to her? Like Charlotte," I mumble. "I couldn't...I couldn't live with myself."

"Now you listen to me, Benjamin Harrison, and you listen good: that woman loves you—"

"How do you—"

"Because I been around a lot longer than you have, son, and I know these things when I see 'em. Besides," she says, stamping her foot, "you two are damn near perfect for each other. You just gotta give yourself permission to love her back."

I shove my hands in my pockets, and take a deep breath, shaking my head as I speak.

"I don't think I can, Annie."

CHAPTER TEN

GEORGIA

S COTT LEAVES LATE FRIDAY NIGHT for the partner retreat, and since he's away for the weekend, Sylvia and I capitalize grandly on the absence of a male in the house.

Saturday morning, we sleep late, and then begin the day with a huge pot of coffee and egg white omelets, as we watch trashy reruns of The Housewives of Beverly Hills. By 1 p.m. we've done nothing but subtly change positions in our respective chairs, getting up only to take Guthrie, or ourselves, to the bathroom. By late afternoon, we begin to feel hungry again, and Sylvia shuffles into the kitchen to raid the refrigerator, bringing back some cold grilled flank steak and tortilla chips. We eat in the living room, still in our pajamas, watching television, bouncing back and forth between celebrity gossip tabloid shows, and horror movies. Although neither of us says a word about it, romantic comedies are definitely not on the menu.

Sylvia takes pity on me and gives me a pedicure, filing and shaping my toenails to perfection, and giving my left foot a vigorous foot massage. She tops it off by painting my nails a vibrant shade of purple, and we each finally take showers after dinner and call it an early night by 9.

I'm grateful for the time alone with my sister, just us two, and although we don't talk about Ben, just having her with me, a physical presence in the house, somehow keeps the hole in my heart from hurting quite so much.

The remainder of the weekend is spent in a similar way, except we focus on chores around the house and trying to keep Guthrie lying down. He's truly feeling better now and has to be watched like a hawk, or he will bear too much weight on his broken leg. I'm beginning to feel the same way. My ankle is feeling so much better, especially while in the boot, and I am walking around the house without crutches for the first time in over a week. It's an incredibly liberating feeling to be able to stand at my full height — not stooped over cumbersome crutches to help guide me from place to place — and slowly, I feel my mood begin to lift.

———

On Monday when Sylvia drops me off at work, I actually walk through the door without using my crutch. Oh, I bring it with me, just in case, but it stays in the back room, leaning quietly against the wall like a child in time-out.

The weather is beautiful outside. It's mid-June, and the flowers are in full bloom. Foxglove, Delphinium, and Bleeding Hearts are planted in huge ceramic containers outside the store-front, carefully shaded by the large Akebono cherry trees lining the street. I know their specific classification because Ed is a walking encyclopedia, always wanting to impart information to customers, and his staff, apparently. The Akebonos shed their soft pink flowers months earlier, and are now covered with a blanket of small, light green leaves. I stand at the front desk admiring the trees and the flowers beneath them...and then sneeze violently.

"Bless you!" Ed's voice echoes from the back room.

I grab a tissue from my pocket and blow my nose. How do I manage to forget my allergies every year? I never even think about what happens every June, until I'm already exhibiting symptoms: constant sneezing, itchy and watery eyes, scratchy throat and feeling incredibly dehydrated from a never-ending post nasal drip. I live in the Willamette Valley, I remind myself, a place that reports some of the highest pollen counts *in the nation*. The place where locals joke and remind each other sarcastically that the name Willamette Valley translates to "valley of sickness".

"I need to move," I mumble to myself.

The bell dings loudly as the front door opens and a UPS driver in an outfit of brown quickly walks in and heads for the back room. He's pushing a hand truck with two large boxes stacked on top of each other. As he passes me a wave of outside air breezes behind him.

"Morning, Georgia," he says, zipping by.

"Morning, Jeff," I say in a hurry. I feel a sneeze approaching.

"Is that our delivery?" Ed comes to the front counter with his hands clasped together in front of him. Ed reminds me of a small child on Christmas morning, so eager to open his gifts. I look at him and nod, and then sneeze, covering my nose with the tissue I still have in my hand.

"Mmm hmm, Jeff just brought in the boxes."

"Excellent! Perfect timing too!"

Ed scampers off behind me, and a moment later Jeff whizzes by in the opposite direction, tipping his brown cap at me.

"See ya, Georgia."

"See ya, Jeff."

The bell dings again as he opens the door, and once more as he closes it hard behind him. The noise makes me wince as I turn back to the computer screen in front of me, my head feeling thick as cement as I lean over the desk.

"We gotta get rid of that stupid bell," I mutter. I recognize the exasperation in my voice and make a mental note to find something positive to focus on,

like a gin and tonic after work.

———

Calvin picks me up around 12:30 p.m. and we drive home to check on Guthrie. I grab a small bottle of Pellegrino out of the fridge and watch through the kitchen window as Calvin patiently follows a limping Guth around the backyard. The dog stops to smell every blade of grass, every fallen leaf, and every branch before he finally finds the spot he likes. As Guthrie finally begins to relieve himself, Calvin opens his arms wide, tips his head back and hollers, "Thank you!" to the sky. I laugh out loud and shake my head.

"You sure were out there long enough," I say, as Calvin comes in through the kitchen, Guthrie in his arms.

"Yeah, well someone here couldn't find *just* the right spot!"

"Maybe he had stage fright."

"Maybe he should remember he's a *dog*."

Calvin walks through the kitchen and into the living room with Guthrie as stiff as a board in his arms. A moment later he saunters back into the kitchen.

"I'm just going to make a quick phone call, and then we can get to physical therapy. Sound ok?" I ask.

"Yep. Sounds fine. Hey, got anything to eat around here?" he says, leaning against the counter.

I open up the fridge and bend down to grab an apple from the drawer. I can feel my linen pants pull across my rear, and I have an awful feeling I'm being watched. I grab an apple and stand up quickly, turning to look at Calvin. He looks like he's been turned into a marble statue. His face is frozen, his gaze locked on the place I have just risen from.

"Hey!" I toss the apple to him and clap my hands.

He snaps out of his trance and catches the apple just before it bounces off his scrawny chest.

"Sorry. I, uh, er...thanks?"

"I hope you're thanking me for the apple and not something else. Now get outta here before I call your mother."

Calvin smiles sheepishly as he turns and heads back toward the living room.

I sit down at the island and pull my cell phone out of my purse, along with Lieutenant Dickerson's business card, and dial the station. As it rings I glance over at Ben's cell phone in the basket near the wall and wonder what he's doing right now. Is he thinking of me? Does he care anymore at all?

"Lieutenant Dickerson please," I tell the receptionist.

"One moment..." Barely audible elevator music fills my ear. "Ma'am, I do apologize. Lieutenant Dickerson is out of the office. May I transfer you to his voicemail?"

"Um, sure. That...oh wait a second, there was another officer that helped me. One minute here..." I reach for the business card again, flipping it over to see Officer Roth's name on the backside along with a string of numbers.

"Here it is. Officer Roth. Is he available?"

"One moment please."

A telephone line begins to ring in my ear.

"Bend Police Department, Officer Roth speaking."

"Hello, Officer. This is Georgia Marks. You might remember me from a couple weeks ago? I broke my ankle at the top of Black Butte..."

"Oh yeah, of course I do. It's good to hear from you, Ms. Marks. How are you feeling?"

"A lot better, thanks. Hey, I was trying to reach Lieutenant Dickerson, but I guess he's out?"

"His unit is out on a call right now. May I help with something?"

I lower my voice and turn away from the doorway. No doubt Calvin is listening.

"Maybe, yeah. I'm not sure if you know, but before I left Bend, I received another threatening text message. Well, it wasn't *my* phone, I was just borrowing it, but the message was about me, and threatening — "

"Hang on. I'm sorry to interrupt you. Did you say you received a threatening phone message before you *left* Bend? Where are you now Ms. Marks?"

I'm silent for a minute, slightly confused.

"I'm in Silverton now. I'm sorry, I assumed Dickerson had filled you in on my...wait a second." A strange thought occurs to me. "You do know about the text messages, right?" I'm aware my voice rises a few octaves.

"No, ma'am, I surely do not. Can you hold a minute while I grab your case file?"

"Yes, absolutely."

What the hell? Dickerson said he had Roth check the number?

Calvin peeks his head around and imitates looking at his watch. I glance at the microwave clock and realize it's just about time to go. I nod back at him and pull my mouth away from the phone.

"Thanks," I whisper, and begin to gather my purse and sunglasses.

I follow Calvin through the living room and open the front door, my cell phone pressed to my ear. I hold the door for him and lock it behind us as we leave.

74

As I click my seatbelt into place, I can still hear the far-away elevator music playing in the background.

"Still on hold?" Calvin whispers as he slides in behind the steering wheel and turns the key.

"Yeah, it's been a while though. Not sure what's — "

"Ms. Marks?" Officer Roth's voice cuts into the phone, the elevator music disappearing.

"Yes, I'm still here."

Calvin starts the car, and as we back out of the driveway, I slide my sunglasses onto my face.

"I'm going to have to take down some information from you and update the electronic file," he says. He sounds frustrated, or maybe upset.

"Um ok, sure, go ahead."

"Let's start with the text messages."

I glance over at Calvin and decide I don't want to discuss all of this in front of him.

"Actually, Officer, could I call you back? I'm just on my way to physical therapy now. I should be done in a couple of hours. Could I call you after?

Calvin turns his head toward me for a moment and then looks straight ahead.

"Sure," Roth says. "I should be here. If you get my voicemail, please leave a message, and I'll get back to you as soon as I can."

"Yeah, ok. No problem. I'll talk to you soon."

We hang up, and I exhale forcefully. It bothers me that he doesn't know about the messages. How could that be? Had I misunderstood Dickerson?

"Everything okay?" Calvin asks.

"Um yeah, everything's fine." I glance at him. The look on his face suggests he wants to know why I was talking to a police officer.

"It's a long story. Basically, when I was hiking, my Jeep was vandalized while I was on the trail, and I had to report it to the police. I was just following up with them now."

"Seriously? Dang, that sucks. Did they find out who did it?"

"No. Not yet, anyway."

———

We pull into the driveway of the physical therapy offices. The front of the building is a wall of windows, and the sun reflects off the glass and momentarily blinds us as we swing into a parking space.

He hustles around and grabs my door as I open it to step out.

"I got that for ya," he says, offering his hand.

"Thanks, Calvin. I'm good." I ignore his hand but smile briefly as I stand up next to him, and then suddenly sneeze.

"Shoot. I'm sorry. It's these damn allergies."

"No problem," he says, laughing. "You want me to walk in with you?"

"Oh no, that's sweet of you, but no, I think I'll be fine. See you back here in about an hour?" I suddenly remember I need to call Roth back. "Uh, make that two?"

He gives me the thumbs up and a corny smile, and all I can do is shake my head in disbelief.

CHAPTER ELEVEN

GEORGIA

CALVIN IS WAITING FOR ME in the lobby when I finish my PT session. At first I'm annoyed to see him; it's only been an hour since he dropped me off, and I still need to call Roth. But as I make my way down the hallway, he stands, and bless his pre-pubescent heart, he has my crutches with him. He holds them out to me, his eyebrows raised in question. I've never been happier to see my aluminum torture sticks.

"Calvin," I say, limping over to him. "You are my new best friend. Thank you so much for bringing these." I lean in, give him a quick peck on the cheek and take my crutches from his hands. He remains frozen in place, his eyes wide with surprise.

Taking the weight off my foot feels immediately satisfying, and a small moan escapes my mouth.

"Ditto," Calvin mutters under his breath, and I pretend not to notice his comment.

"Good Afternoon, this is Officer Roth. May I help you?"

"Hi again, it's me, Georgia Marks. I'm sorry it took so long for me to get back to you."

I am stretched out on the couch, my blue boot on the floor beside me — my foot and ankle resting on a throw pillow. I took three Motrin the moment I entered the house, and I'm finally beginning to feel my muscles relax.

"Hi, Georgia, hey thanks for calling me back. Just one second, I'm going to close my door." I hear chair wheels roll over a mat and the sound of a door softly shutting. "Okay, I'm all set. Thanks for waiting."

"You bet. So, I think you were going to take down some information?"

"Correct. Now, you mentioned you had received, excuse me, the person whose phone you were borrowing, had received some threatening text messages?"

"That's right, yes. And, about that, may I just say I'm kind of surprised you didn't already know? At least about the first message, anyway. When I told Lieutenant Dickerson about it, he said he was going to have you check out the source of the number. A few days later, he gave me information about how it was a solicitation data processing center or something."

Roth doesn't reply.

"Officer Roth? Are you there?"

"Yes, I'm here. I'm sorry, I was just uh...I was just reading a message that broadcast over my computer screen."

"Oh, should I — "

"—We have to keep abreast of all calls that come in. I'm sorry for the interruption." His voice is much stronger now.

"So, you didn't know about the text message then?"

"Ms. Marks, I'd like to start from the beginning just so that I can make sure your electronic file is updated. Would that be all right?"

"Of course." Why is he dodging the question?

"Whenever you're ready, go ahead."

For the next fifteen minutes, we talk about what happened that weekend after my hotel room was broken into. I explain how I borrowed Ben's phone, what I can recall of the text message that came through, and how I relayed all of this information to Lieutenant Dickerson. I go on to explain that Dickerson reassured me the number was found to be a solicitation center of some sort and that it would be virtually impossible to find out who actually sent the text.

"He told me you had checked on that number yourself," I say. "Is that true?"

"Well, hmm. All right, I have everything noted here." He pauses, and I wonder if he's going to actually answer my question. "Uh, Ms. Marks, it certainly is possible Lieutenant Dickerson assigned another officer to investigate the telephone number you provided. I will be conferencing with the Lieutenant later today, and can confirm this information with him at that time."

"So that's a no," I mumble.

"Pardon me?"

"Nothing." I let my voice drop like an anvil.

Roth picks up the conversation as if nothing at all is out of order.

"And then you said you received another text? When did that one arrive?"

"Last Monday."

"And what did that text say?"

"It said something like, *I'd think again if you think you can keep her safe.*" I shudder at the memory.

"And do you know what telephone number that message was sent from?"

"No. It was different from the one used before, but I didn't recognize the number, and neither did Ben."

79

"And is Ben with you now? Does he have the phone?"

"Um, no," I say. "I would guess he's back at work up on the butte. He left the phone here though." I pause a moment. "We kind of had an argument, and he left quickly. He left the phone here. He didn't really seem to care about getting it back." I chew on my lower lip. Why am I telling him this?

"I see. I'm sorry to hear that." He waits a moment. "Do you think you could give me the numbers the texts came from?"

"Um, yeah. I'd need to charge the phone again though. To be honest, I just feel like I'd rather not see it or deal with it again. I'm not even actually sure where it's at." Of course I know exactly where it is — I moved it to a shelf in my closet so I wouldn't see it every time I entered the kitchen — I just don't want to seem like I'm a completely heartbroken mess to Officer Roth.

"I would really like to have the numbers. Could you call me back today or tomorrow with that information?"

"Yeah, I think so."

"All right, so is there anything else I should know or any questions you might have, Ms. Marks?"

"No, sir. I can't think of anything else. I'll get back to you with that telephone number as soon as I can."

"Sounds good. Enjoy your evening."

The line goes dead, and I lay still for a moment, the phone still resting at my ear. Why is he being so elusive? Did Dickerson flat out lie to me? That lazy jerk probably didn't want to follow up on some bogus text message, so he lied to cover it up. I'm sure that's it. Nothing more really to worry about. He was just being an—

IF YOU'D LIKE TO MAKE A CALL, PLEASE HANG UP AND DIAL AGAIN.

I toss the phone across the floor in frightened reaction to the automated voice that booms in my ear, my upper body completely rigid. Even Guthrie barks at the sudden violent movement.

"Sorry, Guth. It's okay, baby. I'm just an idiot." I reach over and pet his head, calmly scratching under his chin and running my hand over his ears. He settles back down on his bed and rests his nose on his paws.

I reach for the phone and click it off — for good this time.

I need to get up and charge Ben's phone, but I'm so comfortable on the couch, it's hard to will myself up. I close my eyes and visualize actually completing the task. I promised Officer Roth I would call him back and the guilt of not doing so begins to settle in. I take a huge deep breath and sit up. Guthrie raises his head at me, watching my movements on the couch with interest. Once he realizes I don't have a leash or food in my hand, he settles his head back down on his bed and closes his eyes.

I grab a crutch from the end of the couch and stand up. As the blood rushes back into my ankle, it begins to throb and ache. The physical therapist warned me this would happen, and that it's normal after performing movements and exercises on the ankle, even as minor and as limited as today.

In my room, I pull open the closet door and take the small, sand-colored basket off the shelf. I grab Ben's phone and charger and make my way back to the kitchen. After plugging everything in, I snag a bottle of water from the fridge and sit down at the island to look at my own phone.

Taking a drink of water, I open my Instagram account and see a gorgeous photograph appear on the screen. It's an aerial view of a forest, the early morning fog lifting off the tops of the trees in thin wisps and clouds. The photo is striking, and I immediately press *like*. I notice the photo is posted by PNWLife — a group I started to follow in the weeks leading up to my Black Butte hike. They share tons of inviting photographs that showcase hiking trails, forests, places to go, and things to see and do, all over the state of Oregon. Of course, I immediately fell in love with their curation and started following them right away. I recall that sometimes they highlight different photographers' work on their feed, giving reference to the original work in the comments section. I quickly jump back to my own photograph of the cabin with the bear hidden in the background and edit the picture to add a PNWLife hashtag reference. Why not?

I study the photo in front of me again. This one, this beautiful photo of the trees and the rising fog tinged with the colors of the sunrise reminds me of what I saw that early morning from the top of the butte. Despite the encounter with the bear and the injury I sustained, I can't help but think about planning another hike as soon as I am able. I love being in the outdoors. I love exploring new trails and working hard to reach rewarding views. And now I know I love high elevations.

It's hard not to circle back around to thoughts of Ben, hard not to imagine the two of us exploring together. Hard not to think of us together in his bed, exploring one another. Had I ever been made love to like that before? Never. Mike was despondent after Jason died, only going through the motions, it seemed. And then, after his drinking became severe, he became rough and unloving. I hated having sex with him and was often relieved when he'd come home too drunk and disinterested to perform.

I had forgotten what it felt like to have true desire for someone, and to be desired in return.

Where Mike was detached and rough, Ben was hyper aware; interested in every aspect of my body, every reaction, every movement. He made it abundantly clear he aimed to please. And judging by the way my traitorous body was tightening at the memory of him, he'd accomplished his goal.

God, I hate the way things ended between us. It isn't right. I should have called him back. I should have at least tried. Maybe he really needed someone to talk to about his past. And what about those threatening text messages? I should have been more concerned about his safety. What if he's been hurt or is in trouble? I stare at my phone and began to pick at my thumbnail. Glancing at the clock, I note the time: 4:27 p.m.

I stand up and hobble back into my bedroom, returning to the kitchen with my wallet in hand. Dropping heavily onto the barstool again, I open my wallet and take out Ben's business card. It's hard to imagine myself calling him and hearing his voice; just the thought of it makes me swallow hard. My heart begins to beat erratically, and butterflies drop into my stomach like cement bricks. I study the card, looking at every letter of his name. I stare at the Ranger Station telephone number listed on the front, daring myself to call.

4:46 p.m. If I wait too long, there's a good chance the station will close.

My pulse is racing as I pick up my cell phone and dial the number, my hands shaking slightly. My index finger hovers over the green "call" button at the bottom of the screen, and I begin to wonder what I will say if he answers. *He's probably at the cabin, Georgia. He won't even be at the station.* I vacillate between feeling relieved and feeling depressed, and before I can convince myself of further negative outcomes, I quickly press the "call" button and bring the phone to my ear. My breath is shallow as the phone rings on the other end. This is a bad idea. I don't want to talk to him anymore. I should just hang—

"Sisters Ranger Station. Annie speaking."

I consider ending the call, but can't bring myself to be so rude to her.

"Hello? Hello? Anyone there, by God?"

"Annie it's me, Georgia."

"What's that? Who's calling?" Annie's voice is loud, and I raise mine significantly to match hers.

"Georgia! Annie, it's me Georgia. Georgia Marks!" I sit up taller.

"Georgia! Oh, honey, how are you? I can't tell you how glad I am to hear your sweet voice!"

My shoulders hunch and my eyes begin to sting.

"Thank you, Annie. It's really good to talk to you too. I'm doing ok. I'm calling from my house in Silverton."

"Well bless your heart, darlin'. Did you get everything sorted out with your Jeep? I just assumed since I never heard back from you that everything turned out just as it should?"

"I think so, yeah. I'm having it towed home tomorrow from Sisters." I pause and clear my throat. "It's at...Ben's house." I can barely say his name without a stab of pain in my chest. God, what is the matter with me?

"Ben? Oh, he's around here somewhere. Just a second, and I'll grab him for you. Great to talk to you, hon. Come see me sometime soon, okay?"

"No! No, no, Annie! Annie are you there?" I yell into the phone. Dammit! I stand up from the stool, placing full weight on my foot before I remember my walking boot is still in the living room. "Argh!" I yell as the pain radiates into my calf and up into my knee. I sit down hard, tears pricking at my eyes.

"Ben Harrison. What can I do for you? " His velvety smooth, sexy voice travels across the line to instantly melt me.

Oh, God.

I swallow and take a slow, careful breath.

"Ben, it's Georgia."

CHAPTER TWELVE

GEORGIA

THIS WAS A BAD IDEA.

"Georgia?" He sounds surprised to hear from me. Ugh. This was a very bad idea.

"Uh...I'm sorry, this was a...never mind. Sorry..." I don't know what to say. My heart is racing so fast it hurts. I want to hang up, but I don't want to be rude.

"Georgia, I'm glad you called."

His voice is quiet.

Soft.

I bite my lip so hard it begins to bleed, and the taste of rust tinges my mouth.

"You're glad?"

"Yeah. I am. I've been thinking about the — Hey, can I call you back from my house? Would that be all right? It's just that, well, I can't really talk here."

"Yes!" I say, too quickly, and then start again, slower. "I mean...yeah, that would be fine."

"What telephone number should I call?"

"Uh. I don't actually know."

"Pardon?"

"I'm calling from my new cell phone, and I don't have my number memorized yet. Story of my life." I laugh nervously. "You can call our new house phone though," I say, and rattle off our number to him.

"Ok. I'm leaving here in about ten minutes, and then I'll call you."

"Ok."

"Georgia?"

"Yes?"

"I'm really glad you called," he says again.

His voice. Oh God, my knees are weak.

I wait for him to hang up before I push *end*. I set the phone down on the counter and wrap my arms around myself, squealing with happiness. Tiny tears spill from my eyes as I gently rock back and forth in my seat. I'm afraid to give his comments too much weight though, too afraid of the pain that might be waiting on the other side of this small bit of joy.

I wipe the tears from my face, blow my nose on a paper napkin and look at the time on my cell phone. It's almost 5 o'clock. Scott and Sylvia will be home soon, and I do not want to be having a potentially serious conversation in the middle of the kitchen when they arrive.

Grabbing Ben's phone and charger from the counter, I make my way back to my room. I don't want them wondering about his phone or asking any more questions just yet.

I plug Ben's charger into the outlet near my bed, and set his phone down on the nightstand, next to the house extension that's sitting stoically in its handset, the green power button staring at me. I can't look away. I watch the screen, waiting for it to display an incoming call. I pick at my fingernails as I sit on the bed. Ashamed of myself for acting like a teenage girl, I grab my cell phone and open my email. Anything for a distraction.

My inbox refreshes and four new emails start to download. The first two are solicitations — a summer sale notification from REI and a reminder from Nordstrom about their upcoming half-yearly sale. I scroll past them while the other two download, making a mental note that I might actually need new hiking shoes soon.

The next two emails appear on my screen; one is from my insurance agent — it looks like an email with a quote for the towing, and possibly the damage repair — I don't even want to open that one yet, and the other is from the Sisters Tribune. The regarding line reads *recent submission*. I suck in a breath. I never imagined I'd hear back from the newspaper. I completely forgot about sending them my photos and my blurb. I open the email with my pulse racing.

Dear Ms. Marks,

Thank you for your recent email regarding your experience on Black Butte. The photographs you submitted and the details of the incident have generated interest within our office. We would like to discuss publishing your story and photographs in our newspaper.

At your convenience, please respond at one of the telephone numbers or email addresses listed below.

Alan Jenkins

Lifestyle Editor

Sisters Tribune News

I stare at the screen and start to re-read the letter in complete shock. The house telephone rings loudly at my side, and I nearly leap off the bed. A fresh wave of anxiety runs through my body as I pick up the phone, waiting for it to ring again before I press *talk.*

"Hello?"

"Hi, it's me," Ben says.

My ears are burning with heat, and my heart is hammering in my chest. *Why is my throat so damn dry?*

"So, about my voicemail to you..." he begins.

"Yes?" *Do I really want to hear the rest?*

He clears his throat and takes a deep breath.

"I've been thinking a lot about how I left things with you, and I just really feel like a total jerk."

"It's ok —"

"—No, I want to say this. It's important to me that I get this out, even if it won't matter now. I don't want to intrude on your relationship, but I do want you to know this."

"Wait, what? Ben, I'm not —"

"No, please hear me out. I don't want to lose my nerve to say this." He pauses and releases a heavy sigh. "Here it is: it really rattled me when you asked me about her...about Charlotte," he says, quietly. "I really feel responsible for what happened to her. And I know I couldn't have stopped what happened, it was her decision, but I've always felt like if I hadn't broken things off, if I'd continued to be there for her, well...she might still be alive." His next words are a whisper. "And the baby might still be alive."

My heart is breaking for him.

He coughs, and it's a moment before he continues. "I don't want you to think I wish she and I were still together — that's not what I want — and it wasn't what I wanted then, either. She was a distraction from a very unpleasant time in my life. She was someone that reaffirmed I could still be...desirable. You have to understand, my confidence level was shit at that point in my life. There's nothing more damaging to a man than finding out the woman he loves isn't physically attracted to him anymore.

And there's nothing more shattering than to discover she's sleeping with someone else. I was crazy with hurt and pain. But at the time, I didn't recognize any of that. I only knew I was blinded by rage toward the guy, and filled with the overwhelming desire to be physical with someone else as quickly as possible."

"My actions during the time with Charlotte are nothing I'm proud of, but my behavior with you is unforgivable. I've been trying to work up the courage to call you, to apologize and explain, but I could never find the right way to say how sorry I am. And I didn't want to intrude on your new relationship. And I realize that's a tremendously lame excuse for not doing the right thing, but it's the truth. All I can say now is that I'm very sorry I didn't stay. I'm sorry I didn't stay and explain to you what happened between her and me or at least answer any questions you may have had. Leaving you was the coward's way out, and I want you to know how much I regret that."

Ben takes a deep breath and I wait, unsure of what to say.

"I screwed up, Georgia. I turned my back on the best thing that's ever happened to me. You mean the world to me, and I'm just so sorry I didn't realize that sooner. I hope one day you can forgive me. Whoever has you now is a very, very lucky man. I'm so sorry it isn't me."

The tears are sliding down my cheeks faster than I can wipe them away, and it takes me a moment to compose myself.

"Of course I forgive you, you silly man," I finally blubber. "But why in the world would you think I'm seeing someone else?"

Ben is silent for a moment.

"You mean you're not?"

"No. Not even close. I've basically been sitting around here feeling like a stupid girl with a broken heart."

"But...but Dickerson said—"

I wipe my cheek and immediately sit up straight. "You talked to Dickerson?"

"Well yeah. I mean, I wanted to make sure you were safe, and I wanted to talk to him about the messages. I assumed you two would be keeping in touch, so I called his office when I got back. But I had to get up to the cabin, so I wasn't able to check in for several days. I finally reached him late Friday afternoon."

"And what did he tell you?" I can feel the spike in my adrenalin.

"Well, I told him how I'd taken you back home, and I explained about the text messages and that I was worried about you. He told me you'd called him and reassured him you were fine. He was kind of a jerk about it, actually. He had this really abrasive and condescending tone, telling me you sounded really happy and bubbly and then he kind of commented under his breath...said it probably had something to do with the new guy."

"What!"

"Yeah. He made it sound like you had someone in your life. So, you're ok? You're safe?" His voice trails off.

Oh my God. I clench my jaw and shut my eyes tightly as I breathe in and out slowly.

"Georgia, are you there?"

"Yeah, I'm here."

"You okay? You sound, I don't know..."

"Yeah, I'm ok. I'm just incredibly angry right now."

"So, what he told me—"

"—was complete bullshit! To answer your question, yes, I'm safe. I haven't had anymore weird things happen." I look up at the ceiling, my pulse racing. "Man! I don't know where this guy gets off! I can't tell you how many times I've gotten into it with him. He treats me like crap, Ben. He's a patronizing, demeaning, arrogant...ugh!"

I am already planning my phone call with his superior.

"Wow," he says, chuckling.

"Are you laughing?" I say, my voice rising. "What's so funny?"

Ben is fully laughing now.

"Nothing. Nothing is funny," he says, instantly calm. "I just haven't ever heard you so mad before."

"You don't know the *hell* this guy has put—" I stop, take a deep breath, and smirk, realizing how childish I sound, screaming through the phone like this. Laughing, I cover my mouth to stifle the noise.

"I'm such a hothead sometimes I guess."

"It's ok. As long as it's not directed at me. Besides," he pauses, "I'm okay with a little heat from you."

I stop laughing immediately as my stomach clenches.

"You are?"

"Absolutely. I'm actually okay with a substantial amount of heat from you." His voice is low, purring almost, and I have trouble catching my breath.

"I really don't know what to say."

"Let's just say I really miss you. And I cannot stop thinking about all the ways I want to...well, maybe we should change the subject," he says, clearing his throat. "How are you feeling? How's your ankle?"

"Um, it's good. I've started physical therapy, just today actually."

"Really? Already? I thought it would be a while before you would be allowed to do that."

"Yeah, me too. I don't know. I guess my x-rays looked good when I saw the doctor. He put me in a walking boot. I'm still using my crutches, but not nearly as much as before. Although after today, it feels like I might be back to square one. Those therapists really work you over." I glance at my foot and lean forward to rub my shin.

"That's good news, Georgia. How long will you need the PT?"

"Well, I'm scheduled to begin with six weeks, twice a week, and then I have periodic check-ups with the doctor."

"Have you been able to start back to work?"

"Yeah, I've been working half-days mostly. Luckily, Ed's pretty understanding. He really only cares if I'm physically present. He doesn't seem to care that I can't really help him do anything besides bookkeeping there."

"Surely you're not driving?"

"Oh, no. I wouldn't even want to try it. No, Sylvia's been dropping me off in the mornings, and then Calvin usually picks me up around noon."

"Who's that?"

"Calvin? He's one of Scott's law clerks." I sense a bit of apprehension in Ben's voice. "Actually, I'm pretty sure he's got a massive crush on me." I can't hold back the start of my laugh.

"Is that right?" His voice is stone cold, which only makes me laugh harder. "I'll be right over," he says.

"I'm completely kidding, Ben. Well, actually I do think he has a crush on me, but he's harmless. I think he's barely twenty-three years old. He's a sweet kid though," I say. "Trust me, he can't hold a candle to you, Ben. No one could."

"I'm feeling a little better. Keep going," he teases.

The door to my room inches open and Sylvia sticks her nose and one eyeball into the room. Her eye is wide with interest, and I wave her in.

"Just a minute," I say to Ben, pulling the phone away and covering the receiver with my hand.

"Hey, sis," I whisper.

She opens the door wider. "Hey, just wanted to see if you were ok. We're home." She steps closer and whispers, pointing to the phone. "Is that *him*?"

I nod, smiling.

She gives me a thumb's up and slowly pulls the door closed again. I take my hand off the receiver and put the phone to my ear again.

"Sorry. You there?"

"I'm here."

"My sister. She wanted to make sure I was ok." I look at the clock on my cell phone. "I should probably get going actually. I need to help her with dinner, or at least try."

"Ok, yeah, I...me too."

"Can you call me tomorrow?" I ask, and immediately feel like I'm seventeen again.

"I would like that very much. But I'll be at the cabin for the rest of the week starting tomorrow."

"I see." I feel like sticking my lower lip out in protest.

"I'd like to call you when I come back into town though, if that's ok? Friday night? I'd offer to come and see you, but I'm not supposed to be out of the vicinity since the weather's changed. We've already had some small fires outside of Redmond."

"No, of course. Yeah, Friday sounds good. I'm looking forward to it."

"Say around 7:00?"

"It's a date."

"Ok. And if you need to reach me for any reason, you can call Annie at the station, and she can get me on the radio."

"Sounds good."

I don't want to hang up.

"Georgia?"

"Yes?"

"It's so good to hear your voice."

A huge smile spreads across my face. "You too, Ben. I've really missed talking to you."

93

———

After we hang up, I throw my body sideways into the pillows on my bed, yelling happily into the pillowcases, and coming up for air with a huge smile across my face.

A moment later, there's a knock at my door, and I sit up and straighten my hair.

"Come in," I say, nonchalantly.

Sylvia pokes her head into the room.

"Everything ok?" She looks at my face, and a small grin appears on her own. "What happened? Tell me everything." She sits down at the end of the bed and tucks one leg underneath her.

I lean forward, smile, and take her hand.

"I'm so in love."

CHAPTER THIRTEEN

MIKE

NO.

NO, THAT CAN'T BE right. Did Georgia just say she's in love with him?

No.

No, she meant she's in love with *me*. I'm her fucking husband! She meant me!

I rip the earbuds out of my ears and pick up the laptop, throwing it hard across the mattress, barely noticing when the tangled comforter blocks it from landing on the floor. I stand up and pummel my fist through the wall, the cheap hotel sheetrock caving and indenting around my cement fist. I turn around, heaving ragged breaths through my lungs as I search for something to destroy. Something to break. I eye the television on the table and march furiously toward it, picking it up over my shoulders as the power cord whips my torso, and smashing it down onto the floor as hard as I fucking can. It feels so good to destroy this room. Not as good as when I tore the shit out of Georgia's hotel room, but close enough. I turn and look around the place, searching for my next target.

———

"You don't understand, Bob," I say, hearing my own words slur as I clap Bob on the shoulder and offer to get him another round. It feels like I called him *Mob*. No, I called him Bob. I'm not that fucked up yet.

"Did I just call you *Mob*, or did I call you Bob?" I ask. "'Cause that would be funny as shit if I called you *Mob*."

I can't see straight, but this only makes me laugh harder.

"Easy now, Mike. Don't you worry at all. We're gonna set things right again. We're gonna get rid of this guy once and for all. Now, I know what you think you heard, but don't you sweat it, son, okay? We're gonna get you two back together, just you wait and see." Bob slides me another shot, and even though it feels like I'm about ready to pass out, I take it and drink it back in one go, slamming the empty glass upside down on the bar.

"Another round!" I holler at the bartender.

Why do my hands hurt so much? I pull them up in front of my face and flip them over, inspecting my knuckles. They're beat to hell, and dried blood has caked in the crevices. Are they larger than normal, too?

"Why're my hands all messed up?" I mumble.

"What? Because you tore the shit out of your hotel room, remember? I had to come over that goddamn pass in the middle of the night to help you get straight."

"We're best friends, huh, Bob? We're better friends than women are, right? Right, Bob? You'll always be a better friend than fucking Georgia."

"You got that right. We don't need our goddamn wives in our lives. All they do is ruin everything."

My forehead hits the shellacked bar before I can tell Bob just how fucking right he is.

CHAPTER FOURTEEN

GEORGIA

M Y ALARM GOES OFF IN the middle of a dream about Ben.

I fling my arm over, hit the snooze button and flop back down against my pillows, trying to sink back into the memory of him. My mind replays what I can most easily remember.

We are upstairs in his barn. It's evening, and the last of the light is filtering through the sliding red door on the second story of the barn. Small flecks of dust dance in the warm, illuminated air. Ben and I are reclining against a few bales of hay, a large blanket strewn out beneath us, my legs intertwined with his. From our perch on the straw, we watch as the sun drops lower behind the mountains; his house below us turning a deep gray as the shadows stretch and yawn over it. He slips his hand into mine as the sky turns a multitude of deep reds and a few birds pass between the trees below. I hear the cows lowing in the distance, their calves answering back, and I tilt my chin up to meet Ben's lips as he rolls me on top of him. He kisses me slowly as one hand slides into my hair, the other around my waist. I am liquid heat against him, he is melting me with one languid slide of his tongue after another.

———

My alarm violently interrupts me again. This time I sit up in annoyance and turn the thing completely off. There's no more delaying — I need to get up. I switch on the lamp next to me and rub my eyes. Raising my hands high above my head, I stretch out my shoulders and yawn. Ugh, I do not want to get out of bed. I want to lie back down into my soft pillows and recapture the wonderful feeling of being with Ben in his barn.

The barn I have never seen the inside of.

I wonder if he even has hay in there?

Suddenly, I remember my Jeep has been stored there for over a week, and a feeling of irresponsibility slices at my psyche. I need to get up, wake up, and make a list of things to do today.

I fling back the blankets and swing my legs over the side of the bed. My foot actually looks pretty good, and from what I can tell there's no swelling. I step down fully on my left foot but only carefully balance the toes of my right foot on the floor. I stretch forward, grab my crutch that's leaning against the closet door, and make my way to the bathroom for a shower.

Fifteen minutes later, I emerge with a towel wrapped around my body and my toothbrush sticking out the side of my mouth. While I showered, I made a mental list of calls I need to make — Dickerson being the one I really don't want to deal with. Just the thought of him makes me bite down hard on the soft bristles of my brush. The first call, however, will be to Vanessa about the towing. I recall seeing an email from her last night but I never got around to reading it, and I need to email the Sisters newspaper back.

I pick up my phone and open my email, brushing my teeth

while my inbox refreshes. I spit into the sink, rinse my mouth and tap the email from Vanessa. She explains to me that her contact in Sisters has been unexpectedly called to Portland for an emergency, so the schedule for photographing and towing the vehicle will have to be pushed back. If I have any questions, I am to call her at the office. She closes the email by wishing me well with my recovery, and I type a quick reply thanking her for the note.

This is probably a good thing, actually. Now I will hopefully have time to contact Ben and let him know about the Jeep. I was so thrilled to talk to him I had completely forgotten to mention that an insurance agent would be stopping by the barn.

The barn. My thoughts drift back to my dream and the feeling of my body wrapped in his arms. A dull ache blooms in my core and I have to clear my throat to focus again.

Clearing my subconscious thoughts of Ben's body from my mind, I reply to the newspaper editor and let him know I am excited to discuss the details of the piece and can be reached by telephone at his convenience. The idea of having my photo featured in a newspaper makes my heart flip over, and I try not to let myself get too carried away with thoughts of the future.

———

Work is largely uneventful, except that a large group of tourists bustle through the shop and buy nearly every wire basket and white farmhouse pitcher we have in stock. Ed is thrilled, of course, and instructs me to order, "twenty more, a.s.a.p!" I do as I'm asked, not wanting to crush his excitement by pointing out that if we can order a quantity of anything, it's not really considered *antique*.

Lunchtime rolls around and Calvin bounces into the shop, punctual as ever.

"Hey, how's the day going so far?" he asks. He's wearing a

soft pink, button-down short-sleeved shirt, open at the collar, and a belted pair of lightweight grey trousers. His caramel penny loafers are, of course, spotless.

"It's going well, I guess. How's life in the legal world?" I hear the lack of interest in my voice and I make a mental note to at least try and focus on his reply.

"It's ok. I'm researching a statute concerning emotional distress right now. It's pretty mind-numbing."

A thought suddenly occurs to me.

"Hmm," I say, narrowing my eyes. "Have you ever done any research regarding harassment?"

"Some." He crosses his arms in front of his chest. "Why?"

"Oh, no reason," I lie. "I was just watching a show last night, and it included a bad cop that was harassing someone. Just wondering if that kind of thing actually happens in real life."

He shrugs. "Yeah, I'm sure it does. But I haven't worked on a case like that before." He looks at me from the corner of his eye, arms still crossed in front of him. "You need some research done, Georgia?"

I touch my collarbone in innocence. "Me? Oh no. I don't need anything." I fiddle with a pencil on the counter. "I was just curious. C'mon let's get home. I'm sure Guthrie is about to burst at the seams."

"After you." He bows out of the way and sweeps his arm out in front of him like I'm the Queen of England.

I roll my eyes at him and swat his arm as I attempt to gracefully hobble by, lobbing a, "shut up" over my shoulder for good measure.

———

Calvin takes Guthrie outside while I grab my laptop, my phone, and Ben's phone, and set everything down in a neat pile on the living room coffee table, preparing to call Officer Roth. The front windows are open, and the warm breeze lifts the linen curtains every now and then. I can see the vibrant oranges and reds of the rose bushes planted in front of the windows, and I know if I walk over, I'll smell their fragrant perfume.

I heel-walk in my boot back into the kitchen to grab a granola bar, a banana and a bottle of water. Before heading back to the living room, I glance outside to check on Calvin. He's crouched down on the lawn petting Guthrie, who's lying on his back showing his belly. I have to give him credit: Calvin is a nice kid who will no doubt become an attorney and make a perfect husband to a very sweet, equally adorable girl.

My smile fades as I think about him doing some research for me on harassment. I could just ask Scott to do it. Or I could do it myself. Isn't that what the Internet is for? Scott will be quicker, and more accurate probably — after all, he's the attorney. But there's something very appealing about the possibility of handling Dickerson all on my own. It feels risky, but also extremely satisfying. Besides, Scott and Sylvia don't need any more distractions or interruptions in their lives. They helped me enormously when I left Mike — heck, they are still helping me -- and I don't want to ask for more.

I'm still standing at the window when I notice Calvin stand up, look at his watch and clap his hands together. Guthrie rolls over quickly and jumps to his feet, resting the toes of his casted foot on the ground. They both turn and head toward the house, Calvin walking slowly and Guthrie limping behind him. I meet them at the back door and hand my unopened bottle of water to Calvin.

"For me?"

"If you'd like it. I just came in to grab some food and something to drink. Thought I'd offer you something."

"Oh, thanks, but that's okay. I'm fine."

101

"Suit yourself then." I twist the top off and take a large sip. The sudden release of carbonation tickles my nose so strongly I choke on the water and cough, spewing my mouthful of Pellegrino all over the front of Calvin's shirt and pants.

Calvin jumps backward and yells while I gag and snort, holding one hand over my mouth and the other reaching out toward Calvin in embarrassment. The sudden commotion causes Guthrie to yelp and limp off to the living room, barking loudly from the safety of distance.

"Hey, man! What the heck?"

He's groaning and wiping the front of his shirt and pants off with his hands, a large dark circle appearing over his midsection, and, to my complete embarrassment, his crotch.

"Oh my God, I'm so sorry! The carbonation — I wasn't prepared! Here, let me get you a towel." I turn and grab the dishtowel from the oven handle and toss it to him. He blots at his shirt and makes a few passes at his pants. I turn away, mortified. "At least it wasn't red wine or something that will stain."

"At least it doesn't look like I totally pissed my pants," he says, his voice dripping with sarcasm.

"You can stand in the sun for a minute. I bet it will be dry in no time. Its just water, after all."

He ignores my comments.

"How much time do we have before your appointment?"

"It's at 1:15...so," I glance at the clock, "about twenty minutes."

"Right. I'll be in the backyard drying out then." He tosses the dishtowel onto the counter, turns and heads toward the back door, mumbling under his breath as he walks.

The door slams behind him and I laugh, shaking my head and trudging back into the living room with my now half-full bottle of water, and snack. I sit down to make the call, and Guthrie settles in at my feet, laying his nose across my toes.

"Officer Roth, please."

While I'm on hold, I wonder if it's a bad omen that I've now memorized the Bend Police Department's telephone number.

"Officer Roth speaking."

"Hi, it's Georgia Marks here. Just calling you back with that telephone number you asked for." I hold Ben's phone in my hand.

"Yes, thanks for getting back to me, Ms. Marks. Go ahead, I'm ready when you are."

I scroll through the text messages, find the two at issue and relay the numbers to him.

"Got it." He exhales deeply. "I'll follow up with these and see what I can find out. Today's a pretty busy day though so it might be a few days before you hear back from me. Be sure to call me though, if anything else should come up, okay? Thanks for —"

"—Hang on. I'm sorry, but while I have you now, could you tell me who I need to speak to about filing a complaint against an officer?"

He's silent for a moment, and my stomach starts to unsettle.

"Uh, sure. Is there something I can help with? Maybe save you the trouble?"

"No, I don't think so. It's not about you, if that helps."

Roth clears his voice before continuing, "We try our best to provide quality service to every member of our community. I'm very sorry if this has not been your experience, Ms. Marks."

"No, you've been great. It's the other guy that hasn't."

"I take it you mean Lieutenant Dickerson?" he asks. Do you feel comfortable talking to me about it? Maybe we can resolve the issue together."

I sigh. "Yeah, I guess so. It's nothing specific really. It's more of a general experience of disrespect toward me. It's like he's got something personally against me. From the beginning, he's been sarcastic and condescending, implying, on more than one occasion, that I have an active dating life and even going so far as to

allude to promiscuity. He's acted completely unprofessionally."
I stand up and pace in the living room. "And now I've found
out that he's suggested, to a good friend, a male, that I'm romantically involved with someone else! He's just too interested in
my personal life, and too quick to make inappropriate
comments."

I hear Roth clicking keyboard keys as I speak, and I begin to
reconsider what I'm doing here.

"You know what, maybe I shouldn't have said anything. I
don't want to get him into trouble and have him take it out
on me."

"Well, it is completely up to you as to whether or not you
wish to pursue a formal complaint against him. I don't want to
dissuade you from that in any way. However, I will let you know
that Lieutenant Dickerson's record is pretty much spotless. He's
highly respected by the Chief and the community. Now, he's not
been with our force for very long, but his service record at his
previous post was also excellent, I believe he had over twenty
years in."

I am beginning to feel anxious.

"Ms. Marks," Roth continues. "In no way am I making
excuses for Lieutenant Dickerson's behavior toward you. In fact,
I completely understand your anger and frustration. I just don't
know that filing a complaint against him will accomplish what
you ultimately want from him, which to me, sounds like a good
old-fashioned apology. Would you say that's correct?"

I consider his proposal. "Yeah. I do want an apology from
him. But more than that, I'd just really like to know why he seems
so hell-bent on me. What did I ever do to this guy?"

"That, I cannot answer. But if you think it will help, I'd be
happy to talk to him, to let him know how you feel and to ask him
to consider apologizing."

"Yeah, I think that would help. Actually, I feel a lot better just talking to you about it. It's really not that big of a deal, I guess."

"It *is* a big deal, and we take our responsibilities very seriously here. Let me see what I can do. And if you change your mind at any time about filing a complaint, please let me know right away, and I will connect you to the right person."

"I will. And thank you. I appreciate you taking the time to listen, and for helping me with those telephone numbers." I'd nearly forgotten the main reason I called.

"Well, I think the crotch of my pants is dry." Calvin's voice booms behind me as he walks into the living room. I whip my head around and point to the phone at my ear. "Oh! Sorry!" he whispers and tiptoes backward toward the kitchen.

"Uh...er, it's my pleasure, Ms. Marks," Officer Roth continues. "I'll be in touch soon." He hangs up, and I drop my chin to my chest, cringing at the thought of him hearing Calvin's comment.

"It's okay, Cal, I'm off now," I call into the kitchen. Calvin reappears hesitantly.

"Sorry about that. I didn't know you were on the phone."

"It's okay, totally my fault." I chuckle. "The Bend police department now officially knows your pants are dry enough."

"Oh, terrific. That's just so...reassuring. C'mon, Chatty Cathy, let's get you to PT," he says, opening the front door for me. "Where I hope they completely torture you." He pinches my arm as I pass by, causing me to yelp and then laugh as I grab my arm in mock horror.

He holds the door for me as I slide into the car. I reach for my seatbelt and realize the metal latch has slid down alongside the door. As I lean down and attempt to grab it with my fingers, my eyes catch an image in the side mirror. At first, I can't tell what it is, and it's only when the sun's reflection changes that I realize it's a heavily tinted windshield.

None of our neighbors have cars with tinted windows.

My fingers find the latch, and I pull it up along the belt and across my chest.

"All set?" Calvin slides in behind the wheel and turns on the ignition.

I glance over my shoulder. "Yeah..." I say, distracted. Parked alongside the curb across the street is a black sedan with matte black tinted windows. I have never seen this car in our neighborhood before.

"Everything ok?" Calvin asks, following my gaze.

"Uh, yeah. Yeah, everything's good!" I face him and then look forward. "What are you waiting for, Grandma. Let's go."

He looks at me for a moment, shrugs, and starts to back out of the driveway. I watch in the side mirror as the dark car lurches away from the curb and accelerates ahead of us. By the time we are on the street, the car is too far away to see the license plate. I pick at my fingernails. It's probably nothing. I'm probably just hyper-aware since I've just spoken to Roth.

"You wanna hear a really funny joke?" Calvin asks.

I smile and look over at him.

"Absolutely."

———

Physical Therapists are trained torture specialists.

Sure, they *say* they're here to help, they *say* their job is to increase mobility, but I secretly believe they are sociopaths that love inflicting pain in new and exciting ways.

I grab two Motrin from the kitchen and make my way to the living room couch with a glass of water. I let Guthrie out of his crate, pop the pills and take a huge swallow of water. He doesn't seem to want to go outside, so I strip off my boot, prop my foot up on a pillow and grab my laptop off the coffee table. Opening up my Instagram app, I'm vaguely curious to see what, if any, activity has occurred in the last twenty-four hours. As my notifications refresh, and I see the activity surrounding my post of the cabin with the bear, I sit up so fast I nearly bounce my laptop off my legs. My mouth drops open as I look at the statistics. My photo has received serious attention. Not only has the PNWlife group chosen to feature it on their own platform, it's also been picked up by several central Oregon outdoor enthusiast groups, as well as a few groups dedicated to tourism. All total the photo has attracted the attention of a few hundred people.

"Guth! Do you know how exciting this is?" I peek around the side of my laptop to find a dozing dog curled up on the floor beside me.

I open up my photo library again and begin sorting through some of the sunrise pictures from that day. I find one I'm proud of, make a few more edits and then post it with the same hashtag references as before. Then I return to my previous post and begin following the people and groups that showed interest in the bear photo, making small comments of thanks to people that took the time to forward, or share the picture, and answering a few questions about the bear. It feels good to be connecting with people, talking to others about Oregon, and exploring the outdoors. And it feels great to receive compliments about the photo from complete strangers. I shut the laptop and close my eyes, now more than ever I am resolved to heal quickly.

I can't wait to get back on my feet, and back outside.

CHAPTER FIFTEEN

GEORGIA

THE REST OF THE WEEK flies by. Between mornings at work with Ed and two intense physical therapy sessions on Monday and Thursday, I feel like I've been beaten to a pulp when I wake up on Friday morning.

My spirits lift considerably when I arrive at work and my cell phone rings. The Sisters Tribune wants to talk about the article, and the editor asks if it's okay to mention Ben and the assistance he and the Department of Forestry provided. I try to contain my excitement and tell him it's probably just fine, but I need to clear it with Ben first, quietly crossing my fingers he will still call me later tonight. The article is due to run the following week, so I agree to get in touch again after the weekend with final permissions.

Upon hanging up the phone, my first instinct is to share the news with my mom. My excitement fades as a dull ache in my chest opens. Will this ever get any easier? I miss her. I miss them both. Every single day. But some days, like today, are harder, when the realization that they are both gone slams into me again.

Will I ever reach a point in life when I don't have to remember all over again?

Luckily, I have Sylvia to share the great news with and she is ecstatic enough for both of us. We agree to a proper celebratory dinner out when she and Scott return from his class in Washington. A small wave of guilt stabs at me as I register relief at having the whole house to myself over the weekend.

Well, Guthrie and me anyway.

———

After work, Calvin takes Guthrie outside while I stand in the kitchen and make myself a strong margarita: fresh lime juice, double shot of tequila, and a splash of ginger ale. I take a long sip and think about what I should make for dinner. I pull out some baby spinach, leftover chicken breast, a couple of hardboiled eggs and some bell peppers, and begin to prepare a chopped salad; the perfect solution to a tired, single girl's dinner on a Friday night.

I am already dreaming about the TV shows I'll watch.

"Guth's all set," Calvin says, coming into the kitchen.

Guthrie trots in behind Calvin; tail wagging, tongue hanging out of his mouth.

"Thanks, Cal. Can you believe how much better he looks? And look how he's walking now."

"I know. It's getting hard to keep him from trying to run outside. I should probably keep him on a leash out back until he gets that cast off."

I finish washing the spinach and dry my hands on the towel at the sink.

"The leash is hanging on the hook by the back door if you need it next time." I pause, realizing something. "Hey, I forgot Scott and Sylvia are away this weekend. I'm not sure, I mean I think I can handle Guthrie, but do you...uh, will you be in Silverton at all this weekend just in case I can't control him?"

Calvin stares at me, no doubt trying to figure out exactly what I'm attempting to say. Ugh, I hate asking for help.

"You know, never mind. I'm sure I—"

"—No, it's fine. I was actually thinking of doing some hiking this weekend at the falls. I could detour through Silverton and stop by on the way up. Maybe 9 a.m.?"

I take a large drink of my margarita and nod, swallowing it down quickly so I can answer.

"Yeah, that'd work. Are you sure it's not too much trouble?" I stick out my lower lip at him. "I'm jealous by the way."

"Of what? My ability to walk like a normal human being?"

"Ha-ha. Very funny. Yes, that too. But the hike! Silver Falls is so beautiful this time of year. Although," I say, dropping my voice. "It's still very muddy on the trails though, so be careful," I warn, pointing my index finger at him. I feel somewhat protective of him — as if he's a younger brother or a favorite cousin.

"I'll be fine. And don't worry. You'll be back on your gargantuan feet again in no time. Then maybe we can go on a hike together." A small grin stretches across his face, and he shoves his hands into his pockets, his head tilting to the side.

A younger brother that needs a girlfriend. His own age. Immediately.

"Ah Calvin, Calvin, Calvin. Ever the optimist, aren't ya?"

He shrugs. "What can I say? You're hot!"

I nearly spit out my drink.

"Okay, I'm not getting caught by that geyser again!" He backs out of the kitchen, and I hear him holler from the front door. "I'll call you in the morning before I head over."

"Bye!" I yell back.

Glancing at the clock, I make a mental note that Ben should be hiking down the butte right about now.

———

After dinner, Guthrie and I curl up on the couch together and turn on re-runs of Seinfeld. I sip my second margarita and laugh as George makes a fool of himself swooning over Marisa Tomei. It's one of my favorite episodes.

Suddenly the phone rings, and I grab it off the coffee table answering it before the second ring.

"Hello?"

"Hi, it's me." Ben sounds tired, his voice husky and deep.

My shoulders relax, and I settle back into the couch.

"Hi, how are you?"

"I'm well. I'm glad it's finally Friday. I've been wanting to talk to you all week."

My stomach starts turning circles on itself.

"Me too. I have so much to tell you."

"Really? Hang on one second — *Charlie!*" His voice is muffled, and it sounds like he's yelling outside. "Sorry, Georgia, Charlie is taking off toward the pasture. *Come on, get in here boy.*" I hear a door shut. "Okay, all good now. Go ahead."

"First the boring thing: turns out my auto insurance wants to photograph the Jeep for the damages claim. My agent has a contact in Sisters, and apparently, he's going to be out next week to take pictures. Is there a way he can make arrangements with Matt to let him into the barn? Oh, and what's your address out there?"

I take down Matt's telephone number and Ben's address, and we talk about it being towed home.

"I gotta say, I'm gonna miss having it in my barn. Reminds me of you." His voice is soft now.

"When can we see each other again?" I ask, pressing my thighs together.

"When can you drive again?" he chuckles.

"Ugh, I don't know. I've only just finished with my first week of physical therapy. I don't even see the doctor again for another three weeks. Can you come over here for a weekend? Or a night..." I bite my lip in anticipation of his reply.

"While there's nothing I want more right now, I really can't. It's been too hot over here, and we've had several small fires already. I spotted two from the lookout just this week." He sighs. "I really miss you though. I miss holding you in my arms. I miss waking up next to you."

The smile on my face could not grow any larger.

"I miss you too. You have no idea. Thoughts of you keep interrupting my day...and my nights."

I quickly change the subject in an attempt to distract my thoughts. "So, some exciting news here...I was editing my photos from that hike and guess what?"

"What, baby?"

"Well, before I came down to your cabin, I took a few photos of it from the top of the butte, and guess what I saw when I zoomed into the background?"

"I—"

"—A bear cub! In the bushes behind the cabin! It was right there, and I had no idea."

"What? Are you certain?"

"Yes! One hundred percent positive. In fact, I sent the photo and a short email to the Sisters Tribune telling them what happened to me. And guess what? They contacted me! They want to run an article along with the picture in next week's paper!"

"No way. That's incredible!"

"I know! And thank you. I'm really excited."

"Well that explains why the adult pursued you so intensely."

"I think you actually suggested that theory after it happened, didn't you?"

"Yeah, but it was really just speculation. Anyway, that's amazing, Georgia! Congratulations!"

"Thank you. Oh," I say, dropping my voice. "The newspaper wants to print your name and mention the help you and the Department of Forestry provided. Would that be all right?"

Ben is silent, which begins to make me feel awkward.

"Or, if you don't want to be mentioned, I'm—"

"—No, it's okay. It...I'm just thinking about the last time I was in the newspaper...with Charlotte I mean."

"Oh. I didn't even think."

"It's all right. This is clearly a completely different thing," he says and takes a deep breath. "Uh, yes, it's fine to mention me, although I don't know I'd add anything of interest to the story. Do I need to sign anything?"

"Not at all. You just need to contact the editor and give him your consent. And you do add interest to the story — you saved my life and took care of me for an entire weekend." I rattle off the contact information for the editor before he can argue any further.

"Is there any other exciting news you need to tell me about?"

"No, I think that covers my checklist."

"Good, because I've had the whole week to think about you and it's been driving me crazy."

"Hopefully in a good way?" My interest is definitely piqued.

"Yes, in a good way. You've been in my thoughts and on my mind every day and every night. Honestly, woman, you've been a serious distraction to my work." I imagine the sly grin appearing on his face, his dark eyes peering out from under his lashes at me.

"I really miss you, Ben," I say, wrapping my free arm around my chest, hugging myself.

"Maybe I can remind you—"

Guthrie suddenly leaps out of his bed and rushes to the front door, barking ferociously. The noise makes me jump, and I immediately sit up on the couch.

"Guthrie! Guthrie, hush!"

"Is everything okay there?" Ben's voice is barely audible over Guthrie's barking.

"I don't know. He's barking at the front door all of the sudden. Guthrie, stop!" I pull the blanket off my lower body, preparing to stand up. "Guthrie, shh!" I'm snapping my fingers at him trying to get his attention, but he won't stop. The hair on the center of his back is raised in a ridge down the length of his spine. I've never seen him like this before.

"Is anyone there with you? Is Scott there?" The tone of Ben's voice is a little frightening.

"What? No, they went to Washington for the weekend." My chest begins to tighten.

"Be careful please, Georgia. Don't open the door without verifying—"

Guthrie is still barking like crazy, and as I approach the door, the barking intensifies. I can't hear Ben any longer.

I flip on the porch light and reach toward the window near the door, pulling back the thin curtain to look outside. The front stoop is empty. I try to see into the yard, but our section of the road doesn't have a streetlight. It's completely black outside. Almost as if on cue, Guthrie's barking lessens and then stops completely.

"Georgia, are you there?"

"Yeah," I say, distracted. "I'm looking out of the window. I don't see anything, but it's pretty dark outside." I cup my free hand around my eyes and look across the yard to where the street should be, trying to adjust my eyes to the darkness. Guthrie begins to whine at my feet. "What, boy?" I mumble as I stare out the window. My hot breath is fogging up the glass. I can make out Sylvia's car in the driveway now, and the sidewalk at the edge of

115

our yard. I'm just about to pull back from the window when I think I notice movement across the street. "Wait. What…"

"What? What is it?" Ben's voice is intense in my ear.

"Nothing. I just thought I saw some—" A quick reflection of light across the street draws my eye, and I hear a small, hollow noise. Is that a car door closing?

"Thought you saw what? Georgia, are you okay?"

"Mmm hmm." I focus on what I can now see of the street, ignoring Ben, my eyes searching for any sign of movement.

"Do you want me to call the police?"

"What? No, I'm fi—"

Then I see it. Across the street, a car moves away from the curb and begins to drive slowly away. There aren't any headlights, only the soft interior glow of the dashboard and the tiny reflection of the front porch light on the shiny exterior as it moves. I gasp and push my cheek against the glass, watching it drive under the streetlight down the road, the light passing smoothly over the sleek black roof.

"What is it? Jesus, I can't stand this." Ben sounds frantic. "Georgia, I'm hanging up and calling the police."

"Wait! I'm sorry. I think it's over now. I just saw a car drive away."

"A car? What kind of car?"

"I don't know exactly. I think it's the same one I saw here earlier this week. It was parked across the street on, oh, was it Tuesday maybe? I can't remember. I didn't recognize it from the neighborhood, so it caught my attention. When we backed out of the driveway, it drove away. I had kind of forgotten about it, but I think this was the same car." I suddenly feel very cold. I stand back from the window and close the curtains tightly.

"I think you should call the police."

I think about it for a moment, looking down at Guthrie, lying in front of the door, his eyes beginning to close.

"No. It's fine. Guthrie is nearly asleep again. Besides, what would I say, *I think a strange car was in my neighborhood?*"

"It would make me feel better."

"But I'd have nothing to report. It would be a waste of time," I say, considering my next course of action. I swallow and then clear my throat.

"Ben, I think I want a gun."

CHAPTER SIXTEEN

GEORGIA

I SLEEP WITH Guthrie in my room and my cell phone under my pillow. Every noise makes my pulse race, and I'm too afraid to turn my bedroom light off. I think I finally fall asleep somewhere after 2:30 a.m.

In the morning, I have burning, red eyes and a screaming headache. My temples throb as I sit up, and it takes all of my willpower to get myself into the bathroom.

I'm showered and sitting in the kitchen nursing my second cup of black coffee when the house phone rings.

"Hello?" I say, my voice thick with lack of sleep.

"Just making sure you're doing ok this morning." Ben's kind voice drifts over the line.

I rub my temples. "Yeah, I survived. Barely," I say, yawning. "I couldn't fall asleep. Kept waking up."

"I'm sorry I couldn't be there with you. If it's any consolation, I didn't sleep well last night either. I kept worrying about you. We need to do something about that."

"I'm not calling the police if that's what you mean. At least, not yet. Like I said, I don't have anything concrete to report."

"That's part of it, yes, but also, I..."

"Yes?"

"I don't like being away from you. You've become important to me. Besides," he chuckles, "worrying about you makes me grouchy."

Even through my sleep hangover haziness, a buzz of excitement purrs through me at his words. "I don't like being away from you either," I say. "I just feel so much more grounded when I'm around you. Like everything is exactly where it should be. I hope that doesn't sound too weird. I'm qualifying my comments with the fact that I'm basically a zombie right now."

"It sounds great to me."

"Hey, I was serious about a gun though," I say, completely focused. "I think I need to learn to at least shoot one. I know nothing about obtaining one or what the laws are regarding ownership, but I think I'd feel safer having one. Besides," I say, "I've decided it's time for me to get my own place, and I want to be safe."

"Oh yeah?"

"Mmm hmm. I've had a good solid year to get my bearings after my divorce. If these experiences — the hike, the injury, meeting you — if all of that has taught me anything, it's that I'm stronger than I thought. That and meeting you feels really, really right."

"It does?"

"Yes. It does. Ben, when you left, it felt like someone had dug a hole in my chest that just kept growing larger. I wasn't prepared for that. I guess I didn't realize how much I enjoy being around you, and how much you mean to me." I take a deep breath. "Is that crazy? We only really spent a weekend together."

"No, I don't think it's crazy. This definitely doesn't feel like anything I've ever experienced. But I also think perspective changes after hard circumstances. I don't know. I certainly don't have all the answers. But I'm not ruling anything out anymore. I know I like being around you. I like it a lot."

"Ditto." I smile and hobble over to the coffee pot, pouring myself another cup.

"So," his voice is louder now. "About the gun...I think it's a good idea too. You don't need a license to buy one, but you will have to go through a full background check. Now, if you want to start carting it around with you outside of your house, then yeah, we'll need to get you into a class so you can apply for your concealed carry permit. But you can buy a gun at any sporting goods store. Do you have one in Silverton?"

"No, but Salem has several, and that's only about thirty miles away."

"I'd recommend getting a small handgun, maybe a 9 millimeter. Even though it's more complicated than a pistol, I'd still suggest taking a look at the 9. It's pretty slim, it's not very heavy, and it's fairly easy to control. But see what you like."

"Hang on. I'm going to grab a piece of paper." I open a drawer and shuffle around, grabbing the back of a take-out menu and a pencil.

"You can just be honest and tell the salesperson you're a beginner and you're looking for something for self-defense. I'm sure they'll show you a couple of different options. I'd probably pick a 9 millimeter for you though. It's likely going to have less of a kick, too."

"Got it. What else do I need?"

"Well, you'll need ammunition. And you'll need to learn how to shoot it. Is there a shooting range in Salem? Or can Scott teach you?"

"Oh no, definitely not Scott. I don't want either of them to know I'm even considering this. They would freak."

"I wish I were there. I'd be happy to guide you. Hey, what

about that kid driving you around? Can he take you to the range? Would he tell Scott?"

"Calvin?" I wrinkle my nose. "Actually, he would probably love the idea. He's all but admitted he has a crush on me."

"That's not funny."

"You've got competition, mister," I tease.

"I'm flexing my biceps right now," he says, laughing. "Also, I have guns. And knives..."

"You have nothing to worry about. Seriously. He's a nice guy, and I really appreciate his help, but he's like a little brother to me."

"I'd like to meet him someday."

"Actually, he's supposed to be here soon," I say, glancing at the clock.

"Oh really?" Ben's voice carries an edge of jealousy.

"To help me with the *dog*." I stand up and hobble into the living room. Guthrie is asleep on his bed.

"Okay, okay. I'm just teasing you anyway. Will you call me tonight? Let me know how things go today?"

"I will. And thank you for your help with the gun. I feel better already."

"I'll feel better when I have you safe in my arms again."

"Me too. A thousand times better."

———

Calvin shows up a few minutes later, precisely at 9 a.m., even though he never called beforehand. I can't complain. At least he's punctual.

To my utmost surprise, he's wearing black hiking shorts, an enviable pair of brightly colored trail shoes, and a dri-fit, short-sleeve hiking shirt. I don't know what I was expecting him to wear, but this is a big departure from his typical preppy look.

I hold the door open for him as he steps inside. "I hope you have a jacket in your car. It's gonna be cold and wet in the canyons up there."

"I do. Thanks, mom." He heads toward the kitchen and looks back at me over his shoulder, grinning.

"Funny, Calvin. Real funny."

He takes Guthrie out on a leash and nearly loses his balance as Guth pulls him hard and fast, trying to get out to pee. They come back in just as quickly, Guthrie leading him through the back door and straight to his food dish.

"Jesus! I guess Guth is feeling better, huh?" He unhooks the leash as the dog bends over his dish and begins to eat ferociously.

"I guess so!"

"All right, well, there ya go." He coils up the leash and places it on the kitchen counter. "I better get going."

"What time do you think you'll be done?" I tilt my head at him and bat my eyelashes.

He stares at me, a blank expression on his face.

"The hell?"

I can't help but laugh. "Okay, okay, so here's the thing: I need you to take me somewhere to buy something that you can't tell anyone about. Not even Scott or Sylvia. I mean it. They can *never* know." I fold my hands in prayer at him. "Please? Could you come back after your hike and pick me up? It won't take very long." I mouth the word *please* at him again as he considers my request.

"Where do I have to take you?"

"Salem?" I say, squinting my eyes at him, bracing for the rejection.

"So, let me get this straight. You want me to drive you to Salem, and back home again, so I can turn around and drive back to Salem? That's like two round-trip trips in one day, Fraulein!" He turns, shaking his head as he walks toward the door.

"I'll pay you!" I shout. "Overtime even."

He stops and turns to me.

"What do you need so badly?"

"If I tell you, you have to promise not to tell—"

"—Scott and Sylvia, I know, I know. Jeez, what are you buying? Drugs?"

"No, I'm not buying drugs!"

"Porn? That's it isn't it?" He waggles his eyebrows at me and nods slowly. "I knew it."

I shake my head and roll my eyes simultaneously.

"You're crazy. I'm not—"

"A gun? Are you buying a...Jesus Christ, you're buying a gun!"

"Shhh! You're yelling!"

He claps a hand over his mouth; his eyes bulging out over the top of his fingers.

"You wanna buy a gun," he whispers, dropping his hand. "How come?"

"It's a very long, convoluted story. But yes, I do want to buy a gun. Would you be willing to drive me?"

"Absolutely." He crosses his arms over his chest and nods slowly.

I'm stunned. This is the exact opposite of what I imagined he would say.

"Really?"

"Sure. I grew up with guns. My family has been hunting and target shooting for generations. It's tradition in the Dorsett family."

"I never would have guessed that. Not ever."

"Why not?'

"Because of the way you...well, I don't really know, actually. You just don't look like the type. Not that there's a type. I just... are you even old enough to own a gun?" I'm only half-joking. I have no idea how old a person needs to be to buy a gun — eighteen?

"I never joke about guns," he says, dead serious.

"Okay, okay. I'm sorry. I'm just surprised you're such a firearms aficionado."

"Apology accepted. Now." He checks his watch. "I'm going to head out, do the hike, and then I'll be back to take you to town. Say, 3:30 ish?"

"Sounds great. Are you sure you won't tell? I don't want to put you in a compromising position."

"It's no problem. I consider it my civic duty." He opens the front door and steps out. "See you this afternoon."

After saying goodbye outside, I glance around the neighborhood. Nothing seems out of place. The strange car is nowhere to be seen, and yet I can't help but feel as though I'm being watched.

Calvin starts up his car and backs out of the driveway. I wave to him and then head back to the house, locking the door tightly behind me.

———

Buying a gun takes a lot longer than I ever would have imagined.

First of all, I have to "try on" several brands and models. There are so many different calibers and names, measurements, and ratings...I lose track of everything pretty much right away.

It probably didn't help that I'd never really been interested in guns. In fact, I was just the opposite: I had always hated guns. After seeing what they did to my parents, I always felt like it was better to just leave guns alone, and let the police handle the criminals that toted them around. But now, feeling unsafe in my own town, in my own home...I'd re-examined my feelings about guns and decided my safety was non-negotiable.

125

Mike's police issue was always present in our house, of course. He always had it — and a shotgun — with him at all times. But his handgun seemed giant next to some of these small pistols laid out on the counter in front of me. They all look like pretty much the same thing to me; some larger, some smaller, some heavy, some light. They all shoot bullets, which is pretty much the only thing that matters to me right now.

The salesman is the exact opposite of what I expect.

Tony is a tall, fit older man wearing silver rimless glasses and a navy blue polo shirt. He has huge Popeye forearms, complete with a USMC globe and anchor tattoo. Staring at it, I wonder how long he was in the service.

Tony takes his time instructing me on the features of each style, and patiently teaches me the basics any firearm owner should know: how to make sure it's not loaded, how to engage and disengage the safety, how to hold it, and how to hand it to someone, which, he adamantly emphasizes, is with the barrel pointed *away*. In the end, Ben is one hundred percent correct: I like the 9 millimeter best. It's light, it's small, and it seems easy enough to use. The ammunition magazines look simple to insert, and they hold seven rounds, plus one in the chamber — plenty. Most of all, it just feels good in my hand. I decide to purchase it and nearly fall over at the sticker price, mentally calculating how many months of payments to my Visa it will require. In the end, I decide peace of mind is worth half a year of interest.

Next, I undergo a criminal background check. Even though I know my record is spotless, I can't help but feel nervous as Tony types in my social security number and politely asks me not to leave the premises. I wonder what kind of information gets reported in a background check. Does it show I'm divorced from a cop? Does it report I went through therapy, or that my parents were victims of a gun-related crime? I have no idea what to expect, and I nervously look at Calvin with a silent plea. He nods and smiles with reassurance, stepping in closer to me.

"Calm down," he whispers. "This is all very normal. C'mon, let's go look at backpacks."

We stroll up and down the aisles looking at backpacks and tent displays and then move on to hiking boots.

"Hey, how was the hike this morning?" I ask, picking up a Salomon trail shoe.

"Oh, it was awesome. It's so beautiful up there, and surprisingly there weren't that many people on the trails. Although..." His voice dies away as he checks the price on a pair of boots.

"Although what?"

"Huh? Oh, nothing. Just, at one point I was hiking along, alone on the trail, when literally outta nowhere, this guy shows up behind me. Like close behind me. Awkwardly close. It was really weird. Eh," he says, shaking his head, "probably just some crazy hippie."

"Ugh. I hate that. No boundaries. Did you just let him pass?"

"No, that was the bizarre part. He showed up just as I reached South Falls — you know, the one you walk behind?"

"Yeah of course. I've hiked that canyon about sixty-five times."

"Yeah, so, I'm starting to go behind it, and I can hear that he's close to me. Like he's only a few steps away, but as we get deeper behind the waterfall, it's getting really loud under there, you know, with the water crashing around, so I don't know if he's still close." Calvin puts down the boot he's holding, and takes a step toward me, his brow furrowed. "But I had this really weird feeling, so I pick up the pace, to the point where I'm almost jogging, and then when I come out the other side of the waterfall, I slow down, thinking I'm gonna step aside and take a picture and let this guy pass me. But when I turn around, there's no one there." He shrugs a shoulder. "Weird, huh?"

"Uh yeah, definitely. Did you see him come out the other side of the waterfall then?"

"Huh-uh. It's like he just...disappeared."

"Hmm. Well, I don't know. You probably just missed him. It gets pretty dark back in there. Maybe he went back to look at the caves..."

"Ms. Marks, we're all set now," Tony says, coming around the corner. "Your history came back good, and we're ready to complete the transaction."

Fifteen minutes later I'm the proud owner of a Sig Sauer 9 millimeter pistol. It's presented to me in a small black suitcase that reminds me of all the James Bond films I've ever seen. Inside the case, precisely outlined rigid blue foam holds the weapon and magazine separate from each other, protecting each piece. A few other areas in the case are empty, and I assume they are for additional rounds or other add-ons. I shut the case, and Tony seals the handle shut with a zip tie, pushing it toward me across the counter.

"Just a sec though," Tony says as I grab hold of the handle. "I'm going to give you a few brochures for local shooting ranges and some information about the next concealed carry class." He looks at me over the top of his glasses and squints one eye at me. "I would highly recommend that you take the class, even if you don't ever intend to carry. And I would definitely get to the shooting range as soon as you are able," he says, glancing at my walking boot. "Get yourself familiar with this weapon. You don't want to need it and not know what to do with it."

He taps the counter twice with the tips of his fingers and walks away. Transaction complete. I slowly turn toward Calvin — my eyes open wide. He shrugs and nods in the direction of the front door.

"I feel like I've just shoplifted," I say as we walk across the parking lot. "I'm waiting for someone to yell *stop!*"

"That's nothing. Try buying a rifle."

Inside the car, I breathe a huge sigh of relief as Calvin shuts the driver's side door and starts the car.

He turns toward me and raises his hand high, palm facing me.

"High five!"

"Thanks," I say, smiling and slapping his hand. "That was really nerve-racking."

"The first time is always the worst. You get used to it after a while."

"After a while? Just how many guns do you own?"

He turns the car onto the main road, and we head toward Silverton.

"Uh...let's see." He silently touches his fingers, counting. Oh my word, he's using both hands. "I guess that makes eight? Yeah, maybe eight or nine." He nods once, apparently satisfied with his decision.

"*Nine?*" I whistle, and shake my head at him.

"There's always something new coming out, and besides, you can never have too many guns."

"Hmm," I say, not really sure how to answer.

"So when are you going to shoot that baby?" He motions to the case at my feet.

"I don't know. I guess I should try it soon, huh? Tony thinks that's pretty important."

"He's absolutely right, Georgia. How about tomorrow?"

"What?" I ask, shocked.

"Tomorrow. How about tomorrow? I can take you to the range back in Salem if you want. The nearest one after that is south, in Albany."

"Oh. Well, I don't know." I calculate what time Scott and

129

Sylvia will likely be home. "Yeah, I guess so. If we go in the morning, I should beat my sister home from Washington."

"Perfect."

"But that's like, another four trips for you. That's a lot of driving and gas. Plus it's your weekend!"

"I don't have anything else to do, and this is the perfect opportunity — no older sister and husband to know what you're up to." He winks at me.

I stare at him for a second, dumbfounded.

"Calvin Dorsett, I have seriously underestimated you."

He taps the steering wheel and laughs. "I'll take that as a compliment."

"Oh my God, you're so weird."

He turns up the radio as he drives me home — the Red Hot Chili Peppers blanketing our ears and filling our minds with rebellion.

CHAPTER SEVENTEEN

GEORGIA

"HOW DID YOU SLEEP LAST night?" Ben asks, his voice is so soft it makes my insides turn to liquid.

It's Sunday morning, but I'm already dressed, lounging in bed. Guthrie is sprawled out across my feet.

"So much better than the night before. It's surprising how reassuring it is just having a handgun nearby, even if I don't know the first thing about actually using it."

"Did you load it?"

"No. I was too afraid I'd screw something up and end up blowing a hole in the wall. Or myself."

"Smart girl."

"But I am going to the shooting range this morning before my sister and Scott get back. I want to learn how to use it." Despite my bravado, I'm still feeling uneasy about the strange car in the neighborhood, and Calvin's encounter on the trail. Maybe it's coincidental. Maybe it's not.

"Calvin taking you?"

"Yep. Turns out he's a gun-toting, card-carrying member of

the NRA." I laugh. "He actually offered. Said it seemed like the perfect chance while Scott and Sylvia are away."

"Why don't you want them to know?"

"Well, for one thing, I don't think they'd approve of having a gun in the house. The subject's never come up, but I just get the feeling, mainly from Scott, that he wouldn't like that idea at all."

"Ah, I see."

"So this is the perfect opportunity to practice with it. Calvin says there's a range in Salem."

"If I didn't know better, I'd say Calvin was making a move on my woman."

"What?" His comment ignites a spark of excitement in my belly. "First of all, he's half my age, well not really, but you know what I mean. And second, he..." trailing off, I remember his *you're hot* comment.

"Well?"

"Yeah, maybe you're right," I say, and we both laugh. "All right, he may have some ulterior motives, but I can promise you, Ben, I'm only interested in his ability to drive, and the fact that he can show me how to use a gun. Seriously, I don't feel very safe anymore."

"I know. I'm really sorry." He's quiet for a moment. "Has my phone received any more text messages?"

"None. Thank God."

"Good," he sighs. "I really believe that was more to do with me than you. Like I said, probably someone connected with Charlotte in some way."

"Yeah, but what about the Jeep? And the hotel room?" Goosebumps rise on my arms at the memories.

"I've been thinking about that too. Bend is a small town, and Sisters even smaller. The vandalism, well, unfortunately, I think that was just bad luck. But as far as the hotel room, it's entirely possible that someone saw us together, driving around with the top down—"

"—Wow, I really miss that."

"You have no idea how much I miss that too." He's quiet for a moment and then clears his throat.

"But if someone saw us, someone that knew Charlotte or knew what had happened, I mean... People can be so crazy, Georgia. Someone with an axe to grind could have easily done that. I told you, she came from pretty rough circumstances. And, no offense, but I didn't get the sense that hotel was ultra secure."

"Yeah, I guess you're right. Still, this weird car in the neighborhood...I'd just feel better if I knew how to operate my gun."

"I agree, and I'm glad you're doing it. I just wish it were me there instead of Clyde."

"You mean Calvin," I snort. "You just need to meet him. He's really like a little brother."

"Maybe I'll make a surprise visit to see you."

I gasp.

"Could you? That would be so good!"

"It would be very, very good," he says, drawing the words out and dropping his voice. I tuck my hand under my thigh, suddenly nervous.

"I don't think I can manage to get away right now, but I'll see what I can do."

"I think you're teasing me now," I say, my face beginning to flush with heat.

"You have no idea. I can't stop thinking about you, Georgia. I can't stop thinking about kissing you. It's keeping me awake at night."

"I know how you feel." My pulse is racing.

"I'm dead serious. I don't think I can stand to be away from you much longer. It's like you've cast some sort of spell on me. I'm not sleeping well. I'm up all night dreaming about you. And during the day I alternate between worrying about your safety and daydreaming about holding you in my arms." He pauses and then groans. "I was a complete fool to walk away from you that day. I will never forgive myself for being so stupid."

"Please, it's forgotten. Don't think another thing about it."

"I wanted to tell you this in person. I wanted to wait so you could see my face. So I could hold you, and you could know just how much I truly mean this...but I don't think I can hold back any longer." He takes a deep breath as I hold mine. "I think I'm falling in love with you, Georgia, and there's nothing I can do to stop myself. Somehow, that weekend together, it was enough for feelings that have been buried in me a long time, maybe even forever, to finally surface and demand recognition. And now I can't get you out of my mind. And the thing is — I don't want to. I don't want you out of my thoughts. Ever."

I am speechless — utterly speechless with huge tears pooling in my eyes. My nose begins to sting, and I know I'm not far away from losing it. I try to breathe calmly and smoothly, but my breath shudders as I rake it in.

"Ah, man, I'm sorry. I should have waited to say any—"

"—No, no! No, please. I'm so moved by what you said. I'm just overcome with emotion right now." I move the phone away from my face as the tears spill over and run down the side of my nose and cheeks.

"Are you all right? It sounds like you're crying. Baby?"

"Yeah, I'm good. Just, I don't know. Surprised, I guess. And happy," I quickly say, before sucking in a long, steadying breath. "It's just that I never thought I would hear those words from someone that really meant them. I never thought I would feel love again, Ben. I really didn't. I pretty much thought life was over for me in that department." Through my tears and runny nose, I smile. "You've been the greatest surprise of my life, Benjamin Harrison."

"When I get my arms around you again, you had better buckle your seat belt, woman."

I laugh, and a few more tears leak from the corners of my eyes. Wiping them away, I stand up to find a Kleenex. Guthrie jolts upright, still half asleep.

"Thank you, Georgia."

I stop walking.

"Thank you? What in the world for?"

"For giving me something to believe in again. For leading me in the right direction. I know that sounds unbelievably corny, but I mean it. With all of my heart, I mean it."

"I seriously do not deserve you."

A sudden knock at the front door sends Guthrie into a barking frenzy as he leaps off the bed and runs to the front door, barking at an ear-splitting level. I spin around in the kitchen, staring at the door.

"Guthrie!" I follow after him, yelling his name and wiping my face.

"What's going on? Is someone there?"

I check the clock on the mantle. "Oh, it's probably Calvin," I say, looking out of the front window.

He's standing on the front porch stoop, staring at the house. He waves when he sees me in the window. Guth sniffs at the bottom of the door and stops barking, his tail slightly wagging.

"Yep, it's Calvin," I say, unlocking the door.

"Morning sunshine! Ready to go shoo—"

I motion to the phone at my ear and Calvin immediately rolls his eyes and clamps his mouth closed.

"I should probably get going, Ben. I want to learn how to shoot before the grown-ups come home."

Opening the door wide, I motion for him to come in. "One second, Calvin," I whisper, and then head back to my room.

"This morning means so much to me, Ben. Thank you for

135

trusting me, and for opening up and being...just so real." I press a hand against my chest. "My heart is bursting right now. Honestly, I'm literally holding it in."

"I meant every word I said. Every. Single. Word."

————

Calvin carries a small black duffel bag — my mini suitcase tucked safely inside — as we walk across the parking lot. The simple white sign displayed high above the facility reads: *Shooting Range*. It's still early in the morning and I only see three other vehicles in the lot. I'm already nervous.

We enter the building through two sets of tinted, heavy double doors. The breezeway in between is musty, and the stale air tickles my nose and threatens to make me sneeze. I anticipate only being allowed through the second set of doors after we flash our IDs to some unseen surveillance camera or something, but Calvin steps ahead of me and pushes the door open easily, allowing me to hobble into the small office ahead of him.

Calvin leads us to a check-in area to the right, and I look around the small room. Different sizes and shapes of guns line the shelves and walls behind the counters. The muffled sounds of unseen shots being fired just beyond the office peaks my senses and a small thread of adrenalin runs through my nerves. Calvin says hello to one of the clerks and we're each given several forms to fill out: a rules and guidelines sheet to sign and date, a liability waiver, and a general information form that asks for driver's license number, address, etc., as well as a section to indicate what type of gun(s) we've brought in. We're asked if we need targets or ammunition, and Calvin taps his duffel bag lightly, indicating we have everything we need. The man verifies our forms, collects the fees, and reaches under the counter to produce two pairs of giant blue headsets — they remind me of what the guys on the tarmac wear when directing airplanes — as well as two small bags of earplugs.

"All right," Calvin says, "let's get in there, eh?"

My stomach sinks with a small wave of anxiety, and I nod and nervously tuck my hair behind my ears.

He leads the way as we step through another set of doors and into the actual shooting range. Inside, the crack of shots being fired in an enclosed facility rings out and echoes against the walls, assaulting my hearing with a piercing *thwack-thwack-thwack*. My hands fly to my ears, and I realize why we've been given two types of ear protection.

The smell of sulfur and hot pencil lead fills the air, and I am reminded of how, as a kid, I used to roll my window down at gas stations, trying to inhale the pungent fumes. Thin clouds of smoke float over the shooting bays, winding and drifting toward the overworked inhalation machines on the ceiling. My heart is beating in my ears, and I notice my hands are clammy.

We pass a few empty bays as well as two that are in use. A woman holding her arms out points a gun at a paper target several yards in front of her as a man in an orange vest stands next to her, shouting instructions and modeling the way she should hold her arms. She shoots several rounds, and the bullet casings fly out and scatter on the floor. The scene reminds me of a slow motion Roman candle firework.

Calvin turns into the bay alongside the far wall of the building, and I'm immediately thankful there's no one next to us. My stomach feels light and a bead of sweat rolls down the center of my back.

Standing in front of the small waist-high shelf that stretches across the width of the narrow bay, Calvin places the duffel bag off to the side. He unzips the bag, pulls out two baseball caps, and two pairs of yellow-tinted safety glasses.

"Here. Put these on, and then put your earplugs and headset

on. After that, you won't be able to hear me very well, so I'm going to shout, but I'm also going to use a lot of hand movements. Just watch what I do and if you have any questions, or don't understand, just signal me with a stop." He holds his hand in the high five position, palm raised toward me, and then quickly closes it, making a fist. "Like that, okay?"

I nod and swallow hard.

I quickly gather my hair back into a messy bun and pull the ball cap down over my forehead. He hands me the safety glasses, and I slide them on — everything around me turning a hazy orange. Calvin put his own glasses on and we both pinch and twist our earplugs into our ears. Instantly, the noise in the building muffles, as if we have suddenly jumped into the deep end of a swimming pool.

He hands me the headset, and I clamp it down over my hat, the flexible cups fitting comfortably over my ears and muting the remaining gargled sounds in the room. In the silence, the sound of my own rapid heartbeat is jarring, and a slight feeling of claustrophobia pulls at my senses.

I look at Calvin, stunned.

He gives me a thumb's up sign and points with two fingers to his eyes and then points them back at me.

Watch me.

I nod in agreement. He turns back toward his bag and removes my gun case, opening up the lid and laying it flat across the shelf. I move forward and stand next to him, watching as he takes out the gun, holds it in his right hand and slides the top back, hard and fast with his left hand. He shows me the exposed barrel.

"See? Empty," he shouts.

I give him the thumb's up and watch as he lays the gun down on the shelf and pushes a button on the wall panel, pointing a finger down the lane. What looks like a huge clipboard attached to the ceiling slides toward us along a track. Calvin releases the button, and the board stops just before us. He reaches inside his bag and retrieves a large thin box, opening it to reveal several paper targets. He pulls one out, leans across the bench and attaches it to the clip. The large black circle in the center of the target is marked by outer rings with numbers, and I wonder if I can possibly hit any of them.

When it's secure, he pushes another button on the wall, and the device retracts down the lane. He releases the button almost immediately, stopping the target at about ten yards away from us. He looks over at me, eyebrows raised.

"Good?" he yells.

I bob my head up and down in nervous agreement.

Next, he pulls out a box of ammunition and the magazine from the gun case. He shows me how to load the magazine, pushing a single bullet down into the track, one on top of the next. The energy inside me buzzes distinctly, and as I watch him, I'm reminded of a Pez candy dispenser from my childhood — except in this case, when you pull the top back, a goddamn bullet shoots out.

Calvin only loads five bullets, even though I know the magazine holds seven. I look up at him and hold up my hand, display five fingers, shrug, hold up seven fingers, and tilt my head at him. I'm playing the world's greatest games of charades inside a shooting range.

He grabs the ammo box and points to the bullets inside. I look down into the box: the ammunition is lined up in rows of five.

"Ohhhhhh."

We turn back to the shelf and Calvin steps next to me and then slightly behind me. I can feel his clothing brush against mine, although this time I don't sense any of his typical flirtations — this is all business. With his arm alongside my shoulder, he reaches forward and picks up the gun, placing it in my hand and closing his own around mine. He raises my arm and points the gun down range. Moving my thumb up and alongside the barrel, he lets it rest on a small latch near the top slide. He presses my thumb down firmly on the latch, and the open slide instantly shoots forward, closing off the barrel with a succinct *slam*. The jolt makes me flinch, and Calvin rests his hand on my shoulder for a moment, reassuring me. He flips another small latch near the back of the gun and waits until I look at him before doing anything else.

"Safety latch!" he says when our eyes meet. "It's on now."

Jesus. My heart is beating out of my chest as he moves around me and picks up the magazine from the shelf, handing it to me and pointing to the open end of the grip. Following his lead, I start to slide it into place slowly and carefully. Calvin immediately flicks my hand, and I jerk my head toward his face and scowl at him.

"No!" he yells. "Be quick!"

He imitates picking up the magazine and slamming it home fast into the grip, locking eyes with me. "Hard!"

I grab the gun again and position the magazine at the mouth of the grip. With one quick movement, I use the heel of my hand to slam it hard into the gun, noting with satisfaction Calvin's proud face.

His smile fades immediately as he points two fingers at his eyes and then at the target. Standing firm behind me he wraps his hands around mine on the gun and raises it to the target, holding it at my eye level. He swings around to the side of me and closes one eye, imitating an exaggerated wink. I nod, understanding he wants me to close one eye while I aim. He pushes my right index finger up and alongside the trigger, resting it in an extended position.

"Find your target!" he yells in my ear. His breath is on my cheek, and I realize I am sweating profusely.

I raise the gun in front of me and look down range at the target, closing one eye and moving the gun until the center of the black circle is between the sights at the top of the pistol. I nod once. Ready.

Calvin raises my thumb alongside the safety latch and lowers it down. Then he taps my extended index finger and yells in my ear. "Squeeze it slowly, but do it deliberately. Don't half-ass it!" I snap my chin down hard to signal I understand.

He slowly folds my index finger back and rests it on the trigger, re-clasping his hands around mine. My heart is racing, and my upper lip is beading with sweat. Staring at my target through one eye, I take a deep breath and slowly exhale. And then I press back on the trigger.

The shot is faster than anything I expected, and I'm thankful Calvin's hands steady my arms and prevent them from flying too far upward. A puff of smoke releases from the pistol and a bullet casing jumps out the right side and bounces off the partition wall. I let out a huge breath, and the corners of my mouth twitch in pride, even though the hole on my target is very far to the right.

I lower the gun, and Calvin increases the pressure on my hands, bringing it back to shoulder height.

"Four more!"

"Okay!"

I close one eye again and attempt to bring the center of the target between the sights. My shoulders are beginning to burn from holding this position, but I don't care. I find the spot I like, squeeze the trigger and release two more rounds. I open both eyes and look at the target: small indentations show in the black of the circle, near the top. I whip my head back, searching for Calvin's reaction. He meets my eyes with a huge smile on his face

"Again!"

Intent on hitting the center, I turn back to the target with renewed focus. Another round lands at the top of the circle, and I quickly aim again and fire, this time hitting outside the black circle, far off to the right. Calvin changes his stance behind me, pressing his chest against my back and squares my shoulders with his own. This time he drops his hands from mine. I'm totally on my own. I focus on the center of the target and hold the barrel pointed there. Out of nowhere Mike's voice trespasses in my mind.

"You think you'll ever be able to do anything on your own? Ha! You wouldn't even survive a day. You were nothing before me, and you'll be nothing without me."

Imagining the target is Mike's chest, I pull the trigger and let the bullet fly with complete satisfaction. The hot casing flies out of the gun amidst a plume of smoke, bounces off the brim of my hat and falls to the floor. The slide at the top of the pistol stays in the open, locked position, showing me the chamber is empty. I lower the pistol to the shelf, my shoulders rejoicing at the release of tension, and shake my hands out. Calvin brings the target toward us and smiles at me. As it glides up, the pattern of holes becomes clear.

The last shot is dead center in the black circle.

"You got him!" Calvin yells at me, holding his hands up for a double high five.

I slap his hands and look back at my target.

"I sure did," I murmur.

CHAPTER EIGHTEEN

GEORGIA

T HE NEXT MORNING, I WAKE up stiff as a board. My upper back and shoulders ache with even the slightest movement, and I wince as I attempt to wash my hair in the shower. Blow-drying is definitely out of the question today.

Calvin and I stayed at the range for almost two hours. In that time, I practiced shooting almost the entire box of 100-round ammunition. When I literally could not hold my arms up any longer, Calvin took over and finished off the box. His aim was incredibly accurate, and much to my chagrin he polished off the remaining ammo in no time. I left the shooting range feeling good, confident, and comfortable holding and handling my gun, and on the way home, I gave it a name for good measure: Betsy. We were a team now, Betsy and I. Kind of like Thelma and Louise...minus the suicide pact.

———

Sylvia meets me in the kitchen, coffee cup in hand as she lets Guthrie out of the back door and watches him from the window above the sink. His cast is off, and he acts like he's never had a broken bone in his body.

"He's getting so much better. I can't believe it's almost been three weeks already," she says.

"I know, I'm so proud of him." I walk over to the window to watch alongside her.

"And look at you! Walking without a limp. When did that happen?" she says, glancing down at my blue boot.

I shrug. "I don't know really. Maybe over the last three days? It just doesn't seem to hurt nearly as much anymore."

She reaches over and pats my arm. "I am so happy for you, and so proud of you, sis. You've really come a long way." She squeezes my shoulder in a kind gesture of solidarity, and I wince in pain.

"You ok?"

"Oh, yeah. I just didn't sleep well last night. Slept on my shoulder wrong or something." My stomach feels sick as I turn away. I hate lying.

"Here he comes." She disappears around the kitchen wall and opens the door for Guth. "You about ready to go then, Gia?"

"Yep. Just let me grab my purse."

My bag is on my bed, and I scoop it up and then check my closet to make sure Betsy is safe on the top shelf. I tap her case with the tips of my fingers, close the closet, and shut the bedroom door behind me.

———

Outside the antiques shop, the weather is a perfect summer day. I take a seat on the sidewalk bench, camera in hand, hoping to soak up some of the sunny views on my break. Tourists are beginning to invade the town now that school is out, and Ed has asked me to work full days when I don't have physical therapy. I'm happy to do it since it means I can earn more money and pay off Betsy quicker. Plus, I've got my eye on a small house outside of Silverton, and I'd like to try and increase my savings account balance. When I think about how I used my half of my parents' estate it literally makes me sick to my stomach. I could have saved it, could have invested it in a place of my own long ago, giving myself such better options after divorcing Mike. But what choice did I have then? Mike and I were newly married and starting our future together. When the opportunity in San Diego arrived, Mike sat me down and explained the only way we could move, and survive while he went through another academy, would be if we used the estate money for the house. This was our chance at a better life. Why wouldn't I want to help? How could I say no? I withdrew the money and turned it all over to Mike with love in my heart and adoration in my eyes.

My stomach churns as I sit in the sun and think back on that decision. I should have never even mentioned I *had* the money. I should have kept it a secret from him, but of course, he knew. He knew my parents had died tragically. I'd confided in him and wept in his arms many nights after we were first married. He comforted me and held me, and wiped my tears, listening to me talk about how much I missed them. He was a good husband back then...before things turned dark.

I shake my head to clear my thoughts and refocus on the future. Fortunately, for the last year, I'd only paid minimal rent to my sister and brother-in-law, and I had almost zero expenses. I managed to save a good amount of my earnings and had the start of nice little down payment for a meager place. Strangely enough, being able to get over the fear of living life on my own seemed to keep me immobile. But over the last three weeks, despite my injury and physical limitations, I have somehow become stronger and more confident. And now, due to the encouragement and support from Ben, I am definitely ready to begin a new chapter in life. My new friend Betsy is no small part of that equation.

I look down the sidewalk, smiling at the tourists casually perusing the shops — the tea store, the art gallery, and the bakery. Children attached to mothers' hips, and dogs attached to leashes. It's a beautiful small town summer scene, and I bring my camera up and focus on the view, snapping a few quick shots of the overall setting and then zooming in on a straw shoulder bag nestled on a bench, tulips and roses peeking out in a show of vibrant violet and tangerine. I lower the camera and play back the images. They seem good, despite the glare from the sunshine overhead. Raising my camera to my eye once more, I zoom in on the far end of the sidewalk and focus on the shadow created underneath the grey and white-striped awning of the bookstore. I move the camera, using it like a pair of binoculars until I find my target: a gorgeous, red-breasted robin seated perfectly on the low-hanging branch of a cherry tree. I refine the camera's focus on the bird, which instantly turns all the colors and shapes in the background into a kaleidoscope. It's a stunning scene, and I snap shot after shot.

A close movement in the background causes the robin to suddenly fly off, leaving the branch to bounce alone in the sunshine. I stay focused on the bobbing twig, hoping to capture the sunlight reflecting off one of the small, shiny green leaves. As I press the shutter button, my entire view fills with a wash of black and grey, and I can't see a thing. I pull the camera away from my face and look up. A tall, dark, and handsome figure stands before me.

My mouth falls open as I push the camera aside and leap to my feet. A huge smile crosses Ben's face as I look at him in disbelief. He ducks his head shyly for a moment, and his shoulders lift to meet his ears. I want to eat him up he's so sexy and adorable.

"I can't believe it!" I stare up at him, taking in the whole of his gorgeous face. "How did you...?"

The corner of his mouth twitches and rises toward his ear. "I may have faked an illness." He glances over his shoulder. "So, shh." He presses a finger to his lips, smiling behind it.

I throw my arms around his neck and jump my legs around his waist, my white jeans stretching across my rear. He grabs hold of my backside and supports me with both hands, pulling me closer.

"I'm impossibly glad to hear you're not feeling well," I say, and without hesitation I gently press my lips to his.

He returns the kiss tenderly, his lips melting into mine. The stubble from his beard tickles the top of my lip as shivers slide down my arms and back. He slowly moves his hands back and forth across my rear as he turns up the heat of his kiss; his tongue teasing the seam of my lips before sliding slowly inside. He tastes like caramel and spice and somewhere deep in my belly a small ache begins to grow. Ben groans from the back of his throat as one hand travels up the small of my back, the other gripping the cheek of my ass. I realize, with slight embarrassment, that we are making quite a scene on the sidewalk, and I slowly pull back, nibbling his lower lip before opening my eyes to look at him. He gives another small moan as I let go of his mouth completely, and watch his dark eyelashes open.

"Mmm. More," he whispers.

I unhook my legs from his waist and drop back to the sidewalk, my hands sliding around the sides of his neck, and flattening against his muscular chest. Looking up at him, feeling his heartbeat under my hands, I'm overcome with emotion and suddenly tears spring to my eyes. I bite my lip, trying to steady my chin and look instead at his chest, focusing on the buttons running down the center of his shirt. He slides a finger along my jaw and gently pulls my eyes to his.

"What's the matter, baby?"

I shake my head, tears pooling in the corners of my eyes.

"I'm just so glad to see you," I say, in a rushed exhale. "You don't know how much I've missed you, Ben." I look up at him and try to smile. He kisses the top of my forehead and pulls me into his chest. For the moment, I'm lost in him. Time stands still as he holds me, and I never want this feeling to end.

"I've missed you too. So very much." He plants another kiss on the top of my head.

I pull away from him and wipe the corners of my eyes, clearing my throat and reaching for his hand to lead him back to the bench.

"How did you know where to find me?" I ask as we sit down, my hand in his.

"It's a pretty small town. I just parked the Scout and started wandering around. I figured I'd find you in one of these shops," he says, glancing down at my foot. "Hey, where are your crutches?"

"I don't need them anymore. Now that I've got my big blue boot." I wiggle my toes at him.

"What? Wow, that's great! Are you in much pain anymore? I just realized you didn't limp or anything."

"No, it doesn't really hurt at all anymore. I'm only really sore after physical therapy, which..." I flip my wrist over to check my watch, "...will be in about three hours."

The chime of the bell draws my attention to the shop, and I glance up to see Ed standing in the doorway, staring at us with his arms crossed.

"Ah shoot," I whisper. "I think I've used up my break time."

I stand and walk over to Ed, leading Ben by the hand.

"Ed, this is my, er..." I stammer and look to Ben before continuing, "...boyfriend. Yeah, this is my boyfriend, Ben. Ben, this is my boss, Ed."

Ed uncrosses his arms and shakes Ben's extended hand with reluctance.

"Nice to meet you, Ben," Ed says, and then abruptly turns toward me. "Georgia, I'm swamped in here. Would you mind coming back in?"

"Of course. I'll be right there."

"Nice to meet you," Ben calls. Ed has already turned his back, the door closing behind him.

"Wow. Is he always so friendly?"

"He's always a little snooty, but I think the tourists are finally getting to him. I better get back in there before he blows a gasket." I turn to face him, winding my fingers in between his. "How long can you stay?"

"I need to leave sometime tomorrow." He pulls me closer to his body. His thighs press against my hips, and my spine tingles with electricity.

"Do you have a place to stay tonight?" I ask, lowering my voice and looking up at him from under my eyelashes.

"Huh-uh," he says, shifting his stance and pressing harder against my hips.

"I know a good place. If you're interested?" I smirk and stand on my tiptoes, reaching up to kiss his lips.

"Mmm. Yes, I am definitely interested."

"I have to go. I'll see you — actually, if you aren't doing anything in about two hours, you could drive me to physical therapy?"

"I'd love to." He raises the back of my hand to his lips and presses a soft kiss on my skin. "See you then."

He backs away as I open the shop door and wave goodbye. I watch him through the glass storefront windows, exhaling a deep sigh as he walks out of sight. Damn, he looks so good in those jeans.

"He's gorgeous," Ed whispers next to me, the sarcasm in his

voice palpable. "But I need your help with these customers," he demands, jerking his thumb over his shoulder, and motioning to the group of women gathered around an old farmhouse table. I cough quietly, compose myself and turn toward the ladies, my head swimming with dirty thoughts of Ben.

———

Will this day never end?

I keep checking my watch and looking at the door, waiting for 2:45 p.m. to finally roll around. I'm so distracted by imagined sexy scenarios with Ben, I enter three sales transactions incorrectly, and have to ask Ed to make the overriding notations.

Finally, in the middle of preparing the bank deposit, the bell above the door chimes, and I immediately look up, my heart flipping in circles at the thought of Ben. The smile on my face changes instantly when I see it's Calvin walking in.

Oh, shit. I completely forgot.

He catches my eye, smiles and walks toward me and I hurriedly look at my watch: 2:43 p.m. Scooting out from behind the desk, I hustle over to Calvin, no doubt anxiety plastered across my face.

"I am so sorry, Calvin! I totally forgot to call you." I pepper the words out.

He stops walking.

"Call me about what? C'mon, we're going to be late." He turns back toward the door just as the bell chimes again, and in walks Ben.

Oh dear.

Ben smiles at me and simultaneously shifts his eyes to Calvin. As he crosses the store toward us, I notice Calvin fold his arms across his chest.

"Uh, Calvin. I forgot to tell you that my boyfriend, Ben,

surprised me today. In all the excitement, I neglected to call and tell you I didn't need a ride to PT." I press my palms together and hold them up in front of my chest. "I'm so sorry!" I rush on, hoping to skirt past the look on Calvin's face.

"Cal, this is Ben. Ben, this is Calvin, my friend that's been helping us with Guthrie and driving me around for the last few weeks."

"Hey, Calvin. It's nice to meet you. Thanks for taking such good care of her." Ben extends a hand toward him.

Calvin hesitates a moment too long before finally shaking Ben's hand. Both of their forearms flex as they lock hands, and it's obvious neither one wants to let go first.

"It's been my pleasure, Ben." Calvin sounds like he's suddenly my father.

"I owe you a debt of thanks. I understand you helped Georgia buy a gun and took her to shoot. Thanks, man. I really wish I could have been here. I appreciate that."

Thankfully they both drop hands at the same time, and I breathe a sigh of relief.

"Absolutely," Calvin says. He suddenly widens his stance, looks over at me and winks back at Ben. "She's a quick learner." He cocks an eyebrow up as he stands there with bravado.

My mouth falls open. *What the hell, Calvin?*

Ben stares at Calvin for a moment, then slowly looks him up and down, a small grin toying at the corner of his mouth. "She's also a fantastic teacher, Calvin," he says with a calm quiet that leaves no doubt as to his meaning. The testosterone practically radiates off of him as the grin spreads across his face like a wildfire.

I step in between them.

"All right, well, we better get going, or I'm going to be late. Calvin," I turn toward him and touch his shoulder. "I'm so sorry I forgot to call you. Can you pick me up tomorrow instead? Same time?"

His whole face glows with happiness as he looks at me.

"You can count on it," he says, and walks past us toward the door, calling out as it closes behind him, "Nice to meet you, Brandon."

I turn to face Ben. He's still watching Calvin walk away, and when he catches my gaze, he closes his eyes momentarily.

"What was all *that* about?"

"That, my girl," he reaches a hand around my waist and pulls me close, "was a pissing contest."

I look up into his dark eyes and smile.

"Who won?"

"Well, since I'll be the one in your bed tonight, I count that as a point in my favor." He runs his thumb in circles around the small of my back as he leans down to my neck, pressing soft kisses on my skin as he travels toward my shoulder. My knees feel like they've melted and it's hard to stand up straight.

"Georgia, I believe you're off the clock now, yes?" I jerk my head toward the sound of Ed's voice and see him staring at us with an unfavorable look on his face.

"Yes," I say, clearing my throat. "Yes, thank you, Ed. See you tomorrow."

He mumbles a reply as we walk toward the door.

"Let's get out of here," I whisper to Ben.

He takes my hand, and we step into the warm sunshine, the sound of the bell chiming behind us.

CHAPTER NINETEEN

GEORGIA

I SIT IN THE SMALL, sterile room — waiting. Waiting for my physical therapist to double check the doctor's order. Waiting so I can be released from the session I've just completed. Waiting, when all I want to do is run into the arms of the handsome man sitting in the lobby, waiting for me.

Annoyed at the possibility of delay, I take out my cell phone and check my email. Inside is a message from my insurance agent. Vanessa lets me know my Jeep has been photographed and is scheduled to be towed tomorrow to the repair shop in Silverton. They will begin work right away and will be in touch with me as soon as it's finished. *Well, that's good news.* I type a quick reply and thank her for letting me know. As soon as I hit *send* my therapist walks in holding a clipboard.

"You're good to go, Georgia. See you next week."

I scurry off the table and out of the door as fast as my legs will take me.

Ben pulls up alongside the sidewalk next to my house and turns off the Scout. Although it's early evening, the day is still bright enough for sunglasses, and the air is filled with the sweet scent of freshly cut grass and rich flowerbeds.

He takes the keys from the ignition and we both turn toward each other simultaneously. His forearm rests across the top of the steering wheel and he's still wearing his aviator sunglasses. I press my thighs together and try to stave off the anticipation I know must be radiating off of me.

"God, you are gorgeous." I whisper. I can't help but shake my head a little.

"Georgia, I cannot wait to get my hands on you tonight."

I think a small whimper escapes my mouth as I turn and focus on getting out of the Scout. My head is swimming and I know I have to keep it together for a little while longer, at least.

To distract myself, I mention the Jeep as we walk into the house.

"Oh yeah, I'm sorry. I completely forgot to tell you someone contacted me from your insurance company yesterday. It was all sort of rushed, but it was good timing — I was home at least. The guy mentioned it would be towed today or Tuesday. I'm sorry, completely slipped my mind. I think I was distracted by the thought of seeing you."

I look back over my shoulder at him and see him slide his sunglasses into the collar of his shirt. The fabric pulls down a bit and I glimpse some of his chest hair.

"I still can't believe you're here," I say, a coy smile dancing on my lips.

"I still can't believe I haven't thrown you over my shoulder and carried you away to a dark corner." He steps closer to me and pulls the corner of his lip into his mouth, gently biting down, never taking his eyes from mine.

Somewhere deep in my belly, a slow ache starts to tug, and I lose my train of thought.

"But they, I mean, they're — Scott, Sylvia, ugh! They're just inside," I say, realizing I've lost the ability to speak in complete sentences.

Ben smirks at my communication blunders. "You're lucky I need to be presentable right now, lady. I'm literally gonna have to sit on my hands at dinner."

I open the door and try to remember how to walk as we step inside.

———

Scott's in the kitchen, sprinkling seasoning over a baking sheet of chicken wings, when we walk in. His red, monogrammed chef's apron keeps his button-down work shirt out of the way as he leans over the raw meat. Just as we enter the kitchen, he drops the jar of spices, and tiny flecks of parsley and oregano spill out across the counter and onto the floor.

"Ah, hell!"

He reaches for a paper towel and crouches to the floor to wipe up the mess.

"Hey, Scott. Need some help?" I offer, laughing at him.

He glances up at us, his scowl shifting to surprise.

"Oh, hey!" he cries, rising to meet us. "You scared the shit out of me." He wipes his hands on the towel hooked through the tie at his waist and extends a hand toward Ben. "Er, sorry, I didn't mean to say th — here, let me begin again: Hi, I'm Scott."

Ben laughs and reaches for his hand. "Ben Harrison. Pleasure to meet you. Hey, sorry about that. We didn't mean to sneak in on you." The two men shake hands and smile at each other. Scott's eyes dart to me for a moment.

Yes, *that* Ben.

"Ben surprised me at work today and then took me over to therapy," I explain. "I invited him to stay for dinner."

"Great! Glad to have you. My wife, Sylvia, is just outside with the dog." He motions behind him to the backyard. "Hey, what can I get you to drink, Ben? I've got beer — Deschutes, Ninkasi, Boneyard..." He turns and walks across the kitchen to the liquor cabinet above the microwave. "Gin, Vodka...you name it, we can probably make it."

"A beer sounds great, Deschutes if it's handy."

Scott pulls out an India Pale Ale and slides it, and a bottle opener, across the counter to Ben. He picks up his own beer and raises it to Ben's.

"Cheers!" the two men say in unison.

A few hours later, we're sitting around the kitchen table with empty plates and empty beer bottles in front of us, our bellies full with Scott's incredible chicken wings, laughing over stupid things we did in school. Ben and Scott bond quickly over the unequivocal excellent music of the 1980's — namely Aerosmith — and their shared love of dogs and the outdoors. I haven't had a moment to talk to Sylvia alone yet, but I can tell she's already wrapped around Ben's finger. The deal was sealed when he crouched down on the floor to play with Guthrie. He didn't even hesitate, just set his beer down on the counter and got down on all fours, patting the ground in front of Guthrie with his hands. Of course, Guth responded immediately, quickly lowering his rear end and wagging his tail ferociously, looking at Ben with expectant eyes.

As I sit back in my chair and watch him interacting with my family, it occurs to me that it feels like he's known us forever — sharing stories, laughing and smiling in our small farmhouse kitchen — and I realize, with a sort of softness, that I want this moment, this cocoon of happiness around me, to last forever.

———

Ben and I offer to clean the kitchen so Scott and Sylvia can take Guthrie for a short walk before calling it a night. It's only just after 8 p.m., but we all have an early morning. Besides, the sexual tension between us is so thick it's almost palpable.

I can't wait to be alone with him.

I place the last dishes in the dishwasher as Ben wipes down the counters, and joins me at the sink to rinse the washcloth he's holding. I close the stainless-steel door with my hip; push the *start* button and turn to dry my hands. Ben is standing at the sink, staring down at me with a small, teasing smile on his face.

"What are you thinking about?" I ask, already knowing the answer.

He stands there for a moment, looking my body up and down.

"I'm thinking about the last time you and I were in this kitchen. This counter..." He grips the edge of the tile and waggles his eyebrows at me — my face flushing as I recall the memories.

"Mmm. Yes, this counter...it could tell some stories about us."

He moves closer to me, placing one hand on the side of my waist and sliding it firmly around my hip and back, pulling me closer, inch by inch. I catch my breath as he reaches alongside my neck with his other hand and slides his fingers up into my hair, gently tilting my head backward into his waiting palm, and exposing my throat. I relax into his embrace, my breath becoming quick. My desire for him is overwhelming.

His lips touch the hollow of my throat, and he licks and kisses his way across to my collarbone. My body shivers and goosepimples rise along my arms and chest; hardening my nipples under the thin cotton bra I'm wearing. I hook a finger through one of his belt loops, pulling myself even closer to him and tilting my chin up. I want his lips on mine immediately.

I have barely closed my eyes and all at once Ben's lips press down hard on mine, taking me by surprise. My body is desperate for his kiss, and I immediately respond, opening my mouth and accepting his offered tongue. My hands slide up from his belt loops and across his torso, along every contour of his abdomen and over his broad chest. I grab hold of the lapels on his collar and curl my hands into small fists, pulling him into me, physically begging him to deepen his kiss. Ben moans into my mouth and presses his hips into me. I feel his arousal through his jeans and my hips gently sway back and forth around his center. He suddenly pulls away from my mouth and steps away from me, leaving me disheveled and confounded.

"What is it?" I ask, breathless. My cheeks are burning with heat.

"I'm sorry. I just didn't want them to come back and find me standing in the kitchen, obviously...excited." He presses the back of his forearm to his mouth and then slides both hands into his pockets, subtly pulling his jeans away from his body and shifting his feet from side to side. I smirk as I approach him and cradle both arms around his neck.

"You seem to be having a crisis over here," I tease.

He lifts a hand to my breast and with two fingers begins to trace small circles around my nipple.

"Crisis diverted," he counters, and I catch my breath.

"More," I whisper.

He suddenly leans over and whisks me up into his arms in one large swoop, and I squeal with delighted surprise.

"I'll give you more. So much more," he growls, and heads out of the kitchen and down the hallway to my bedroom, kicking the door closed with his heel.

He lays me down on the bed roughly, but I don't mind in the least. It's all we can do to keep our hands off each other. His fingers find the button on my jeans, and he deftly unhooks it, pulling down the zipper and revealing the white lace underneath. I lift my hips off the bed, and he slowly slides my jeans off, tossing them quickly into a pile on the floor. He leans over me and kisses the tops of my thighs, sending shivers up my body.

He pulls back to look at me and smiles.

"You are exquisite, Georgia. Absolutely stunning."

I sit up on my knees with confidence, taller than he is now, and grab his shirt, unbuttoning it as quickly as possible and folding it backward over his shoulders. The white t-shirt he's wearing underneath pulls across his chest, and small curls of dark hair peek out from the V-neck. I run my hands over his chest and down his abdomen, grabbing the seam of his shirt with my fingertips and pulling it straight over his head. His bare chest is before me, and the smell of his warm skin reminds me of fresh laundry and soap. I lean down and plant kisses across the center of his chest, along the muscular hollows between his pecs, exploring each curve and valley of his torso. His breath increases, and he wraps his arms around my hips and rear, settling me down on top of him. I straddle his hips as his embrace holds me in place, and the thick denim of his jeans pushes upward against my thin cotton underwear. I unbutton my blouse and pull it off my shoulders, throwing it in Ben's face as I sit astride him. He chuckles, bunches the shirt between his hands and brings it to his face, inhaling deeply before tossing it across the bed. He stares at me, in my white bra and underwear, sitting on top of him, and smiles seductively, his dark eyes hooded with desire. He moves his hips slightly, and his erection pushes against my skin, the material rough against me. I catch my breath and slide slightly forward onto his belly, his bare skin immediately increasing the heat between my legs. He reaches forward and around me, and quickly unbuttons his pants and slides his zipper down. When he lifts his hips to pull his pants off I have to quickly brace myself on the bed, my hair falling over my shoulders and bra, my breasts nearly in his face. He lowers his hips, and I sit back on his stomach. His jeans are around his knees, and I feel his briefs tent upward behind me.

In one quick movement, he rolls me over onto my back and stands up, removing his pants completely and standing in front of me at the side of the bed, his arousal clearly visible in the strained fabric of his underwear. He crooks a finger at me, smiling.

"Come over here, baby."

I crawl toward him and sit up on my knees, wrapping my arms around his broad shoulders, trailing my mouth up the side of his neck and biting gently at his earlobes. He tilts his head to the side and groans with pleasure.

With my mouth busy at his neck, I run my hand alongside his waist and over the top of his hip, sliding my fingertips under the waistband of his briefs, and lower, slowly taking hold of him and caressing his length.

"Oh," he gasps, tilting his head back, mouth slightly open. I kiss the underside of his jaw as I stroke him. The sound of him in utter ecstasy instantly turns me on, and I grab his chin and pull his mouth down toward mine, kissing him passionately. With one hand, he takes hold of the back of my neck and pulls me closer, deepening the kiss — his tongue sliding alongside mine, filling my mouth with the taste of him. With his other hand, he runs his fingers up the inside of my thigh, reaching for me. My pulse starts to race, and I pull away from his mouth to breathe. Throwing my head back, I cry out in pleasure as he pushes aside the thin material separating me from his fingers, finding his target and beginning to move.

He buries his head in the center of my chest, his teeth pulling at the cotton fabric of my bra as he continues working — my hips beginning to sway with the increased pressure. At some point, I'm aware of him putting a condom on, and this realization only makes me more excited. He reaches for me again and again, and I moan in ecstasy at the feelings he is creating in me, coming closer and closer to orgasm. I look down at him, my hair falling over the swell of my breasts. My breathing is ragged and deep, and I quickly unhook my bra and let the rise and fall of my body naturally work it off my breasts. Ben grabs the material with his teeth and pulls it away from my chest completely, slipping it down my arms. I toss it aside and push my torso into his face, the stubble of his beard rubbing against the tender, pale skin of my breasts. I shiver and know I am close.

"Mmm. Oh, Ben, stop. You have to...oh God...oh God. You have to stop. I don't want to yet..."

"Why not, baby?" He breathes against my nipple, his teeth biting down gently. "I want you to come, beautiful girl." He suddenly pushes the center panel of my underwear completely aside and firmly lowers my hips down, entering me completely in one quick motion.

I come immediately — my body shaking under the waves of pleasure rippling over me. It's impossible to contain my cries as he continues to push and pull, raising and lowering my hips with each thrust. Another, stronger orgasm crashes through me, and my body erupts in electrified nerve endings.

He stops moving and holds me close to his chest, encircling me with his strong arms and planting soft, loving kisses all over my body.

"You are simply perfect, Georgia. A beautiful, *beautiful* woman and I adore making love to you."

I open my eyes and run my hands through his hair, at a loss for words to describe the incredible feelings flowing through me. He closes his eyes as my fingers twist in his hair, and I feel him, still hard inside me. I tilt my hips backward and lower myself fully onto him again, grinding slowly back and forth against his erection. He catches his breath and rolls me quickly over onto my back; bringing my legs up to rest on his shoulders as he positions himself deeper. My hips tilt upward, and I gasp in pleasure as he works, again and again, and yet again.

Ben's momentum increases, and the sight of his open mouth and closed eyes is nearly enough to send me over the edge again. I grip his forearms as I realize he is nearing his own release. Suddenly he opens his eyes and stares at me.

"You feel so good. I don't want to stop..."

"Please...don't...stop," I whisper. My mind is breaking apart. I've completely lost control.

"Oh God!" he cries, thrusting into me as he reaches his own orgasm. He continues to press himself into me, slower and slower until he lowers my legs and lies on top of me, overcome with exhaustion.

Completely enraptured with one another, we curl our bodies together, physically spent. Ben's arm over me draws me close to his chest, protectively fitting me into the perfect contour of his body, and just as I drift off to sleep, I hear him whisper.

"You've given me something to believe in again, Georgia."

Squeezing his hand, I slip into a sweet, blissful oblivion.

CHAPTER TWENTY

MIKE

E ACH SCENARIO FEELS BETTER THAN the last.
I imagine slamming his head through the windshield of
my car, crushing his skull and smashing each and every bone in
his perfect fucking face. Maybe running him off the pass would
be better. Watching his ridiculous vehicle skid across the road
and through the barrier, flipping over and over and down the side
of the mountain. It would be easy to make it look like an accident,
and it would take hours to retrieve him, hours in which he would
suffer miserably before finally suffocating in his own thick blood.

Or, even better, I could just sneak into Georgia's house right
now, stand over him with my gun pointed right at his forehead,
wait until he wakes up and then blow a hole the size of a baseball
through his head. This is the option that appeals to me the most. I
know Scott won't have a gun in there, and if it weren't for that
damn German Shepherd, I'd do it.

The possibilities are endless.

I slam my hands against the steering wheel, staring at the
seductive silhouettes moving in the dim light of Georgia's room.

This motherfucker is going to pay. One way or another. You can't just sleep with another man's wife and expect to walk away.

I let that stupid little prick Calvin get away the other day. It was a moment of weakness, but I won't let that happen again. Not when I can see this asshole *actually* fucking her.

My wife.

Fucking her.

I want to scream until my lungs bleed.

I hold myself together with thoughts of *his* lungs bleeding.

CHAPTER TWENTY-ONE

GEORGIA

B EN AND I SIT NEXT to each other at the table the next morning, our legs touching, feet intertwined, smiles plastered across both of our faces. The plush bathrobe I'm wearing suddenly feels too warm as the heated glances we share makes my blood rush. My sister pretends not to notice, but I see her rolling her eyes at us. The aura of new love swirls around the kitchen like the wisps of steam from our hot cups of coffee, and I can't help but smile.

We decide that Ben will give me a ride to work before heading back over the pass to Sisters, and I'm thankful for the small amount of additional time I can spend with him.

"It was really nice to meet you, Ben. I hope we get to see you again soon," Sylvia says, reaching her hand toward Ben. He stands up from the table, sidesteps her hand and instead embraces her in a giant hug.

"Likewise. And thank you for opening your home to me. I really appreciate it." He smiles at her and then turns to shake Scott's hand.

"Come back anytime, Ben. And bring your dog. We'll take Charlie and Guthrie hiking at the falls."

They shake hands firmly and clap each other on the back.

"That sounds great, man. And hey, you both are welcome at my place anytime. I'll cook us a nice meal, and we can check out some great breweries, or float the river or something in Bend. Sky's the limit over there."

I beam with pride as I watch the interaction between them.

Scott and Sylvia head into the morning as I hold the front door open for them. The air smells strongly of flowers and damp grass, and I sneeze three times before I shut the door.

"Bless you!"

I turn around to see Ben with his arm outstretched, bringing me the box of Kleenex from the kitchen.

"Ah, thanks. It's hay fever. Sometimes I'm all right, and then other times it just hits me out of nowhere," I say, pulling two tissues from the box.

"You know, a lot of people from the valley move to Central Oregon for that very reason. We don't have the grasses over there." He grins at me. "I mean, I'm just stating a fact."

Is he suggesting I move? I try not to read too much into the comment and instead change the subject.

"Well, I need to finish getting ready," I say, and head back toward my bathroom. "Would you mind taking Guth outside?

"You bet, no problem."

"Thank you, the door's through the kitchen," I call out over my shoulder.

I hear Ben talking to Guthrie, his voice playful and high, as I pick up my hairbrush and begin to smooth out the wild mess on top of my head.

A moment later, a shirtless Ben steps into the bathroom behind me and slowly closes the door, locking it with one hand as he stares at me in the reflection of the mirror, a coy smile on his lips.

I pause mid-stroke, the brush raised above my head.

"What's this?" I ask, slowly lowering my arm. My stomach starts to swirl at the anticipation of his plans.

"You know, we have a little time before you need to be at work," he says, trailing a finger down the center of my spine. I'm wearing my robe, but the pressure from his touch sets my nerve endings on fire.

He gently pulls the hairbrush from my hand and sets it down on the counter, holding my gaze in the mirror, as he bends and slides his hand under the hem of my robe, running his fingers up the back of my leg. I catch my breath as I feel him behind me, pressing himself into the space between my legs. I slowly close my eyes, relaxing into his touch.

"Open your eyes Georgia. I want to see you." His voice is suddenly commanding and confident, and it instantly turns me on. I open my eyes and watch his face in the reflection. His eyes are intent, smoldering, staring at me with a look of need I haven't seen before.

And I am thrilled.

He holds my gaze for a moment before pulling the collar of my robe down from the back of my neck, and for a moment I can't see his face as he plants hot kisses across the top of my back, his tongue tracing the invisible circles his lips leave behind.

He moves his mouth to the side of my neck as his hand inches up the back of my thigh. He's watching me; watching as he kisses my skin, watching my face as his fingers cup the cheek of my ass. He squeezes a handful of the soft flesh and then slides his hand in between my legs, his fingers reaching for, and entering me. I close my eyes and roll my head back. The feeling is so overwhelming.

"No, baby," he whispers. "Keep watching me." I slowly open my eyes again and look at him. His cheeks are flushed, and his dark eyes are hooded. He exudes pure lust, and the knowledge that it's me that is causing this physical desire in him turns my blood to fire. God, I want him so much.

"*Ben*," I whisper.

He reaches his other hand around the front of my robe and slides it inside, taking hold of my breast and tugging at my nipple in the way he now knows will make me crazy.

"Oh God," I say, my knees beginning to buckle.

He's still moving inside me, and I can feel myself becoming more and more aroused. My eyes start to close against the building sensation and he pinches my nipple between his fingers. I can barely stand.

"Look at me, Georgia. Watch what you do to me."

He removes his hand from my breast and pulls the hem of my robe up and over my rear. His foot gently pushes against my ankle, spreading my legs apart and I instinctively grab onto the countertop.

He grins at me as he puts the corner of a condom packet in between his teeth and begins to unbutton his pants. A moment later I hear his jeans and belt hit the floor.

He rips open the foil with his teeth, and I watch him as he glances down at himself, rolling the latex over his length. His tan forearms are taut, the veins raised over the thick musculature underneath, and a small shiver of anticipation runs down deep into my belly. A moment later he grips both sides of my hips and looks at me in the mirror.

"Now, Georgia. I want you right now."

My pupils are dilated in the dim light and my mouth is slightly open. I am completely his.

"Yes," I gasp at him.

"I'm afraid this is going to be fast," he warns, and my nipples harden in response to the naked desire in his voice.

He enters me quickly from behind, and I can't help but lean

farther over the counter, pressing back against him as he moves, fast and deep, his hips pushing hard into mine. I begin to close my eyes in pleasure and a sharp slap against my rear jolts me.

Ben is grinning at me in the mirror, his lips parted, a sheen of sweat across his brow.

"Don't make me spank you again, sweet girl," he coos. He's holding me tight and the feeling is even more delicious than ever.

He slowly rubs his palm against the spot he slapped as he continues making love to me, and I nearly collapse in ecstasy. I am a shaking, trembling mess, and when he increases his tempo, I know I am close. I shut my eyes as the waves begin to roll through me, and this time he lets me retreat into my mind as he too reaches his release, both of us falling against the cool tile of the counter.

Unable to speak, unable to breathe.

———

In the shower he holds me against his chest, stroking my back with his fingertips and kissing the top of my wet hair.

"Did that bother you?"

I slowly look up at him in confusion, and then smirk at him. "Did *what* bother me? If you mean the incredible sex we just had, yeah, I'm very bothered. Can't you tell?"

A thin smile pulls across his mouth, but it doesn't reach his eyes.

"I mean, did it bother you I told you to keep your eyes open? Did it bother you I slapped your extraordinarily perfect ass?" He grabs ahold of my flesh to make his point, this time slowly massaging me.

He looks at me and then tilts his head to the side, suddenly shy. Oh God, how I'd like to wrap my legs around him again, right here and now.

"I loved it, Ben. I love it when you take control, when you tell me exactly what you want. And watching you losing yourself with me...oh yeah, it's an incredible turn on. And besides," I say, putting my finger to his lips, "I deserve a spanking every once in a while."

He opens his eyes a little wider and suddenly takes my finger into his mouth and begins to suck. I know my mouth drops open in response, but I don't care. I pull my finger from his mouth and bring my lips to his, grabbing the back of his neck and drawing him closer to me.

This man will surely be the glorious death of me.

CHAPTER TWENTY-TWO

GEORGIA

Saying goodbye is hard.

Harder than I'm prepared for.

I try and will the Scout to travel slower into town. I pray for parking spaces to be unavailable. I silently wish for Ed to call me and mysteriously grant me the day off — anything that will prolong our parting. I feel like a teenage girl, sulking and sad because I'm not getting my way.

"But when am I going to see you again?" I whine as we sit in the Scout.

"I'm not sure. Unfortunately, I *really* can't come back until fire season is over. It's just too risky, especially with the tourists that are hiking the butte now, and the thunder and lightning storms that will come."

I sigh. "I know, I know. Well, maybe I can convince my sister to drive me over soon. Or maybe Calvin could bring me." I shoot him a glance, testing his reaction.

"Uh, no."

"Why not?" I tease. "After all, you could be pretty lonely by this weekend." I slide my hand along the top of his thigh and up his inseam. He sucks in a quick breath, shifts in his seat and places his hand on top of mine, bringing it to his lips, and kissing it softly.

"Mmm, I'm already lonely. Maybe I can hire a driver to tie you up and bring you to my bedroom." He narrows his eyes at me as his lips play along my fingertips.

"I'd prefer a blindfold," I say.

Ben pauses his kisses and clears his throat, staring at my mouth.

"Is that so? Hmm, I will definitely put that to memory."

He puts his arm around my shoulder and pulls me close, kissing the top of my head.

"I enjoyed this time with you so much, Georgia. I don't think you understand how happy I am when I'm with you."

I tilt my chin up and look at his dark eyes, trying to memorize his features: the thin crow's feet at the corners of his eyes, his dark, full eyebrows — the crooked scar just above his left one — the shape of his lips, the color of his beard, and the small bits of grey at his temples. I reach up and touch the side of his face, holding his gaze.

"I love you," I whisper.

The tips of Ben's eyebrows rise, and three tiny frown lines appear at the top of his forehead. He draws his lips into his mouth and shakes his head slightly from side to side. I'm about to speak, but before I can say anything more, he places both hands on either side of my face and pulls my mouth to his, kissing me with newfound intensity. I wrap my arms around his neck and breathe him in. I want to remember this moment forever, the way he smells, the way his skin feels next to mine...I don't ever want to leave.

He pulls away and takes a deep breath, staring into my eyes.

"You are quickly becoming the greatest thing that's ever

happened to me," he says, kissing my forehead. "I love you too, sweet girl."

I reach over and gather up my things, preparing to leave. Opening my purse, I hand Ben his cell phone, and a huge smile erupts across his face.

"What's this? Man, it feels like I haven't seen this thing in years!" He turns it over in his hand as I place the charger on his thigh.

"I just thought it should probably be with you again. After all, it is *yours*," I laugh. "But seriously, you might want it. Besides, now I have a new phone, so I don't really need it anymore, do I?"

He puts the phone down on the seat and takes my hand in his, kissing it once more.

"Thank you. So many memories wrapped up in this small piece of technology."

I move toward the door and place my hand on the handle. I have to do this now, or I'll break down.

"Goodbye, Georgia. I'll be at the cabin for the rest of the week, but plan to hear from me Friday evening, ok?"

I nod and swallow hard as I slide out of the Scout, angrily fighting back the stupid lump in my throat. Shutting the door behind me, I cross in front of the truck to the sidewalk and stand in the shade of the tall buildings. I turn and wave once to Ben. He starts the Scout, slides his sunglasses on, and gives me his thousand-watt smile.

Damn, he's so flippin' gorgeous.

I wave again as he pulls into traffic and drives around the corner; honking the horn once before the truck disappears down the street.

Sighing, I walk on auto-pilot to the end of the block and turn to push the heavy door of the antiques store open — the bell chiming as I step inside.

———

Work drags on for what seems like a small eternity. Although it's a gorgeous sunny day, we have few customers, and I spend the majority of my day dusting the myriad of odds and ends we keep scattered throughout the shop. I'm lost in thought, and Ed actually has to snap his fingers at me a few times just to get my attention.

I never thought I'd be so happy to see Calvin.

He waves at me as he walks through the door, and I check my watch: 3:30 p.m. Hallelujah. Finally, I can leave for physical therapy. I'm due to recheck with the doctor in a week, and I want my findings to result in an immediate removal of this big blue boot.

"Be right there, Calvin!" I practically run to the back of the shop and grab my things. "Bye, Ed. See you in the morning," I shout over the store, Ed nowhere in sight.

"Don't be late," he huffs back, peeking his head out from behind the door of a chipped armoire.

Calvin raises his eyebrows at me and tips his head toward Ed. I roll my eyes and shrug.

"What can I say?" I murmur. "He's a cranky old coot sometimes."

———

As we head across town toward the clinic, I slouch down in my seat and watch the traffic and houses go by. I'm dreaming of pine trees and high mountain air, not the dullness of this valley that surrounds me.

"You okay?" Calvin's voice startles me out of my trance.

"What? Oh yeah, sorry. Just lost in thought."

"I bet I can guess about what," he mumbles.

I stare at him for a moment, watching his face tighten up as he drives.

"Hmm, do I sense a small bit of jealousy?" I tease.

He looks over at me quickly and then back to the road.

"Me? Jealous?" he guffaws. "Hardly."

I'm silent. Waiting...

"I mean, I'm the one looking out for you here, but whatever." He glances over at me, straight-faced.

Oh dear.

"Oh, Calvin, come on." I place my hand on his shoulder. "Really now. I'm so much older than you. You can't possibly be serious?"

He stops at a red light and examines his fingernails.

"No, I know," he starts. "It's just that, well, what can I say? You can't help who you're attracted to, right?"

"Nope, that is definitely true. Hey, if it helps at all, I'm completely flattered by it," I say, pausing. "But I'm in love with Ben. Really in love. But I'd also really like to keep my friendship with you, if that's ok? And anyway," I say, patting his shoulder, "you *are* the one that taught me to shoot. I'll never forget that."

A small smile creeps across his face.

"Hey, I'd actually like to get some more practice in. Do you wanna go this weekend?" I ask.

"Yeah. That'd be cool. I could do Saturday. But what will you tell Sylvia?"

"I won't need to tell her anything. They plan to go hiking all day."

"Perfect. We can do some target shooting, and then maybe lunch afterward?" He looks at me with a hopeful expression, but then registers the look on my face, and quickly holds up both hands in front of him. "Hey, no, I'm not trying anything. Not a date. Just two friends, right?"

I smile slyly at him. He *is* making me feel a little better; at least I feel like laughing now.

"Ok sure. Deal."

We pull into the parking lot, and he drops me off near the front entrance.

I get out of the car as he opens the passenger window. "See you in about an hour?" he calls.

I nod and wave, and head inside for another round of torture.

———

Surprisingly, I'm not that beaten up after physical therapy. The exercises are much easier this time, and I'm even allowed to walk around without my boot. At first, it feels very odd, and I'm afraid of hurting myself all over again, but after some weight testing and small steps, I feel much more comfortable and even work up to a very light walk on the treadmill. Although I'm not officially released from my boot until the doctor gives approval, I take it off once I'm in the car again and walk barefoot across the lawn to my front door. We never walk in the grass — Sylvia, Scott and I — always using the pathway instead, but I can't resist the smell of the earth and the sun glinting off the freshly mowed lawn. The soft green blanket feels wonderfully warm under foot; the earth molding to my heel with each step, and I realize how much I've missed simple activities like this.

I'm almost to the door when I notice what looks like the imprint of a boot heel, or at least half a boot heel, in an area not covered by grass. I stop and bend over, staring at it, trying to think of a reasonable explanation for what would make that impression. My gut tells me it's potentially connected to the same person driving the suspicious car, but my head decides it's probably the mailman or UPS driver, or someone dropping something off that I hadn't noticed.

Guthrie barks from inside, snapping me out of my thoughts, and I stand up, pushing away my suspicions and heading in to deal with the dog.

———

As I stand in the kitchen, leaning against the counter, I consider my options for dinner. I feel like putting together something nice for Scott and Sylvia, and I open the fridge to pull out a package of ground beef, a container of spinach, ricotta cheese, and a few eggs. Soon I've whipped up the filling for stuffing some large pasta shells and begin to gently fill each thin cylinder. Once I've lined the pan with the pasta, I pour a marinara sauce over the top and sprinkle torn basil over that. Sliding the dish into the oven, I turn my attention to the green salad ingredients I find in the fridge and quickly toss that together.

I'm in the back room selecting a bottle of wine when I hear the door open.

"Hello!"

"Back here, sis," I yell, bent over a low rack filled with local Pinot Noir.

"Hey, there you are. Something smells good."

I stand up with the bottle in my hand and walk over to give her a hug.

"What's the occasion?"

"No reason. Just wanted to do something nice for you and Scott. And I'm craving pasta," I say, braving a smile.

"Miss Ben, don't ya?"

I nod, and my face crumples a bit, embarrassing the hell out of me.

"Oh, sweetie. Come here. I'm so sorry. It's gotta be hard."

I take a deep breath.

"It's okay, really. I'm just being silly. PMS probably," I joke, and then make a mental note to check the calendar.

"When will you see him again?"

"I don't know. Not until I can drive myself over there, I guess." I look down at my foot and stick it out a little.

"Hey! You're wearing an actual shoe!"

"Huh? Oh, yeah. I'm not officially supposed to until I see the doctor next, but it feels fine so far. A little tight, but no pain."

"That's amazing! What a quick recovery. You're the ideal patient."

"I guess? I think my break must have been in just the right place or something."

"Well, whatever the reason, I'm happy for you. Maybe you'll be getting over to see him sooner than you think. By the way," she lowers her voice as she wraps an arm around my shoulder, leading me back into the kitchen. "Scott and I love him. I'm serious. We really, really like him, Gia. You two are a perfect couple."

I lean my head on her shoulder.

"C'mon," she says. "Let's eat. I'm starving."

———

After dinner, I escape to my room and put my feet up while I open my laptop and check my email. I'm surprised to see a note from the Sisters Tribune again. I hesitate and then open it, bracing for a negative report. Maybe someone has seen the story and is upset. I say a silent prayer that Ben isn't slandered.

To my happy surprise, it's completely the opposite. The editor is writing to let me know he's been contacted by a local magazine. They've seen my article and the photographs, and they want to talk to me about writing a piece regarding summer hiking in the Bend and Sisters area. He's writing to ask my permission to forward my contact info along.

I re-read the email three or four times before finally squealing with joy and excitement.

A moment later I hear footsteps jogging down the hallway. Sylvia rounds the corner into my room, eyes huge.

"I heard you scream! What's the matter?"

"Don't worry. It's good news! You will never believe this!" I say, swiveling the laptop around for her to read.

I watch her face as she reads each line of the email, her smile growing bigger and bigger until her hand covers her mouth in disbelief.

"Georgia! This is ah-maze-ing! Do you know what this means? You could become a featured photographer, or a regular columnist or something!" She sits down on the edge of the bed and stares at the wall, still talking. "This could lead to so many more opportunities. Magazines, newspapers...we'll have to get you set up with a social media platform, and you'll need a publicist..."

"Ok, ok, calm down, sis. You're getting *way* ahead of yourself. Let me just call him back first, okay?"

"What? Oh, yeah of course. I'm just brainstorming." She reaches over and gives me a tight hug. "I'm *so* proud of you! Can I tell Scott?" she asks, clapping her hands together in anticipation.

"Um, sure, I guess?"

She leaps off the bed, already bolting for the doorway.

"Scott! Scott, you will never believe this!" she bellows down the hallway.

I turn back to my computer and type a quick reply to the editor, letting him know it's perfectly all right to release my information, and that I will be calling him in the morning.

That night as I lay in bed, I reflect upon how fortunate I am to have so many wonderful people in my life and so many opportunities presented to me.

Finally, it feels like my life is headed in the right direction.

CHAPTER TWENTY-THREE

GEORGIA

A WEEK LATER, I EMERGE from the doctor's office victorious; wearing two sandals and carrying a small blue paper that indicates my full ability to return to all normal activities.

Even driving.

I walk out of the building at a hurried pace, feeling as if I've just mistakenly been released from prison and any minute the guards will notice and sound the alarm. I hurry out to meet Calvin. He's leaning against the passenger side of the car, feet and arms crossed in front of him.

"Well, well, well," he says, grinning at me. "Where's Big Blue?"

"Big Blue sleeps with the fishes," I say, running my finger across my neck in a slow, vertical line.

"No way!"

I nod and laugh. "Yep. She is no more. And good riddance. She was a little wench, that Blue."

"God, I think having your foot free has somehow short-circuited your brain." Calvin feigns mild distress and hurries to open the passenger door. "Get in the car before it gets worse."

He slides in behind the wheel and starts the car. It's only 11 a.m., and already it's blazing hot. The air conditioning kicks on, and the engine throttle increases to accommodate the demand. Strangely enough, we continue to sit in the unmoving car, silence falling upon us. Finally, I look over at Calvin and raise my eyebrows.

"Well?"

"Oh. Sorry, I just realized..."

"That?"

"Well, it's lame I guess, but I was just realizing I won't be needing to drive you around everywhere anymore or help with Guthrie. Although, I guess he's been fine for a while now. Such a stud."

"Hmm, no, I guess not. I hadn't thought about it really." I pause for a moment. "You're the only one here that knows I have a gun though, and I'm going to need to keep practicing. Just because nothing weird has happened lately doesn't mean I shouldn't stay ready, right? Besides," I say, "I'm sure I'll be taking the concealed carry class soon enough, and I'd like to ace it." I stick my palm out toward him. "What do you say? Shooting partners?"

He reaches over and shakes my hand.

"Yes, definitely."

We smile at each other, sealing the deal.

"C'mon, take me home already, I'm starving! If you're nice, I'll even cook something for you."

Calvin slams the car into gear, and to my utter embarrassment, burns the tires exiting the parking lot.

———

"So, how come you don't have to work today?"

Calvin and I are sitting next to each other at the kitchen island, homemade BLT sandwiches and citrus salads in front of us.

"I took the day off because of my doctor appointment," I say. "But after work tomorrow, I have the rest of the week off. Every year, Ed takes a 4-day weekend around July 4th. He just tacks on a Monday, Tuesday or a Thursday, Friday to the week where the holiday falls. It's actually nice."

Calvin nods and bites into his BLT, mayo squeezing out from the side and dripping onto his chin. I smirk and hand him a napkin.

Across the counter, my cell phone rings in my purse. My mouth is full, so I raise my arm in front of Calvin, wiggling my hand and pointing to my bag. He leans over and yanks my purse by the strap, dangling it in front of him like a dirty sock as he passes it to me. I swallow the huge bite, grimacing as I choke it down.

"Hello?" My voice cracks and I try again. "Hello?"

"Georgia? It's Vanessa from Assurity Insurance. Catch you at a bad time?"

"No, not at all."

"Ok, great. Listen, I wanted to let you know your Jeep is all set and waiting to be picked up. You'll just be responsible for the deductibles on the towing and the repair. The repair falls under the comprehensive portion of your policy, so there's a separate claim for that."

While this news thrills me, it also makes me nervous. Add this to my growing pile of bills to pay, including my new health insurance policy that is now *twice* as expensive.

"That's great news, Vanessa, and really perfect timing too." I stand up and grab a pencil and notepad, writing down the shop information, and thanking her once more, before hanging up.

I glance over at Calvin. He's bent over his plate, elbows out to the sides, digging into the last of his sandwich like an animal.

Switching off my phone, I press my hands together.

"My Jeep is ready to be picked up. And I can actually *drive* it!"

Calvin shoves a bite of grapefruit and fennel into his mouth and drops his fork onto the plate. It rattles and bounces off, clattering onto the counter.

"What are we waiting for?" he says, holding his arms open wide.

His happiness is contagious, and I smile and hustle around to sit beside him again, picking up my sandwich and taking another huge bite.

"Mmm, just one more bite."

———

Climbing into my Jeep again feels surreal.

Nearly a month has passed since I last sat in it, and I no longer recognize the scent inside. It smells different — like new leather, air freshener, and strange chemicals. I have to adjust everything — the seat, the rearview mirror, the outside mirrors — even the radio stations have to be re-programmed. The front windshield and both front windows sport small white stickers on the outside, showcasing the logo of the glass company.

Calvin opens the passenger door, admiring the interior of the Jeep.

"Whoa. Ok, from now on, we drive this," he says, running his hand across the seat.

"Hop in. We can go for a quick—"

The door slams as he pulls the seatbelt across his body.

"—ride."

We drive around through town and then head up toward the

Silverton reservoir. The day is bright and warm, and we roll the windows down and open the sunroof to enjoy the sunshine. As we pick up speed, the wind snaps my hair around my head and across my face. Out of habit, I open the console to grab the nylon running cap I keep inside, my hand reaching in, feeling around for the hat while I look ahead on the road.

"What are you looking for? I can help," Calvin hollers, leaning over and reaching into the console.

"There should be a black Nike hat in there," I yell back and put my hand back on the wheel. Driving feels so awkward. It's almost like I've forgotten how to do it.

"I don't see a hat. A few hair ties...some Chapstick...deodorant?" I glance over at him. His face is scrunched up.

"What...sometimes I forget," I say, smiling sheepishly. "Really, no hat?"

"Huh-uh. What's this?"

He pulls out a small, sealed red envelope and holds it up, flipping it side to side as the wind whips the top of it back and forth.

"What's that?" I holler.

Calvin shrugs. "Thought you'd know."

I hold up a finger to him. "One sec!"

We near the entrance to the reservoir, and I slow the Jeep and pull onto the gravel road. The wind dies down as we bounce along, trying to avoid the majority of the potholes.

"I don't know what that is," I say, pulling strands of stray hair from my mouth. "But I'll take a look once we get to the parking lot."

We come out of the trees and descend the bumpy gravel road toward the parking area. Below us to the right, the reservoir water sparkles, reflecting the early afternoon sun.

I pull into a spot near the dock and shut the Jeep off. A small cloud of dust blows past us toward the water.

"Wow, this is cool," Calvin says, looking out at the water.

Near the far end of the lake sits a canoe with two people in it, fishing poles arcing into the water. Close to the dock, a woman and a toddler sit at a picnic table in the shade of a fir tree, eating from packed lunches. A child's fishing pole and plastic red bucket rest on the seat beside them.

"Let me see that envelope," I say, holding my hand out.

Calvin tips it into my fingers, and I look it over. I don't remember leaving this is my car. It feels like nothing is even inside. I run my fingernail underneath the flap and open the rest with my thumb. Pulling it apart, I look inside. I almost don't see anything at first, but then realize I am looking at the white back-side of a photograph.

"What is it?" Calvin asks.

"I don't know," I murmur.

I pull the photo out and turn it around, and what I see makes me gasp.

"Oh my God," I whisper, slamming the photo upside down against my legs.

"What? What is it?"

I shake my head. "This can't be happening."

"What can't be happening? What's going on Georgia?" Calvin unbuckles his seat belt.

I turn in my seat and look behind us, searching for any strange cars.

"Georgia!" Calvin raises his voice, his eyes wide. "What the hell is going on?"

"It's a photo, okay!" I yell back. "It's a photo of Ben and me. Kissing. In Silverton. Just outside my work." I lower my voice and look him straight in the eye. "This was just last week, Calvin."

My hands start to shake, and I wrap my arms around myself. I don't know what to do.

"Hey, calm down. It's going to be all right. Let's just think about it for a second," he says. "Do you have any idea who might have taken this?"

I shake my head, staring at my steering wheel. My mind is racing.

"No old flames around town that might be jealous?"

"No. I didn't even grow up here."

"Really?" He seems surprised by my answer.

"No. Sylvia and I grew up in Vancouver. After our parents passed, we both got married. I moved to San Diego, and Sylvia moved to Salem, and then Silverton. I've only been back here for a little over a year," I say, stumbling over the words. I'm shaking and sweaty.

"You were *married?*"

"Yeah. For about seven years. But none of that matters, Calvin. Who the hell is stalking me?"

"Well, one picture...I don't know that it's stalking just yet."

I turn toward him, my voice loud and angry. "This Jeep was vandalized at Black Butte while I was hiking there. Two days later my hotel room was broken into, and the word *bitch* was written on the bathroom mirror. Then Ben's cell phone started getting weird text messages about me, crazy shit about keeping me safe, Calvin." I pause as I take stock of the surge of adrenalin racing through my system. After a few deep breaths, I continue. "Then, about a week ago, I noticed a weird car in the neighborhood. You were there. It was a day you took me to work. And the other night — the night before I decided to get a gun." I breathe deeply, but too fast, and I choke a little on my words. "Guthrie, all of a sudden, started barking like crazy and ran to the front door. *The front door,* Calvin!" I bury my head in my hands as my shoulders shake, my lip trembling.

"Jesus Christ, Georgia. Do the police know all of this?" He reaches over and rubs my shoulder.

I nod. "Bend PD knows about the stuff that happened over

there. No one knows about the car, or this note, obviously," I say, through hiccuping sobs.

"What about Ben? Does he know?"

"Yes, except for this." I hold up the photo.

Calvin is quiet for a moment. I sniff loudly and open the console, grabbing a lone coffee shop napkin to wipe my face.

"All right. So, no one here would have any reason to stalk you or bother you, right?"

I swallow and clear my throat, "No. I can't think of anyone."

"What about past boyfriends? Dates, even. Any weirdo dates?"

"I've only been on about two dates since I moved here, and neither of them were serious. One was only a single date and the other guy...I think we dated for about three weeks. We just mutually stopped contacting each other."

"Does he live around here?"

"I don't know. He lived in Salem when I knew him. His name was Jake something."

"Maybe try to remember his last name, and we can look him up on social media at least. And we should go to the police station, right now, so you can report all of this."

"Ok," I say, wiping my nose. "Ok, yeah. I need to call Ben, too." As soon as I say it, I realize I can't reach him. "Shit! I won't be able to. He's at the cabin all week, and there's no cell service up there."

"What cabin? Where the hell is he?" Calvin pulls his seatbelt across his chest, and I turn the Jeep back on.

I reverse into the parking lot and start back up the gravel hill.

"On top of Black Butte, near Sisters. He works at the fire lookout tower up there and stays in the cabin."

"He lives at the top?"

"No. Well, kinda. He works for the US Forest Service. He mans the tower during fire season, and also during summer thunder and lightning storms. He lives in the cabin up there when he's not in the lookout."

"And there's no cell service?"

"No. Just radio. I can call the ranger station in Sisters, and they can relay a message up to him, but that's about it."

I steer the Jeep around the larger potholes, bouncing along the gravel as we near the gate and main road.

"Okay, so you can call Sisters when we get to the police station. And what about Scott and Sylvia? Do they know?"

"No!" I say, whipping my head toward him. "I mean, no," I say, my voice quieter. "They don't know. At least not all of it. They know about the Jeep being vandalized, and about the text messages, but that's it. And I want to keep it that way. You don't understand, Calvin. Scott could handle it but Sylvia? No way." I shake my head and swallow hard.

"Why? Why not?"

We reach the main road and stop. The trail of dust catches up with us and billows around the front of the Jeep. I look at him and then drop my gaze to the floor.

"Because," I say, shaking my head. "If she thought I might be in danger, or that someone might be trying to harm me, I know it would..." I can't finish my thought.

"It would what?"

I shake my head again and sigh.

"I know it would remind her of our parents' deaths."

CHAPTER TWENTY-FOUR

GEORGIA

THE SILVERTON POLICE TAKE MY statement, my fingerprints, and the photograph, to be examined for evidence. An officer there also performs a quick print dusting of the inside of my Jeep, and the door handles. Even though he says most people are smart enough to use gloves, he doesn't want to overlook a step that could potentially reveal the perpetrator.

Another officer, a pretty young woman with shiny black hair pulled back into a tight bun, sits down with me and helps me reconstruct an outline of the events, beginning with the vandalism. She takes down the names of Officers Roth and Dickerson, and indicates she will check in with them as soon as possible.

She exhibits a warm, friendly tone as she asks me about my history.

"All right, Ms. Marks. While we wait for the officers to finish with your Jeep, I'm just going to pull up your record and enter in this new information today."

Calvin and I sit quietly next to each other on the opposite side of her spotless desk. He already called Scott and told him he was helping me pick up the Jeep and taking a test drive, and would be back to the office in a bit.

"Ms. Marks, I see you have recently purchased a handgun. Do you currently have the gun in your possession?" The officer asks, her left eyebrow rising as she peers up from her screen.

"Yes, that's true. I bought it after all these things started happening. I don't have it with me now if that's what you mean. It's at home."

"And is it in a locked safe, or other secure location?"

"It's—"

Calvin suddenly leans forward.

"—Officer, if I may? Ms. Marks is not under investigation at this time and is not required to disclose the whereabouts of her handgun. She has confirmed it is not currently on her person."

I slowly turn my head toward Calvin, eyes widening. *What the hell?*

"And you are?" She sets down her pen and folds her hands together in front of her, setting her jaw.

"Just a friend. But I am aware of Ms. Marks' legal rights."

She looks him up and down and blinks her eyes. Twice. I have the distinct feeling people like this exasperate her every day.

She turns back toward me, a thin smile on her face. I want to die from embarrassment.

"Ms. Marks, indeed you do not need to answer the question. We are only concerned for your safety and the safety of others around you. We see a tremendous number of injuries — even deaths — each year from accidents caused by guns in the home. If you have not already, I would highly recommend purchasing a gun safe, and also taking a firearm safety class, or classes, on a regular basis."

I open my mouth to tell her about my planned class, but she holds up her hands in front of her. "No need to comment," she says, glancing over at Calvin. "I just want you to be safe."

"Thank you, Officer..." I scan her badge for a last name. "Sanchez."

She advises me to keep a journal that lists all of the events, as well as anything that occurs from this point forward, including the date and time of each incident. She gives me explicit instructions to notify the police immediately should anything else occur, and tells me to save every message, every phone number, and every shred of evidence that might possibly lead to the identification of the person. I am warned not to endanger myself, or others, but am encouraged to try and document as much as possible without provoking whomever it is. She indicates if we can determine who is behind these events, we can obtain a restraining order, and, more importantly, possibly press charges.

Another officer approaches the desk and hands me my keys.

"You're all set, ma'am. I apologize for the dust residue. We did try to wipe everything down well, but do be careful of your clothing. You might want to give it a once-over with a damp cloth when you get home."

I thank him, and Calvin and I stand up to leave.

"Ms. Marks, if I may?" Officer Sanchez motions for me to follow her.

I look at Calvin. He crosses his arms in front of him and opens his mouth to protest. I furrow my brow at him and shake my head, and he snaps his mouth shut.

Officer Sanchez and I walk a few steps away and stop. I clasp my hands and turn to face her, preparing for the worst.

"I just wanted to tell you something else, in private." She reaches out and touches my elbow. "Nine times out of ten, in cases like these, the person doing the stalking is romantically involved with the victim — or has been. Usually, the perpetrator has had his or her romantic intentions rebuffed." She glances down for a moment and then looks me directly in the eye. "I don't want to make any assumptions as to what your relationship is with him," she says, sliding her glance sideways toward Calvin, "but I wouldn't rule anyone out. I just want you to be safe, Ms. Marks."

I stare at her for a moment. She seems completely sincere. Behind her eyes is a look I can't quite fathom, but I get the feeling she's speaking from experience.

"Okay, thank you, Officer. I appreciate the insight and the consideration."

"My pleasure, ma'am. Here's my card. Call me if anything else should happen, or if you remember anything else."

We walk back toward Calvin who has shifted his stance to a wider position.

"As soon as we hear back from forensics, we will let you know, Ms. Marks."

We shake hands, and she walks us to the front door.

———

I drive with caution, watching every car around me, scanning every corner we pass, noting each passerby with interest.

"If you keep this up, you're going to crash before we even get there. Want me to drive?"

I take a deep breath.

"Sorry. I'm just on high alert now. I feel like I can't trust anyone. Like any one of these people could be the person following me around." I shiver and accelerate back toward the repair shop.

"So, I know there's probably no good time to talk about this kind of thing, but I wanted to tell you..." he trails off, and I look over at him.

"Yeah?"

"I wanted to say that I'm really sorry about your mom and

dad." He looks at me with caution. "I can't imagine how awful that must have been for you and your sister."

I swallow hard and keep my eyes on the road.

"Yeah. It was. But thank you." *Please don't ask me what happened, Calvin,* I silently pray.

"Was...I mean, did the police ever...never mind, I'm sorry. It's none of my business." He looks out of the window, and I breathe a sigh of relief.

"It's just...," he starts again.

"They were mugged, Calvin. Out on a date in Seattle. A horrible case of being in the wrong place at the wrong time. Shot. Both of them. The asshole was never caught. Sylvia was in her second year of college, and I was in my senior year of high school. Because of our ages, we were allowed to stay in the house. Their assets paid it off." I look over at him. "Okay?"

He drops his chin and looks at his lap.

"Yeah, okay. I'm sorry."

After a few blocks of silence, I can't take it anymore. He's like my little brother, and I feel guilty for snapping at him. I reach over and touch his shoulder.

"Hey, I'm sorry. I shouldn't have been that way."

"No. It's my fault. I...I should have kept my mouth shut."

"It's fine. Really. It's just been a tough day." I pull into a parking spot in front of the repair shop. Calvin's car is just a few spaces away.

I put the Jeep in park and look over at him.

"I'm glad you were with me today, Calvin."

He slowly reaches for the door handle, head down.

"I mean it. Thank you for coming with me to the police station."

He looks over at me and smiles thinly. "You bet." He slides out of the Jeep and stands next to the door. "This might be an awkward time to ask, but if you want to go shooting again this weekend, I'd be happy to go with you."

"I would love to do that. But this weekend I'm going over to Sisters." *And I can't wait to get away from this town.*

Calvin sticks his hands in his pockets, and I feel I need to elaborate to spare his feelings. "I'm meeting with a newspaper editor on Monday — I might have a writing assignment," I say, trying to sound cheery. "But how about when I get back? Rain check?"

He smiles and looks down the street before glancing back at me. "Sounds great. Have a good weekend. You know how to reach me if anything comes up between now and then." He winks and shuts the door, and I breathe a sigh of relief as I watch him walk over to his car.

I lock the doors and sit in the parking space for a moment, pulling out my cell phone from my purse and looking up Annie's number.

Fifteen minutes later I turn off my phone and sit back in my seat, relieved to have passed the information on to her. She assured me she would notify Ben the moment we hung up. When I told her I would be in Sisters over the weekend, she made me promise to come and see her, which I happily agreed to. She told me to try and relax, let the police handle the problem and to just go about my normal routines, albeit keeping a careful awareness of my surroundings. Her motherly advice somehow made me feel a little better, and I hung up feeling slightly less anxious.

———

Turning the Jeep onto my street, I slow down and scan the road, searching for the strange car, or anything unusual. It's nearing five o'clock, and our neighbors are beginning to return home from work. Front yards are scattered with children playing with their dogs, elated at no longer being cooped up in school or in the house. Nothing appears out of the ordinary, so I pull the Jeep into the driveway, lock it, and head indoors.

Guthrie is waiting at the door for me, his tail wagging back and forth so hard it stings as it slaps my legs. His ears stand straight up, and he won't sit still, running ahead of me toward the kitchen, and then stopping and looking back to see what is taking me so long.

I open the door, and he dashes outside, leaping off the stone patio and jumping into the yard to immediately drop his hips and relieve himself.

So what if he pees like a girl. I actually find it endearing.

I close the door and let him play outside for a bit while I go back into the kitchen and open the cupboard. I pull out a box of crackers and open it, mindlessly filling my mouth with one after another while leaning against the counter. I hear my mother's words reminding me not to eat standing up, and not to eat directly from the package of anything. I compromise with her and sit down on the bar stool, my hand still inside the box. The memory of her still aches in me. What I wouldn't give to have her put her arm around me now, and assure me everything will be all right. How many nights have I cried myself to sleep, torturing my thoughts by playing the movie of our lives on repeat in my head? Sylvia and I didn't have the perfect childhood, not by any means — our dad's career as a prosecutor left the three of us alone many nights at home — but we knew we were one hundred percent loved — cherished is more like it, by both of our parents. There was no safer place on earth than snuggled down in our side-by-side twin beds, our mother's goodnight kisses still warm on our cheeks, me staring at Sylvia as she stared back at me, softly singing our made-up songs to each other as we drifted off to sleep. We lived our entire lives never once considering that it might all come to a screeching halt one day. It never occurred to us that curled up in a dark corner of Seattle was a slumbering, sinister monster, just waiting to take our happiness, and rip it to shreds.

Life is like that sometimes I guess: just when everything feels soft and good and safe, something or some*one*, horrible comes along and destroys it all.

CHAPTER TWENTY-FIVE

GEORGIA

THE FARTHER I DRIVE FROM Silverton, the better I feel.

I leave town around 3 p.m. on Friday, not making one stop as I head for the highway. I want to put as much distance between the town and me as quickly as possible. Although I have no way of proving it, I have a gut feeling that whoever is watching me is still in the town I'm now leaving behind. I feel like I'm escaping from a trap, fleeing to the safety of the mountains, to the safety of Ben's arms.

The plan is to meet at his house tonight, and then head up to the cabin tomorrow morning so he can work over the weekend, with both of us returning to spend Sunday night at his house so I can meet with the editor on Monday morning. It's a whirlwind weekend, but I'm excited to see him and relieved to be away from home.

I try to push thoughts of going back to Silverton on Monday afternoon out of my head completely.

The drive over the pass is slow going. The summer weekend traffic bunches up in between passing lanes. RVs and trucks with campers slow down the flow of cars, motorcycles, and SUVs. A small bit of road construction brings everyone to a halt just past Detroit and nearly causes an accident as everyone tries to pass at the first available opportunity.

Even though it's cooler at this higher elevation in the pass, I still have the windows cracked for air — my shorts and oversize sweatshirt keeping me perfectly comfortable as I listen to the radio. As soon as I reach the summit, I send Ben a text message, letting him know my whereabouts. He's probably already on his way down from the butte, heading for home.

I anticipate arriving in about thirty minutes, and my stomach flips as I think about seeing him again, breathing in his scent, and standing in his embrace.

———

I pull into Sisters, smiling as I drive through the tiny blocks. People spill out from the shops, the sidewalks and walkways overflowing with meandering tourists. Kids with giant ice cream cones bounce along next to their parents, holding hands as they stroll through town. It's such a friendly place — Sisters — and I find myself thinking it's a town in which I could easily live and be very comfortable.

At the third block, I turn right and head out of town on the long, paved road and my insides begin to somersault.

By the time I pull up to Ben's house, it's fully dark. Moths and mosquitoes dance around his front porch lights, unable to break away from the bright glow. Turning off the Jeep, I slide outside into the cool night air and listen as the crickets orchestrate the evening around me. As I step onto the porch, the door opens, and Charlie bursts out, barking like crazy and wagging his tail, circling me and pushing his nose into my legs. Ben appears in the doorway behind him, drying his hands on a dishcloth, a sexy grin spreading across his face. He tosses the towel over his shoulder and opens his arms wide for me.

"Welcome home, baby."

———

We wake up early the next morning, practice thoroughly enjoyable, albeit indecent, acts in his shower, and make a quick breakfast before packing up his work truck and heading out of town. As much as we both want to laze around, wrapped in each other's arms, a fire south of town has kicked up, and Ben is anxious to get back up in the tower. He's also received reports that a thunder and lightning storm is predicted to come through Sisters later tonight, and into Sunday morning.

"Won't that help the fires though, the rain?" I don't understand his anxiety.

"No. It's just the opposite. Many times these storms are dry. There's no rain up here in the high desert, just a lot of charged electricity in the air. Next to human oversight and arson, lightning strikes are the most common cause of fires around here."

I'm starting to feel a little nervous.

We pull past the entrance of his driveway, and he hops out of the Scout, closing and locking the gate behind us.

I think about the tower and the storm. By my estimate, it stands at least sixty feet above the summit of the butte, sticking out like a giant antenna in the sky.

"Won't the tower be an obvious target for a lightning strike though?" I say, as he slides behind the wheel and pulls out to the main road.

He looks over at me and nods.

"Yes, exactly. They are giant targets. Which is why you see them grounded with copper cables. It's actually pretty interesting: the cables attract and absorb the strikes, disbursing the charges deep into the ground."

"But you won't be in the tower during the storm, right?" My eyes feel huge. And they must be because Ben glances at me and laughs.

"Well, it just depends on how intense the storm is."

"You must be kidding me."

"No, I'm actually not. Like I said, lightning strikes are the second most common initiator of fires. We need to be able to respond right away, even to a small strike. It's been so dry, even a relatively small fire can quickly get out of hand."

"But...the electricity! You could be electrocuted!"

"If the storm gets too close, I have a special stool up there I sit on. No, really." He begins to laugh, no doubt in response to the look on my face again. "It's wood and has glass insulated feet on it. Wood and glass are very poor conductors of electricity. I mean, it's not a perfect guarantee, but at least it's better than nothing."

"Oh my God, Ben. There's no way I'll be okay with you being up there during a storm."

We come to the 4-way stop in town, and Ben looks over at me, staring for a moment.

"Well, if it gets too intense, I'll get out of there and head for the cabin. Would that make you feel better?" He lays his hand on mine and gently squeezes.

"Depends on what your definition of *too intense* is. I have a feeling you'll be up there much longer than I'm comfortable with." I look out of the passenger window; two yellow labs tied up outside the bookstore wag their tails as people walk by.

We turn left, and I look at him again.

"I just don't want anything bad to happen to you. I...I would be devastated, Ben. I really would."

"Come here." He pulls his arm across the back of the seat, and

I quickly unbuckle and slide over next to him, clicking the lap seat belt across my hips. I tuck my body in next to his and rest my head on his shoulder. My arm crosses his chest, and I hug him tightly.

"Don't ever let go," he says, stroking my hair.

"I never will," I whisper.

———

The parking area is empty when we pull up, and Ben parks the truck in the shade of the pine trees. A moderate breeze drops dry pine needles all over the hood of the truck and windshield and swirls them through the air like minuscule chopsticks. I open my door and step out into the crisp morning, catching some of the twirling sticks in my hair.

We lug our packs to the end of the tailgate and shrug them on. Ben's exposed frame pack is massive, and tightly jammed with all sorts of gear — food for the weekend, extra radios, an extra blanket, a parka, small propane canisters, and water containers — and of course, his first-aid kit.

"The only thing you're missing is an upside-down saucepan on your head," I say, hiding my laugh behind my hand, my shoulders beginning to shake.

"Do not judge the pack, female." He runs his fingertips up and down the sides of his waist, displaying in admiration the length of the pack, trying not to laugh.

He slams the tailgate shut and locks the doors, turning toward me.

"All set? How's your foot feeling?" he says, pointing to my ankle.

I'm wearing an ankle brace, and I wrapped an Ace bandage around it before we left the house just as a precaution. I've been practicing moderate incline walking at home on the treadmill, and feel pretty stable, but I don't want to risk anything. "Yeah, it feels good. I'm ready if you are."

"All right then, after you." He motions toward the trailhead, and we set off.

———

Midway to the summit, my foot begins to ache. I don't want Ben to worry, but I can't ignore it any longer. We stop for a rest, plunking down on the edge of the trail. The view around us takes my breath away — Black Butte ranch and the pastures lie far down below us to the east and nestled in the trees, Highway 20 winds and twists like a flat shoelace, placing a thin break between the forest tree lines on either side of the road. To the south, the mountains majestically loom over the valleys, and although only a month or so has passed since I was here last, much of the snow has melted from the base of the mountains, leaving exposed areas of dark rock and pumice now visible. Faded jet streams reflect against the clear sky, forming crisscrossed highways above us, and the soft sounds of nearby birds chirp in my ears. I close my eyes and lean my head on my pack, the sunshine warming my face.

A wave of anxiety passes through me as I am suddenly reminded of the bear. I sit up in shock and grab Ben's arm, squeezing very hard.

"What about the bear, Ben?"

He places his hand over mine.

"You don't need to worry. First of all, I haven't seen that bear, or any bear, up here since that day. And remember, that was a very rare occurrence. Don't forget: she had her baby nearby at that time — also a rare instance." He removes his hand from mine and taps the side of his pants. "Besides," he continues. "I'm prepared."

My gaze follows his hand to the holster at his side, the butt of the pistol sticking out. I breathe a sigh of relief and drop my shoulders. I hadn't even realized I was so tense. My own handgun is securely stowed in my pack, but it would be hard to reach in an emergency. Even though I don't have my concealed weapons permit yet, I still brought it along. With everything that's happened, and continues to happen, I didn't want to take any chances. Still, knowing Ben's pistol is easily accessible relieves my anxiety.

"Well, that does make me feel a little better," I say, holding my fingers together to measure the small increment.

He smiles, reaches over and pulls my hand away, leaning in to kiss me, soft and slow. His lips are salty from sweat but his mouth is sweet and delicious. I could strip his clothes off right here.

"Hmm, I guess I feel *somewhat* better now," I say, closing one eye and shrugging off the kiss as uneventful.

"What!"

He launches himself in full force over me, smothering me with his body and kissing me hard on the lips and throat, biting softly at my neck. I kick my feet in surprise, laughing underneath his exquisite touch, knowing I am finally safe.

———

We arrive at the summit around noon, the hike having taken longer with my ankle and the amount of gear Ben hauled. I down the last of my water as we climb the last bit, and promptly sit down on a large boulder by the base of the lookout tower. The huge rock is covered in scratches — names, dates, pointed hearts, and other angled drawings make up a totem of sorts. I make a mental note to carve something significant on it over the weekend.

"Let's get inside, and get that foot up." He motions toward the cabin across the butte.

I stand and nod, heading downhill. I cannot wait to get inside and relax.

Stepping onto the porch, I wait as Ben unhooks the padlock, and pushes the door open. As we head inside, I note the hole in the porch where my foot crashed through is now repaired. The replacement wood is bright and new against the graying, older areas. I glance down at my ankle, also repaired and new, and I recognize a similar effect in my heart. This cabin, and the man that occupies it, holds so much of my love, of my heart. It almost aches to realize how much I care for this man.

"C'mon in," he says, holding the door open for me to pass through. "Come in here and let me take care of you."

CHAPTER TWENTY-SIX

GEORGIA

THE CABIN SMELLS LIKE WARM wood, wool blankets, and pine trees. The scents are familiar, welcoming, and I immediately feel a sense of protection wash over me.

Ben drops his shoulder, and slides his heavy pack off his body, resting it on the kitchen table before heaving it to the ground near his desk. He turns and walks over to where I'm still standing in the open doorway.

"You okay?" he asks, stepping closer. He hooks his fingers under the straps of my pack, pulling them outward and off my shoulders.

"Oh, yeah, thank you," I say deftly, shaking my head. "Sorry. Just so many memories here."

"Mmm hmm, some not the best, I'm sure. Time to make some new ones, huh?"

I look up into his eyes and see only tenderness there. Leaning into his chest, I rest my face against his warm body.

"New memories are good," I murmur.

He rubs my lower back and brings his hands to rest on either side of my arms.

"C'mon, let's get you horizontal."

"And people say chivalry is dead," I say, grinning and turning to walk over to the low bed.

The Aztec-print blanket lies folded across the foot of the bed, and I smile as I sit down and stretch out. I feel instantly better and breathe a huge sigh of relief, closing my eyes. Ben gently lifts my ankle and places a pillow under it as he unties the laces of my trail running shoe, loosening it across the top of my foot.

"Oh, sweet mother," I moan.

"Okay to take it off?" he asks, chuckling.

"Yes, please. Hurry!"

He pulls my shoe free of my foot, and I wriggle my toes in ecstasy.

His hands knead the center of my foot firmly, working his way slowly down to my heel.

I roll my head back against the pillow and close my eyes.

"Oh God. I would marry you in a heartbeat if you asked me right now," I say, groaning in pleasure.

His hands suddenly stop moving.

My eyes spring open, and I lift my head up from the pillow, horrified.

His face holds no trace of emotion.

"Oh shit, Ben. I'm sorry. It was just an exp—"

An enormous smile cracks across his face, his eyes gleaming at me.

I sit up and slap at him, my face burning with embarrassment.

"Hey, hey now. C'mon. It's not every day a guy gets proposed to like that." He holds up his hands, feigning protection against my blows.

I lie back down and throw my arm across my face, laughing.

"Sorry. It's just, well...that felt really good."

The mattress sinks down next to me as Ben's body presses

over mine. I pull back my arm and look up into his eyes. He's resting on one elbow while his other hand lazily traces up my side and under my chin. He holds my mouth with the tips of his fingers, our eyes locked in each other's gaze.

"You've captured my heart, Georgia." He stares at me a moment longer. "Please don't ever let me go."

I pull him close to me and wrap my arms around his body. I want to protect him from all the sadness that has crept into his life over the past years. I want my love for him to drown out all the anger and ache. I want to bring alive in him the feeling of loving, and being truly loved in return. I kiss his temple and run my hands over his shoulders.

"I love you, Benjamin Harrison. I love you with all of my heart. There's no other place I want to be than right here, right now, with you." My lips whisper the words beside his ear.

He's quiet for a moment, and then tucks his head into the empty space of my neck and nuzzles me.

"I don't deserve you." His tone of voice suggests he wants to say something else, but he doesn't.

After a moment I shift next to him.

"Hey, is that your holster, or are you just happy to see me?" I ask, a smile teasing my face.

Ben rolls off of me, laughing. He stands up and removes his holster, placing his gun in the nightstand drawer. I pretend not to notice when he quickly wipes the corner of his eye as he turns to look out of the window. I know exactly how he feels; finally finding someone you love is like being lost for days, for weeks, for months. Being lost, and then, miraculously, being found.

Ben clears his voice. "I should get out there and check the equipment in the tower. Make sure the propane is turned off, etc."

I sit up quickly.

"Why? Is the weather changing?" I stretch to see out the

window. The sky seems slightly darker, cloudier maybe, but not by much.

"No, no. It looks okay now, but these storms can blow in without much warning. I just want to be safe."

He walks over to the desk and pulls the hand-held radio out of the receiver, tucking it into his belt loop. He scoops up the lantern off the table and sets it on the wood stove, next to the pack of matches. Walking over to the kitchen, he rustles around in a cabinet below the sink before pulling out a handful of half-burned candles in holders. He places all of them on the kitchen table.

"You need anything before I head up there?"

I shake my head, trying to think of something.

"No. I don't think so."

"Here, I'll bring you a water bottle. There's more in the fridge but try not to open the door too often. If a storm hits, we'll need to shut down the generator too."

He places the bottle on the nightstand next to me, and sits down on the edge of the bed, picking up my hand.

"If I don't tell you this right now, I might lose my nerve. So, here goes," he says, clearing his throat. "It sounds crazy, but I knew then, the last time you were here in this bed. I knew then there was something different about you. Something unique." He drops his chin.

"I tried to dismiss it, the pull you had on me, even then. But I couldn't. I couldn't stop thinking about you, wanting to know more about you." He traces slow circles on the back of my hand, and it feels like my heart doubles in size.

"That night you slept here, I told myself to stay away. I convinced myself not to open up or even think about letting you into my life." He shakes his head at me, and pulls my hand to his lips, planting soft kisses.

"Somehow...and I don't know why, I just felt safe around you.

The more time we spent together, the more I found myself opening doors that had been locked shut for so long."

I swallow hard, a huge lump forming in my throat.

"You have given me so much, Georgia. You've given me direction again, a purpose, and a reason to keep moving forward."

He looks at me, tears beginning to pool in his eyes.

"I was so lost before I met you. I can't begin to tell you how much pain..."

He swallows, and a single tear slides slowly down his cheek. My heart feels like it is breaking in half.

"You have re-centered me, you've given me hope again — something I never thought I'd find. You've become my true north, and I'm not the least bit ashamed to say I'd probably follow you anywhere. I hope you can understand what I'm trying to say here —I love you very much, Georgia."

He takes a deep breath and slowly raises his eyes to mine.

"And I would be honored if you would share my home with me. I don't want us to be apart ever again."

I can't hold back any longer, and I throw myself forward into him, wrapping my arms tightly around his neck and planting myself firmly in his lap. I hug him, and then pull my head back and kiss him in rapid succession over both sides of his face. He begins to laugh, begins to try to talk but I smother his lips with kisses, too. He mumbles something under my lips, and I pull back, pausing in my barrage to look at him for clarification.

"I said, 'does this mean that's a yes'?" He runs his hands up my back as I nod my head repeatedly.

"Yes! Absolutely, yes!"

I look back down at him, love and desire pooling in my belly. He's staring at me with the most beautiful smile on his face, and all at once I know. I know without a doubt that my future centers around this man.

And I'm not the least bit afraid.

———

The cabin windows are open, and a cool breeze over my forearm raises goosebumps and causes me to shiver. I look up and realize the light has significantly faded, and I hadn't even realized. I was so absorbed in my book. I put it down across the arm of the chair, and take a deep breath. I'd thrown on Ben's shirt after we'd made love, and the soft flannel brushes against my naked breasts as I stand up and stretch, raising my arms above my head and pulling the tension in my muscles free.

My watch says it's just after 7 p.m. Ben must still be up in the tower.

Walking over to the bed, I snag my jeans off the floor and drag them on, the denim, cold against my skin. I walk over to one of the windows and reach to pull the sash down. It's old and weather-beaten and doesn't budge when I pull. Wiggling it from side to side I gradually work it shut. Breathing a sigh of relief, I dust my hands off and prepare to move onto the next one.

And then I stop, mid-reach, and gasp.

To the west of the cabin, the sky is literally churning. Thick, dark blues and muddled grays look as though they've been swirled together in a blender. Beyond these colors, the sky is black as night. Although I've never personally experienced a tornado, the TV shows I've watched all depict the sky in exactly the way I'm seeing now — it's like the moment before the funnel cloud forms and strikes the earth. I hurry and shut the other window, hustle back to the wood stove, and light the propane lantern. Gathering up the candles from the kitchen table, I light each of those as well and place them throughout the interior of the cabin.

As I set a candle down on the nightstand, I glance out of the window toward the lookout tower. I can see a dim light on inside, and I watch for a moment, looking for evidence of Ben's movement inside the glass-paneled crow's nest. The wind begins to pick up, and suddenly I hear the soft rumble of thunder in the distance. Standing perfectly still, I begin to whisper the protocol my mother taught me as a child.

"One alligator...two alligator...three alligator...four al—"

A giant crack of lightning streaks across the sky — illuminating the interior of the cabin in an impossibly bright flash. My shoulders jump around my ears, and I scream in shock.

"Ben!"

I turn and quickly make my way across the cabin to the front door, pulling my parka from the kitchen table and shrugging it on as I grab the door handle.

Another thunderous rumble breaks out across the sky, this time supplemented by a deafening boom that seems to split my stomach in half. I reach for the handle of the front door and yank it open as hard as I can.

Suddenly I can't breathe anymore. I can't move or make a single, solitary sound. I have no air left in my lungs, and my feet are planted in cement. Standing in front of me, half concealed in the darkness, is the face of my nightmares.

"Hello, Georgia," he sneers. "You've been a very, very naughty girl."

CHAPTER TWENTY-SEVEN

GEORGIA

A STREAK OF LIGHTNING CRACKS across the sky, and illuminates Mike's shadowed face for a fraction of a second. I'm too stunned to speak. Too shocked to think. My mind is an empty slate, my mouth suddenly bone dry. All I feel is the overwhelming sensation of the enormous danger standing before me.

"What's this? No kiss for your husband?" A wicked smile crosses his lips for a moment before turning into a deep, sinister frown. "No? No hug!" He raises his voice and reveals only his bottom teeth. The overpowering smell of alcohol radiates from him, filling my nostrils.

Suddenly I snap out of my trance, my brain directing all available force in my body toward slamming the door closed. It's too late, of course. Mike thrusts his arm out in front of him like a concrete barrier, blocking the door with his thick boot and locked elbow. My strength is useless against his, and he easily pushes his way forward into the cabin. I backpedal into the center of the room, trying to put as much distance between us as possible.

"Aren't you going to invite me in? Tsk, tsk." He clucks his

tongue at me. "Remember what I taught you? Manners, George. Manners."

His syrupy sweet voice turns my stomach sour, every word churning in my belly.

The heel of my shoe catches on the braided rug near the wood stove, and I stumble and right myself, gasping. There really isn't anywhere for me to go. I can't look for usable weapons without taking my eyes off Mike — and that is something I learned never to do. Ever.

I clench my fists, my palms cold and clammy with sweat.

I swallow hard and square my shoulders.

"What are you doing here, Mike?" I stammer.

I have to tell myself to breathe, to remain as calm as possible. The old playbook comes back to me: *Keep him talking. He won't hurt me if I keep him talking.*

He looks around the room, and I follow his glance to the bed; the disheveled ruins of Ben and my passionate lovemaking evidenced by the rumpled sheets and pillows and — I gulp — my bra, strung over the footboard. His focus lingers there, and he steps forward, picking it up and bringing it to his face, burying his nose deep within the fabric. When he pulls the lace away, all I hear is an evil snicker.

"What do you want?" I repeat, louder.

His eyes instantly snap back to mine, and a shiver slides up my spine. I've seen that look before. I take a small step backward, and my hands feel the familiar corner of the wood stove. I step slowly to the side of it, keeping my hands on it the entire time.

"What do I want? What I've always wanted. I want what's *mine.*" He slowly follows my steps, closing the distance between us.

"I'm not alone here, Mike."

I say the words slowly, wondering if I've made the right move in doing so.

He narrows his eyes at me for a moment, the side of his mouth curling into a sneer, and then it all disappears, his face unreadable again.

"Oh, you mean Ben? He won't be around anytime soon." He chuckles softly under his breath.

"What? What do you mean? Where is Ben?" The panic in my voice is unmistakable, even to me, and the taste of bile floods my mouth.

"Such an incredible view from that tower, don't you think? Oh, wait, I forgot. You haven't actually been up there yet." Mike rubs his hands together in front of him and inspects his nails. Immediately I notice the dark red-black stains across his knuckles, streaking down the sides of his hands.

"Jesus Christ, Mike, what the hell have you done!" I scream at him and try to back up toward the chair.

He flattens one of his hands out in front of him; examining the dried blood, and brings it to his mouth, slowly dragging his tongue across the stains. I watch this display in horror, too stunned to speak. Suddenly he drops his hands and lunges at me, crossing the space between us in two quick leaps.

I take a huge gulp of air and scream as long and as loud as I can, but it's lost in the simultaneous explosive rumbling in the sky above the cabin. The ground shakes as the thunder echoes off the mountains and reverberates down through the valleys.

I close my eyes, and put my arms up in front of my face, bracing for the impact I know will come from Mike's hands. The blow sends me flying backward into the nearby wall, crashing into the corner of the windowsill. I fall to my knees, the side of my face exploding into an accordion of pain. My vision blackens for a moment, and my head rings with the noise of the thunder, or is it the throbbing pain? I bring my hands up in front of my face and curl my legs up to my body as close as possible, keeping my face tucked into my chin. *Only show the elbows and head, only the hardest parts of me. Protect everything else.*

"Fuck! God dammit, sweetheart! Now look what you made me do!" he wails. "All I wanted to do was talk to you. I just wanted to show you how much I still love you, how much you still mean to me. And now look. Look what you've gone and done!" The hairs on my arms suddenly stand on end, and the room erupts in two blinding flashes of light. I shut my eyes hard against the erratic streaks.

I taste blood in my mouth, and I run my tongue along the side of my molars, tasting more. My heart is racing, and my hands begin to shake. Panic starts to set in. I'm having trouble breathing. *Think, Georgia. Calm down and think. You're still conscious. Play along.*

I slowly raise my head and look up to the level of his steel-toe boots.

"I'm so sorry, baby," I soothe, my voice soft as a lamb's ear. "I deserved that. You were only trying to show me how much you love me." I pause, waiting to see if he will bite.

Mike emits a deep sigh and shuffles his feet.

"You know how much I hate it when you disobey, George. I don't like to punish you," he says, his voice high and playful, like a child. "But you didn't leave me a choice, did you? You were very bad. You left me — you left *us*. And for what? For that piece of shit?" His voice thunders, and he stamps a boot hard on the ground.

I immediately look up at him, praying my risk will pay off.

"I was very, very bad, and I deserve your punishment," I quickly say. "I promise I won't ever do that again. I'm so sorry. I can come back. I can fix this. Please...please forgive me." My stomach swims with nausea, and I pray I won't vomit and break the small window I'm slowly gaining.

He sighs again and relaxes his posture. Tears run down his

face, and he closes his eyes, swaying a moment, no doubt from the alcohol.

"First Jason, and now you. I can't live without you, sweetheart. I've never been able to live without you, ever since I met you."

"Here," I soothe. "Can I help you lie down?" I ask, coming up slowly from my submissive crouch.

His eyes fly open.

"*No!*" He roars at me, his canine teeth glinting in the dim glow of the candles.

I tuck my head back down and curl up protectively.

"Ok, ok, I'm sorry," I plead. *Please God, do not let him crush me.*

"Shh, why are you crying, George? It's okay. Come here." His voice is tender now, soft and sweet. Ben's face flashes into my mind, and I nearly lose my breath. *I've got to get to him.*

I crawl over to Mike's feet, gingerly extending my hand toward his boot. Another thundering explosion breaks open over the cabin and my body jerks in fear. I whimper as my hand begins to shake.

Mike crouches down and takes my hand, petting it with his calloused palm. I lift my gaze to his hand, the dried blood and open cuts inches away from me. Is Ben lying dead in the tower?

I bite back another scream of terror as a white explosion of light illuminates the room. For a moment I lose sight of Mike, my eyes blinded by the bright electricity. The wind suddenly picks up again, howling through the seams in the log walls, and rattling the windows and door.

"I'm so scared," I whisper. "I'm so scared and so cold."

"I've got you, honey. Here, let me wrap you up."

Mike pulls me to my feet with great care, wrapping his arm around my shoulder. The smell of him sickens me — a biting mixture of alcohol and sweat. I am repulsed by him, but I can't show it. I must be careful, playing along with his game of husband and wife.

My balance is completely lopsided as we begin to walk, my head swimming with agony. I close one eye against the throbbing in my temple and stumble forward as he leads me across the room. Toward the bed. *Oh no. No, no, no, no, no.*

I slow my steps and resist against Mike's arm. He twists my parka in his hand and pulls me closer to him, cooing in my ear.

"What's the matter, George? You like the bed, remember? You liked it just a few hours ago, *didn't you?*" His voice slices my veins open, and I swallow back the blood and bile.

I nod from under his arm, even though I'm desperately trying to think of what I can use against him. *Think, Georgia!*

He forces me to a seated position on the edge of the bed as another wave of thunder crashes over us, causing me to flinch. *One alligator...*

"Shhh. It's okay. It's just a storm. You're safe now," he mews, roughly stroking my hair with bloodied hands. "It must have been hard, pretending to like him." A split second of rage flashes over his face, and I wince as he grabs a section of my hair and rips backward, snapping my chin up to meet his bloodshot, black eyes. "I know you don't love him like you love me." He pauses, lets go of my hair and then crouches down to look me straight in the eye, his putrid breath covering my face. "That's why you bought the gun, isn't it?"

My heart stops beating. A bolt of lightning splits open the sky above us. *Less than one mile away.*

"Oh, I know all about you," he sneers. "I've always known about you, baby. Ever since you were sixteen."

What? I didn't even know Mike when I was sixteen. This is madness.

"You've been a very busy girl lately, haven't you?" He stands up and begins to unbuckle his belt. "Did you happen to check your little gun before you packed it yesterday? No?" His evil smile tells me all I need to know: he's been in the house. The gun is probably unloaded, or broken, or both. Either way, I know it's useless to me now.

"I'm happy you know about it," I lie. "I knew I would need it for him. He wouldn't leave me alone, and I had to be safe. Just like you taught me."

His hands pause on his now-open belt.

"You were such a good teacher, Mike. Nobody could ever teach me like you," I say, slowly reaching my shaking fingers toward his jeans, circling the button at the top. "I'm so glad you found me." I close my eyes as the thunder breaks over us, rattling the window beside me.

Mike takes a step closer to me, grabbing the back of my head and twisting his hands in my hair until it is agonizingly tight against my scalp.

"You're hurting me," I whisper, leaning my head back to ease the pain. "I can't please you if you're hurting me," I reason.

He uncoils his hands slightly, easing the slack, and simultaneously pulls my head closer to his crotch. I work hard not to resist what he wants, counting in my head. *Three, two, —*

From the corner of my eye the lightning forks across the sky, and I turn my head to follow it, my pupils dilating as the bolt of energy surges through the sky and strikes the top of the lookout tower, a spray of sparks erupting in slow motion against the dark night sky.

"*Ben!*" I scream.

I don't even have a chance to defend myself. Mike knocks me sideways across the end of the bed and over the log footboard. My body flops onto the braided rug like a rag doll.

"DON'T YOU EVER SAY HIS NAME AGAIN! Do you hear me? He's dead, Georgia!" Mike screams from across the room.

I try to argue with him, try to tell him that Ben's alive, but I can't seem to make my mouth move correctly. My brain feels fuzzy, and my vision is spotty. All I can manage to say comes out in a quiet plea.

"Liar," I groan, my eyelids shutting against the pain.

"You stupid bitch. You stupid, lying bitch! You're just as bad as those two fucking idiots that raised you — coddling you and filling your head full of ridiculous ideas about love and relationships and happy-fucking-ever-afters. Guess what, Georgia? You had happily ever after with me. You had the storybook romance with me!" Mike yells and beats a fist against his chest. "Tell me I didn't take care of you, George. Tell me I didn't love you and give you everything. Your worthless excuse for a father was wrong, wasn't he? He said I could never take care of you the way you deserved, could never love you or provide for you the way he wanted. Said I was too young and didn't have a good enough job. Well, *fuck him,* Georgia. You had it all!"

I try to say he's mistaken. That he never knew my parents, never met my dad – but I can't. I am overwhelmed with pain. Every inch of my body is crying out, crumbling under the weight of what he's done to me, crashing down and splintering apart.

Mike is screaming so hard at me that I can actually see spit coming out of his mouth. I try to roll onto my shoulder to get up and away, but the pain in my head is debilitating. The thunder and lightning are on top of us now, and the noise when the thunder claps is almost deafening. My mind is rolling, and I can't focus on any one thought.

A flash of lightning streaks across the window and illuminates the sickening grin on Mike's face. He's staring at me, smiling, and suddenly he breaks out in maniacal laughter.

"You know what, Georgia?" Mike whispers, coming closer. "I enjoyed killing them."

"Yeah," he laughs, "that's right. I enjoyed it. No one tells me who I can or can't love. No one. I did the honorable thing. I asked that fucking waste of a father of yours, *permission* to date you. You never even knew, did you? 'Course not. You were still just a kid in high school. Well, let me tell you, sweetheart, it was love at first sight. I loved you the moment I saw you, Georgia. The very moment your parents' car backed into mine. You remember, don't you? That day in Vancouver? Oh, it was a gorgeous day, wasn't it? Remember? You and your parents were shopping, and your dad accidentally backed his shiny Navigator into my shitty-ass car in the parking lot, remember? As soon as I saw you, I wasn't even mad anymore. I just took your father aside, and explained it would be no big deal as long as I could ask you out on a date."

No. No, this can't be right. My parents were innocent victims of a horrible tragedy. An accident. Nothing premeditated. Not by Mike. Not by the man I called my husband. No. No. I can't think straight.

"Do you know how ashamed of myself I was for sinking to that level? *Do you?* When he looked me up and down and told me there was no way his daughter would be allowed to date *someone like me*, someone that looked like he had a questionable past, well...well, that just wasn't acceptable, Georgia. I was going to make you mine. I was going to make you love me like I loved you, whether he and your mother liked it or not," Mike says, suddenly slamming his fist on the footboard.

"I set you free! Your parents were suffocating you, don't you see? You and I could never have been together if they weren't out of the way! You were *mine*, Georgia! No one was going to take you away from me. With them gone, we could be together. Just the two of us."

"And what do you do in return? You fucking betray my love for you!" Mike's voice booms across the room; he is screaming, hollering, throwing a tantrum.

And I don't care.

I feel nothing as I slowly open my eyes. I can't hear anything anymore. I see the lightning flashing around us, and I can see Mike's mouth moving, but I can't hear a thing. My mind is a house of pain and horror as I process his words and insults. I can't think straight.

My mother.

My father.

Ben.

All of their faces flash in front of me as the room flips on its side, and I feel something warm and wet under the side of my face. I roll my eyes up and around. I see Mike's feet pounding toward my head, but I still can't hear anything. It feels like I am suspended underwater in my own cocoon of noiseless existence. My parents. My poor, beautiful parents. How can this be possible? How could I have let this murderer into my life? How could I have been so incredibly stupid? I want to die. I don't want to go on living knowing this horrible truth.

I feel the floor tremble beneath me, and I lazily try to look up to see what's happening. Everything moves in slow motion. The toe of his boot drives toward my chest as if it's dragging through drying concrete. I want to pull my legs up in front of me, but I can't seem to remember how. All the fight has gone out of me.

"You will be mine again!" he bellows.

All at once my rib cage explodes in shattering pain, and the room fills with blinding white light. As I look around in desperate fear, eyes open wide, I realize I am hearing the sound of my own painful screams. I squeeze my eyes shut against the pain in my side and grind my head against the rug.

"Ben," I moan.

Mike's face is in my face, and I can feel his breath on my skin. His hands lift my head off the ground as he spits through his teeth at me.

"Don't you ever say his filthy name again! Do you hear me!"

He furiously lets go of my head, slamming it down against the floor, and I cry out again as I listen to his sarcastic laugh above me.

"You're nothing but a whore. A trashy little bitch whore. That message I left for you on your mirror? It was the fucking truth!"

Another deafening roll of thunder rocks the cabin, and I silently pray for salvation.

"You thought that guy up there was better for you than *me*? Better than me, Georgia! You're so stupid! You didn't even know this guy's past."

He turns and stomps toward the back windows. He passes by the nightstand, Ben's books stacked neatly on the side, the candle burning softly. He stops, staring at something there, and then suddenly picks up the table and throws it sideways across the room, the books scattering across the floor, the candle rolling out of sight, and the contents of the drawer sliding under the bed and across the floor toward me.

I close my eyes as the lightning cracks across the back windows. The electricity in the air lifts my hair off the floor in front of me.

"You think you're so fucking smart," Mike yells. "Did you know he killed a woman? Drove her to swallow a whole bottle of pills!" He turns back toward me, his arms flailing in all directions. "You think he served time? Hell no! You let a goddamn murderer into your bed, *our* bed!" He works his way around the cabin, pulling down pictures and throwing furniture across the room.

I roll onto my back, trying to follow his movements, and my head lolls to the side as I face the dark underside of the bed. I can't seem to take a full breath, and my ribs feel like a fire is ripping through them.

My parents. Ben. The agony of what I'm realizing is pulling me under.

Another clap of thunder momentarily drowns out any noise around me.

"But even he wasn't enough was he? You spread your legs for that idiotic child, Calvin! You really lowered yourself into the sewer with that one, didn't you, you worthless tramp." He yells the words from across the room. I try to speak a word of defense, in an attempt to calm him, anything to make him stop, but my jaw won't work — the words won't come. I am numb from the pain, and the realization this sociopath murdered my parents.

"And to think of all that I gave you, all I provided for you. How *perfectly* I loved you."

The volume of his words increases. He's coming closer.

My ears begin to hum, and the hair on my head rises off my scalp as the lightning flashes against the darkness. The entire cabin is momentarily illuminated, and an object under the bed catches my hazy attention. Before I can put the cognitive pieces together, the room darkens again, and the smell of sulfur drifts into my nostrils.

I feel the weight of his boots beside my head. He stands still for a moment next to me as I lay on the floor, motionless, silent, tears sliding across my nose and into my ear.

"Look at you now," he whispers, slowly coming around the side of me. "Disgusting."

My arm is bent under the bed, my fingertips making contact with hard, rough edges, gaining purchase and drawing it into the palm of my hand.

"The only thing you're good for now is one, last, worthless fuck." Through the haze in my eyes, I watch as he unzips his pants and drops them to his knees. He is fully aroused, and I pull in a tiny breath, trying to move my legs closer together, preparing to hold off what I know he will do next.

The thunder breaks again as he rips my legs apart. The pain is excruciating, and somehow I find the air to scream. The biting smell of smoke suddenly fills my nostrils, and I choke and cough violently. Something is on fire! The thunder bellows against the cabin roof, and the lightning pops and snaps, electrifying the room once more. Smoke billows across the floor and around my hair.

Mike kneels down in front of me and takes hold of my pants and underwear, pulling them down from my hips.

"No!" I try to yell, but my throat is burning. The smoke is traveling across the floor and into my mouth and throat.

"Shut up! You know you want this!" he says, pinning my flailing, free arm down under his knee. I look into Mike's eyes as he lowers himself over me. He is pure evil. There is nothing good left of him...there never was.

"You," I choke. "You are...finished here," I whisper as his face draws closer to mine. The stench of his breath and body fill my senses, and I am suddenly filled with an overwhelming feeling of rage. "You have hurt me...for the...last time," I say, struggling for air, and then, somehow, I suddenly find my voice. "You sick... twisted...pathetic, *fuck* of a human being!"

My throat shreds with each word I scream at him, but I don't care. I don't care about anything anymore.

"Shut up!" He rears back on his heels and draws back his fist in the air.

And that's all I need.

At that moment, I hear nothing. I feel nothing.

Time stands still as my fingers firmly close over Ben's gun underneath the bed. My thumb automatically reaches up and lowers the safety latch in one deft movement as I bring it out in front of me, reach my right hand to meet my left, and pull the trigger as hard as I can.

The shot causes the gun to recoil in my hand, but still, I hear nothing. I look at Mike's face as his fist slowly relaxes, his fingers opening like a child's releasing a toy in sleep, and I notice the grimace on his face, the angry lines across his forehead — all fading, little, by precious little.

"George," he gasps. "Georgia, I love — "

I close my eyes and pull the trigger again, and again, and again until all I hear is the quiet *click, click, click* of the empty gun.

CHAPTER TWENTY-EIGHT

GEORGIA

I DROP THE GUN TO the floor as Mike's bloodied, disfigured body crumples, and sinks to the ground. I vaguely register the sound of his skull smacking the wood floor as it echoes through the room.

I feel nothing.

I have no words.

I realize the room is filling with smoke, and I can see flickering shadows of flames reflecting on the wall across from me, but I don't care.

My head feels so thick, and suddenly I'm overcome with utter exhaustion. Every breath feels like a knife slicing through me — every slight movement produces merciless waves of pain. My world without Ben is a silent, never-ending wasteland. My world without him isn't worth living in.

A terrible trick of my mind allows me to hear his voice, muffled and echoing, calling me by name. I want to follow his voice, to hurry and find him, to join him and never look back. I want to close my eyes and never wake up again. I want to be with him, wherever he is.

Maybe that's exactly what I will do. To continue to fight feels so hard, so exhausting. I don't want to do it any longer. I just want to surrender to the peaceful unconsciousness that's beckoning me.

CHAPTER TWENTY-NINE

GEORGIA

P AIN.
 THE DULL ACHE AND heaviness of pain envelop me like a blanket of lead I cannot push aside. My senses are dulled, and muddy. I cannot put the pieces of the puzzle together.

I am sinking.

I am falling and flailing into a pit of agony.

Everything hurts, and I cannot breathe. I have no air.

I am choking on the strangling smoke as it wraps its tendrils around my lungs, scorching and burning alive everything it touches.

CHAPTER THIRTY

GEORGIA

M Y BODY IS BENDING. MY legs are weightless. I cannot feel my hands.

I am moving. I am floating.

I open my mouth to scream in pain, but I have no voice. I am dying. I am dead already.

Ben.

My name.

Ben is saying my name.

I want to see him. Where is he?

I can see a sliver of light in the distance. I can see a shadow. Am I being carried? The shadow moves to the light.

I am nothing.

CHAPTER THIRTY-ONE

GEORGIA

H USHED VOICES ARE NEARBY. WHISPERS and murmurs, the voices raise and lower, but I can't understand what they are saying.

Where am I?

I don't know.

Everything is black. It is too hard to focus.

I realize I'm cold, and I want a blanket, but I can't seem to make my vocal cords work, or even move my mouth.

I am laying on something soft. I feel pressure on my back, and I want to roll over. I try to move, but I am too heavy. It feels like a mattress is on top of me, pressing down without mercy, against my chest.

I want to scream. I want to pound my fists and wake myself up out of this nightmare. I want to open my eyes and make all of this stop. I know I am alive because I can feel my heart racing, feel it ready to burst out of my chest. *Why can't I open my eyes? Why can't I talk?*

Voices again.

It feels like someone is moving close to me.

Help! I scream, in silence. *Please help me!*

I smell the floral scent of cheap perfume, and I want to vomit.

And then, suddenly, I am absolutely painless.

I am floating above the clouds, soaring peacefully across the treetops. My body is below me somewhere I can no longer see. I feel nothing, I see only the landscape of the earth before me, and I am in no rush to go anywhere. I am so peaceful. I am completely comfortable and utterly relaxed.

I drift across the water as the tide pulls me out.

CHAPTER THIRTY-TWO

GEORGIA

A M I ALIVE?
MY LEFT eyelid flutters open, and then immediately slams shut again. The light is too bright.

I cannot seem to operate my right eye at all.

Where am I?

I try to feel my body. I bend my toes and try to move each finger individually. It feels like a month passes while I attempt these simple tasks. A soft sheet is covering me, and my toes scrape against it when I try to move them.

I hear the sound of a machine near me. The periodic *blip... blip...blip* sounds like an alarm that won't shut off.

In a faraway place, I think I hear people talking. It sounds like they are talking without opening their mouths. Everything is muffled and garbled.

I try to open my mouth and speak, but the pain is so great I have to bite my tongue not to cry out, and I feel a tear slide down my cheek.

I will myself to open my eye again, prepared for the light this time. I open it to a thin slit and stop as the light assaults my cornea. I want to close it again, but I am so curious to know where I am. The struggle to keep my eye open is too great, and it snaps back down. I am in blackness once again.

I hear a toilet flush nearby, and then the sound of running water. I hear paper towels being pulled from the holder, wadded up and tossed away.

The smell of hand sanitizer floats into my nostrils.

Am I in a hospital? I must be in a hospital.

I force myself to open my eye again, and this time I am able to slowly tolerate the light. The sunshine is pouring through the window to my right, the thin mini blinds making the shards of light flicker and dance across the wall. I turn my head slightly and look away. Even though it's a minuscule movement, pain shoots across my forehead, and I have to close my eye again and wait.

I try to take a deep breath to relax. As I begin to expand my chest, a scathing pain shoots across my side, and I am left unable to breathe, unable to speak. It is fire, scorching my skin alive. It is ten thousand needles all piercing my lungs at once. I feel my mouth open but, only a small squeak ekes out.

The machine near my head begins to make a louder noise. The *blips* become loud, persistent *beeps* that go off in rapid succession, sounding an alarm. My heart thuds in my chest, increasing as I listen to the machine. Will this pain ever stop?

I squeeze my eyes closed and pray for release.

I hear someone's shoes rubbing against the floor near me. A moment later, a coolness spreads through my arm, and up into my shoulder and across my chest.

The pain is slowly receding.

Suddenly my hand is lifted, and I flinch against the touch, my left eye springing open.

"Oh, I'm sorry. I didn't realize you were awake." A young woman is standing over me, holding my wrist in her hand. She has kind brown eyes and a pretty smile. Her shirt has a black stethoscope tucked into a chest pocket. She has a name tag...does that say Shellie? Staci? It's too hard to focus. Instead I try and concentrate on the feeling of her warm hand on my skin.

The beeping machine slows to an easy rhythm, and my breathing relaxes. I stare at the woman, unable to speak. She looks at something just above me and checks her watch, slowly setting my hand back down on the bed.

"Are you cold, Georgia? Can I get you another blanket?"

I want to say yes, but my voice still isn't working. I muster as much strength as possible and try to nod instead. I close my eye as I do so, hoping she has noticed my attempt.

"Okay, hon. One second, okay? I'll be right back. I'm going to get you a warm one."

I try to follow her with my eye as she walks away from my side but the pain in my forehead is like a concrete barrier, and I focus instead on keeping my breath shallow.

A moment later I hear her shoes on the floor again.

A heavy warmth begins to envelop me from my feet to my neck. My arms are gently raised and tucked underneath the heat, and I think I might die from pure happiness. This is the most wonderful feeling on the planet. It's as if I have just stepped into the hottest shower after walking in the snow for hours without a coat.

"There. That's gotta feel better, huh?" These soothing words are like little anchors to me, and I cling to each one, slowly crossing this sea of fear as I head toward dry land.

"How's your pain level, Georgia?" Her voice is soft, slightly raspy. She speaks with a slow, measured cadence.

"I know it's hard to talk right now, and I don't want you to worry about that. Your voice will come back soon. Your throat was badly damaged by the smoke, and you've only been here three days, so don't worry about rushing anything," she says, typing something on a keyboard next to me. "If it helps, your family has been here non-stop," she says, smiling. "And your friend seems pretty interested in your well-being..."

My heart stops. Calvin. She thinks Calvin and I are romantically involved. I don't have the energy to correct her.

Her words only bring up memories of Ben, and a wave of nausea passes through me as I realize, once more, that I will never see him again. I could drown in this pain — this overflowing ocean of depression that surrounds me.

"I'm going to pick up your hand again, okay?" She pulls back the blanket and gently takes hold of my hand, gently patting the top of it and then massaging my palm.

"We'll start with this. If you need more pain medication, try and squeeze my finger, okay?" I blink my eye as many times as I possibly can and try to nod. I don't want to feel anything anymore. I focus on moving my fingers around hers, and I manage to grab her thumb and squeeze it as hard as I possibly can. I feel tears escape the corner of my eye and slide down the side of my face.

"It's okay, love. You're doing so well. Let me get that for you right now." She gives me a gentle squeeze and replaces my hand under the warm blanket before she steps away from the bed.

A moment later I feel the tension in my body release and begin to evaporate completely. I can breathe easier, and the pain in my head is slowly letting go.

"There you go. Is that better?"

I slowly open my eye and look up at her. She's smiling at me, and her eyebrows lift slightly as she asks the question. In my drug-induced daze, I notice she has the smallest space next to a canine tooth, and it's somehow soothing to me. Her face is full of kindness, and I attempt to smile at her, not sure how much movement is conveyed.

I close my eye again, suddenly overwhelmed by drowsiness. I

listen to the soft rhythm of the beeping machine as sleep swiftly pulls me under.

———

There's an indentation on the bed near my feet. My foot seems to be angling to the right, following the impression of the weight. The weight shifts slightly, and my toes touch something firm. I can't quite shake the sleep from my head, even though I want to open my eyes.

Someone is touching my foot through the blanket, rubbing my toes and pressing on the top and bottom of my foot with simple, soft movements. I feel very comforted, very safe — which only reminds me of how I felt with Ben. The crushing weight of the realization that Ben was left in the tower overwhelms me. He was murdered. Murdered by my — I can't think straight. The pain in my chest explodes again as my body begins to shake. I feel my face wet with the tears that will not stop. I want to die. Why was I not left to die?

The weight at my foot shifts and suddenly releases.

"I think she's in pain again, Scott. Go get the nurse!" I hear my sister's panic, and I cry harder. I don't want to open my eyes. I don't want to face anyone or hear the horrible news. I want to slip back into unconsciousness and never wake up again.

I turn my head to the side, the pain kills me, but I don't care. Tears flood across the bridge of my nose and drip down onto the pillowcase.

My body is broken. My heart is crushed.

I don't even respond when I hear the nurse's voice ask me how I'm doing.

I just quietly sob and wait for the sweet release of the medication.

CHAPTER THIRTY-THREE

GEORGIA

"NO. YOU DON'T UNDERSTAND. SHE is in no condition to talk to anyone right now, Sheriff."

"I understand your concern, Ms. Sorenson. However, it's been nearly a week now, and we need to at least attempt to speak to her about what happened."

"I'll tell you right now what happened. Her psychopathic, abusive, asshole of an ex-husband stalked her, followed her to the top of that mountain, and beat her — nearly to *death*— and she shot him in self-defense! That's what happened!"

Sylvia is screaming at a police officer. And she used a cuss word. She must be really pissed.

I am semi-awake, listening to the people in my room talk. I'm touched by my sister's indignation on my behalf, but otherwise I don't care what's being said. All I care about has been stolen from me.

I blinked, and the small piece of happiness I'd found vanished. All that wasted time. All those suspicions. I should have followed up more carefully. I should have pressed the police

243

for more information about Mike. I should've investigated on my own. The realization that none of it matters now tears me apart again.

As I lie in this miserable hospital bed thinking about how messed up my life has become, I decide, with finality, that I will never tell Sylvia the truth. I will go to my grave keeping this secret. Knowing it was Mike that killed our parents would absolutely destroy her, and I won't be the one to do it. I refuse.

I want to go back to sleep. I want these people out of my room. I want total darkness, and quiet.

I want Ben.

"Calm down, sweetheart. He's just trying to do his job."

"I won't calm down, Scott! Georgia nearly died up there!"

"Ma'am, I give you my word, if Ms. Marks begins to show signs of distress I won't press any further. Besides, her doctor has her well-being at stake here. He's not going to let me get her all riled up."

I hear Sylvia exhale a long, slow breath.

"All right, fine," she says, lowering her voice. "But you listen to me: I'm going to be standing *right* outside that door. If I see my sister getting upset, you're done. Got it?"

"I appreciate your cooperation, ma'am. I shouldn't be long at all."

"Thank you, sir," Scott says. "We appreciate all that you are doing. My wife is just very upset."

"I understand completely. I'll try to be quick."

I hear the door shut, and the sounds of the hallway fade to a distant murmur. The room is quiet now, and I hear the machine next to me emitting a low hum that drifts across the room.

The officer walks closer to the foot of my bed and stops. I don't want to talk to anyone. I don't want to hear the details of that night. I don't want to hear about how they found Ben's body.

"I know you're awake, Ms. Marks."

I flinch, and then attempt to open both eyes.

To my surprise, I find I can now open my right eye as well as my left, although my right eyelid feels incredibly thick and heavy. My vision is impaired on that side, and I can tell my eyelid is either damaged or severely swollen.

I lift my gaze to the officer standing before me.

He reaches up and tips the end of his cap toward me. His radio crackles as a voice booms out into the room, relaying call information and codes. He quickly turns the radio volume down.

"Ms. Marks, I'm with the Deschutes County Sheriff's office. I'd like to ask you a few questions about the events of last Saturday night — the night you were attacked. Would that be all right?"

I roll my eyes to the side and focus on the tubes taped to the top of my right hand. Even if I had something to say, even if I knew my voice could actually work, what difference would it make now?

The officer walks around to my side of the bed and pulls the pastel upholstered chair up underneath his legs. He sits down, crosses his leg over the top of his knee and places his clipboard in his lap. His black socks are too short, revealing the pale white skin of his lower leg.

"I know this is going to be hard for you, remembering what happened that night and all. But you should only have to go through this once. We just need your statement before we can move forward."

I lift my gaze to meet his and stare at him for a moment.

"Can I get you anything, Ms. Marks? Water? Juice?"

Yeah. You can get me my goddamn life back. How about that?

I look away, staring instead at the wall beside me.

"Look, Georgia," he begins, scooting his chair closer to the

245

bed. "I know you've been through a hell of a lot lately. I've read your file, and I've had a long talk with Officer Roth here in Bend, and Officer Sanchez in Silverton. I'm up to speed on everything, and I know the last thing you want to do is talk about what happened up there, but you have to understand: your fingerprints are all over a gun that killed a man. We need to know more about how that happened."

I close my eyes and repeat the words in my head, *killed a man.*

It all happened so quickly, and yet now it seems like it's replaying in my mind in slow motion. I will never forget the look on Mike's face as the gun fired and the first bullet struck him in the throat. For a split second, I was in shock. I had done something terribly wrong, and I felt sick. I wanted to take it back, wanted to save him.

And then I remembered the horror of my parents' death.

Nothing else mattered from that moment on, not the mind games and manipulations — not even his beatings. As I watched him grab his throat, blood spurting between his fingers and beginning to flow down his arms, I remembered all the nights I lay awake crying for my parents, wishing more than anything I could have them back again.

And then I remembered his hands covered with Ben's blood.

As I watched him bleeding in front of me, I pulled the trigger again and again without hesitation, until I couldn't fire the gun any longer.

I open my eyes and look directly into the Officer's face.

"I don't regret killing him," I whisper. My throat is on fire, but I don't care. "And I would do it again in a second."

He suddenly reaches forward and takes my hand. He has a kind look on his face, and his eyes are fatherly. Protective. He clenches his jaw, takes a deep breath and lowers his voice.

"I don't blame you in the least, Georgia."

He replaces my hand on the side of the bed, gives it a pat and sits back in his chair. He clears his throat and double clicks the end of his pen.

"Let's start at the beginning."

CHAPTER THIRTY-FOUR

GEORGIA

I AM LYING NEXT TO Ben in the cabin. It's midday, and we are still in bed. He's sitting up against the headboard, shirtless, wearing black-rimmed glasses as he reads a new book on hiking in Central Oregon. I am lying on my side, alternating between memorizing every detail of his face and upper body, and closing my eyes to doze. I am enormously happy and content; there's no other place in the world I want to be, and there's no other person I want to be with. I reach over and lay my arm across his exposed abdomen, snuggling my face into his side. He takes a hand off his book and sets it over mine, gently tracing circles with his thumb.

"I love you, Ben," I whisper, slowly becoming conscious.

My eyes are still closed, but I smell the acrid, sterile hospital room.

No. I don't want to regain consciousness. I want to slip back into this dream.

Tears slide down my face as I realize, with every new waking, all that I have lost.

I am not comforted to learn from the Sheriff that Mike was placed on administrative leave over a month ago for drunken and disorderly conduct. I don't care that two women pressed charges against him for assault, and I am not appeased to learn that Officer Dickerson and Mike worked together in San Diego. Dickerson's wife left him, and he moved to La Pine where Mike apparently met up with him and started stalking me again. It also doesn't help much to hear that Dickerson has been arrested and charged with aiding and abetting for his role in Mike's actions. I am actually unmoved to learn he was funneling information about me to Mike all along — my injury, my hotel, the cell phone I was using, my relationship with Ben — all of it. Not only did Mike have information about my whereabouts all along, but Dickerson apparently left out information from my file.

The Sheriff explains that through several conversations with Officer Roth, they were able to piece together what truly happened, arresting Dickerson just after he reported to Mike that Ben and I were back in Sisters. Not that it was even necessary. The Sheriff informs me a quick search of Scott and Sylvia's house revealed transmitting devices in our home phone — Mike's equipment, of course.

The Sheriff tells me, quietly, that lightning struck the cabin, igniting the generator outside and starting a fire near the front of the house. The flames were spotted from another tower south of Bend and called in to the Sisters' Ranger station. He tells me how paramedics and firefighters risked their lives in a helicopter, flying around the tail end of an electrical storm to land at the top of the butte.

I stop him there and cover my ears, even though doing so causes me excruciating pain. I don't want to hear any more. I don't want to hear the words I know are coming next. I can't face it.

He tries to calm me down, tries to reassure me everything is all right, but I sit up as much as I can and try my best to scream at him to leave. My throat feels like it's splitting at the seams, and I clutch at it before slamming my head back into the pillow. The machine behind me emits a steady stream of loud, continuous beeps, and all at once, several people rush into the room.

A moment later, I slip into sweet unconsciousness.

———

I can tell my room is dark as I lie in my hospital bed, eyes closed, trying desperately to grasp the last fragments of my subconscious life with Ben. My dream is slowly slipping away as I unwillingly become more aware of my surroundings. The smell of the sterile room, the sounds of activity in the hallway, a telephone quietly ringing somewhere...I want to shut it all out and slip back into lying next to Ben.

I want to go back to sleep and never wake up.

My face is wet with tears as I quietly cry. My body shaking as the pain across my chest intensifies with my heaving sobs.

A noise across the room alerts me, and I realize I might not be alone. I don't even care who it is. I don't want to see anyone. I don't care if anyone sees me.

Soft footsteps approach the side of my bed and stop. I turn my head away, unashamed of my rude behavior.

"Go away," I whisper. My voice is raspy but getting slightly stronger.

The bed indents, as whoever it is sits down. I lift my hips and move away as much as my broken body will allow. I wince as pain shoots up my ribcage.

"Just go," I hiss through my sobs.

I am furious as I realize the person is carefully lying down next to me. I breathe in, preparing to mutilate my throat as I yell at the intruder, and then immediately stop.

I smell pine.

I smell pine trees and fresh air.

A hand gently presses on my hip, radiating warmth through my thin blanket.

I open my mouth but am speechless.

I am too afraid to open my eyes.

"I will never leave your side, Georgia." His voice is soft and deep. His words pierce my heart and break me wide open.

I turn my head toward him, and slowly open my eyes. It's dark in my room but the machine behind me gives off a dim light, and I can see the side of his face, the ridges of his beard and the outline of his long eyelashes.

"Ben?" My voice is barely a whisper.

"I'm right here." His voice breaks on the last word as he chokes back a muffled sob.

I am so stunned. I literally have no words to use. I feel my face crumple as I turn over as much as my shattered body will allow. His hands help me as much as possible, and he gently wraps his arms around my shoulders, testing each point of contact for signs of pain.

I bury my head in his chest and cry openly for a long time. He holds me as tight as possible and softly runs his hands over my hair, down my back, stopping just above the beginning of my rib cage. He continually hums in my ear, melodies I've never heard before but that are soothing to me, nonetheless. Afterward, I am reduced to the involuntary accordion sobs that always follow a hard cry.

"Shhhh. It's okay now. I'm here. I'm not going anywhere. You're safe, baby."

I pull my head back from his chest and look up at him. He's really here. I reach up and touch his chin, the side of his face. I want to throw my hands around his neck, but I can't move my arms any higher.

"I thought," I swallow hard. "I thought..." I cannot make myself say the words.

"I know. Shhh. I know, I thought the same about you." He closes his eyes and shakes his head. "I never want to feel that again. Not ever. I want you by my side. I want you forever."

He leans forward and kisses my forehead, and I close my eyes and breathe in the scent of him. His body radiates heat into mine, pressing against me, and I begin to feel whole once more.

"How?" I squeak. "What happened?"

"Don't talk. I know your throat is damaged." He moves the hair that has fallen over my eyes.

"It was...Georgia, it was awful. When I finally got down to the cabin," he begins, "it was in flames, and I couldn't find you right away. When I saw you lying on the floor, well, I thought I was too late." He stops, and it's a moment before I hear his voice again. "I thought I had lost you forever. Thank God the helicopter arrived almost as soon as I brought you out..." He trails off, his voice breaking on the last words. My heart aches for him. I can't even imagine had the situation been reversed and it was me that found him. I can't stand the thought any longer, and I lean into him again and breathe deeply against his chest.

"But his hands...there was so much blood."

"Yeah. He was waiting for me when I climbed into the tower. Completely blind-sided me. Hit me on the back of the head with something heavy. I only remember a few punches after that. I think it was a lightning strike that woke me up. I don't know. I just knew I had to get back to you..." he says, wiping the tears from his eyes.

"I love you so much," I whisper, my voice raspy and hoarse. My throat is on fire. My body is broken and bruised, and I don't even care.

None of it matters.

The only thing that matters in my world is lying next to me in this dark hospital room, wrapped around my body like a harbor of safety — a shield against the darkness.

And I know, deep in my soul, I know that I am no longer lost.

EPILOGUE

I AM CURLED UP IN the corner of the leather couch editing my latest writing project for the Sisters Tribune — a story about how an avid hiker, one Calvin Dorsett, recently proposed to his girlfriend of only three months, on a hiking trip through the Three Sisters wilderness. Staring at the photo of the two of them on top of South Sister, I'm struck by how perfectly life works sometimes.

All at once, I am aware that a heavy stillness has descended over the house. The wood is crackling in the fireplace, and I glance up from my laptop, wondering what has changed in the atmosphere. The sky outside is thick overcast, and varying shapes of heavy grey clouds fill every direction I'm able to see.

The front door shuts, and the sound of boots stomping on the slate entryway breaks the silence.

"Brrrr! Whew, it is definitely getting cold out there!" Ben says from the hallway.

Charlie's ears perk up from his bed by the fire, and we both turn our heads in the direction of Ben's voice. A moment later he appears in the living room. A thick wool hat covers his head, and the tops of his ears and the tips of his cheeks are bright pink. His dark winter beard is thick and full, and his mustache covers the top of his upper lip. He's wearing his black barn coat, and his arms are loaded with firewood. I can't help but bite my lip as he smiles at me — my heart leaping all over the place.

"I think you're even sexier in winter," I say, setting my laptop on the cushion next to me, and standing up to meet him.

I take some of the wood from his arms, and we walk to the fireplace, dumping it all into the iron grate. He dusts himself off over the hearth and pulls the jacket off. Taking a step closer to him, I run my hands over his thick, plaid shirt. The small diamond solitaire on my ring finger glints with the reflection of the dancing flames and I smile at the memory of his proposal.

Looking up into his eyes, I reach toward his hair, pull off his hat and let it drop to the floor.

"Come down here, fiancé," I murmur.

He grins slyly, leans down and kisses me slowly, but firmly. I melt into his arms as he holds me tighter, no longer worrying about broken ribs or collapsed lungs.

Charlie's bark from across the room causes us to break the kiss and turn toward him. He's looking outside, and as I follow his gaze, I notice movement at the top of the windows. I gasp gleefully as I realize what I am seeing, and turn quickly back toward Ben, a huge smile on my lips

We stand facing the windows — Ben's body behind mine as his arms fold around me, watching the first December snowflakes circle and twist in the sky above us before floating down to blanket the frozen earth. Ben leans his head down and presses his lips softly to my ear.

"Forever," he whispers. "I will be by your side, loving you forever, my beautiful, soon-to-be wife."

I can feel his cheek rounding against my temple, and I know

his mouth is beginning to curve with that incredibly sexy smirk I've come to love so much.

I close my eyes at his words and smile softly, turning my face to meet his.

"Forever and ever, Ben. Forever and ever."

The End

You have just finished reading *Lost and Found*.

If you have a moment, please help other readers find this book by leaving an honest review online.

If the idea of writing a review is daunting, don't worry! Even just a star-rating (1-5 stars) is helpful on any of the sites below.

Goodreads

Amazon

Barnes and Noble

iBooks

Kobo

Instagram

Facebook

AFTERWORD

One of the questions I am often asked is, "what inspired you to write this story?" The truth is I don't really know. It just sort of happened.

The one thing I *do* know is that I've always respected the writing advice, "write what you know." So when I began this story with just a character that was escaping an abusive marriage, I stuck her in the place that I know. A place that always makes me feel centered and alive — central Oregon. To me, there is something a little magical about hiking to the top of a mountain, and elevating yourself closer to the sky. So I guess I thought, if it works for me, why not make it work for Georgia, too?

After graduating high school I worked over the summer for the Department of Forestry as a wildfire firefighter. That meant my co-worker and I worked in the woods, drove a huge four-wheel-drive, manual transmission truck filled with water, wore steel toe boots, had fire retardant clothing and an emergency shelter in a bag that we carried at all times. I had zero training, zero prior experience, and zero references. But I was willing to work hard and learn, and I think that's what landed me the job.

During our days in the forests, and on the logging roads of backcountry Oregon, we came upon fire lookout stations and watchtowers, and I immediately took an interest in them. They just seemed so remote and quiet and just...cool.

The first time I hiked Black Butte and saw the lookout tower and the log cabin at the top, I was thrilled. The cabin was abandoned at that time but I was still intrigued by it, and began imagining the Forest Service workers that used to live there while they worked in the tower. It just seemed like a neat, albeit lonely, job. One that would suit only the right kind of person...maybe someone with a troubled past.

And with that Ben's character was born.

———

Maybe there's a place you've visited, or lived, that inspires you. Maybe there's a unique spot that only you know about. Maybe take a chance, take a risk, and write a few ideas down. And then write a few more.

See where it takes you.

If I can do it, anyone can.

ACKNOWLEDGMENTS

Thank you to everyone who encouraged me to keep writing and supported this crazy dream. Without your constant feedback and encouragement, I know this story would still just be rattling around inside my brain.

Thank you to my friend Micayla Lally (author of "A Work of Art") for giving me the push I needed to start writing. You continue to inspire me, make me laugh, and generally just make the world a better place. Cheers to you, lady!

Special thanks to Korrie Kelley and the outstanding group of ladies she has gathered around these books. Everyone deserves a friend like Korrie in their lives. My only regret is that we didn't meet sooner. I love you, girl.

To my sweet friend Staci Studley, who supported the creation of Ben and Georgia from day one. Without her early positive feedback on chapters — one in particular — I never would have pushed on to completion. Thank you for always being a shining ray of positivity in my crazy, crazy life.

Finally, I would like to recognize and thank my advance reader team. Thank you all for leaving the much-needed reviews when a book is released. Thank you for your honesty and love of reading. Without you guys and your dedication and loyalty, these stories would never get off the ground. You are all so precious to me and I wouldn't trade you for the world.

———

To anyone who has ever felt lost: I see you.

I've *been* you.

And my most sincere advice is: keep going.

Keep searching for the thing that makes you feel alive; whether that's writing, drawing, hiking, organizing, reading, leading, following, or supporting...just keep going. Don't let what other people think stop you from pursuing what makes you happy. Give yourself something to look forward to every day, and then encourage someone else to do the same.

Find your happy. Be found.

Lost in the Right Direction

———

Hey you, let's stay in touch!

I love to hear from readers. I love feedback about stories, sharing book recommendations, tips and tricks, and just finding out what's going on in your life.

The best way for us to connect, the best way to find out when I release new books, launch a pre-sale, or offer free advance review copies of upcoming novels, is by joining my mailing list.

It's called the *5-minute newsletter*, and every month you will receive one short email about novels I am working on, music that inspires me, food, exercise, podcasts, and products I can't live without.

The newsletter is easy to read, easy to reply to, and gives us a way to connect.

Here's how to sign up:

http://eepurl.com/deRUg1

ABOUT THE AUTHOR

Megan Carr is an emerging author of romance and romantic suspense. *Lost and Found* is Megan's second book.

Connect with Megan on any of the social media channels below. She would love to hear from you.

f facebook.com/megancarrauthor

🐦 twitter.com/megancarrauthor

📷 instagram.com/megancarrauthor

📌 pinterest.com/megancarr

g goodreads.com/megancarr

a amazon.com/author/megancarr

Made in the USA
Middletown, DE
02 December 2018